SURFACING

First Paperback Edition: October 2015

For information on subsidiary rights, please contact the publisher at rights@jollyfishpress.com. For a complete list of our wholesalers and distributors, please visit our website at www.jollyfishpress.com.

For information, address Jolly Fish Press, PO Box 1773, Provo, UT 84603-1773.

Printed in the United States of America

THIS TITLE IS ALSO AVAILABLE AS AN EBOOK.

Library of Congress Cataloging-in-Publication data is available.

ISBN-13: 978-1-631630-54-5

10 9 8 7 6 5 4 3 2 1

To Molly,
for everything.

SURFACING

MARK MAGRO

JOLLY
FISH
PRESS
Provo, Utah

BALTAZAR

I realized I loved her sometime in between jumping off the top of the building and hitting the ground.

My class was in Level F's underground testing arena for an experiment when I first saw her. We were idling on top of a make-shift structure that stood approximately thirty stories high. The other classes were safely working on projects on the arena floor, but they made sure to take a moment to stop and watch when any of us jumped. I assumed the sight was more entertaining from the ground.

The control group had gone first. As all evidence indicated, we confirmed that if you fall three hundred feet, you leave a sizeable splat upon impact. The mess never remained long, though. Giant robotic wipers gave the target area a clean sweep after every jump, restoring it to a pristine condition. After fifteen equally brutal trial runs, an experimental gel cushion was applied to the landing target. The substance, designated Substance 37X, foamed up into a blue puffy material that resembled pillows from afar. The goal was to show that this substance could help a free-falling body land with minimal damage, despite the force produced by such a long fall. Normally, I would find an experiment like this fascinating, taking extensive note of every conceivable observation with my datapad.

This time, though, I didn't really give it too much thought. I was too busy staring at the girl standing next to Dr. Douffman, and I was noting how she made me feel like my skin was on fire.

I went with the usual observations first. She was about my height, although that doesn't prove much because I'm below average for a sixteen-year-old male. Her skin was as light and pale as her full white hair, which hung to her shoulders. Nothing completely out of the ordinary.

It was her eyes that really stood out under the fluorescent lights of the arena. I had seen plenty of people in video torrents with blue eyes, but never up close like this. They almost appeared to glow. One glance from her had me so entranced that when the line moved, Tern had to push me along because I hadn't noticed.

"Who's that?" I whispered back to my roommate.

Tern tucked his thin arms under his bony armpits and stole a few glances at her, pretending he had something in his eye to cover up his staring. "I don't know. A transfer, maybe?"

"Who are you malfunctions talking about?" Zeke asked, turning around from his spot in front of us. I sighed and subtly nodded toward the girl, hoping not to draw any attention. Unfortunately, subtlety was not one of Zeke's stronger attributes.

"Pretty thermal, boys," he barked loudly. "Pret-ty thermal."

She looked toward us immediately and we darted our eyes in other directions as though convinced the sterilized steel walls of the arena were the most interesting things in the world at that moment. If she thought something was amiss, she didn't show it and looked away after a few seconds. I elbowed Zeke in his ribs when we were clear. The sweat under his grey t-shirt made my skin moist. "Way to make it obvious, quark."

Zeke rolled his eyes. "Oh, please. A new student joins our class and we're *not* supposed to stare? We're scientists, for crying out loud! We're supposed to be nosy."

Tern shook his head. "I think the word I'd use is 'inquisitive.'"

"The word I'd use for you . . . I can't say: there are children nearby."

"Will you two solder it up?" I whispered harshly. Dr. Douffman was staring at us disapprovingly.

Our professor cleared her throat, tapping on her datapad with her ruby nails. "As we begin the experimental portion of this exercise, class, take note of the gel's form upon impact. Remember Protocol #248."

"*Studious notes can make or break an experiment,*" we recited in unison. With our datapads at the ready, my class huddled closer to the jump point. I was still struggling to fake an interest in what we were doing. This mystery girl had my full attention, and any attempt to reclaim it was futile. The force of attraction was just too much to resist.

Once the gel was ready below, the scientists monitoring the impacts gave us the signal to begin. Freedman deposited his datapad in the safety bin and took a deep breath before jumping. I didn't see the landing, but the sound of his bones breaking echoed throughout the arena. My class let out a collective groan. The wipers got to work shortly after, cleaning up what was left of him. It was just the first trial run, but the early evidence seemed to indicate that Experiment #114165 was going to be unsuccessful.

I pretended to take notes as my classmates leapt one after another. Each run sounded the same: the clang of a datapad being deposited into the safety bin, the thud of flesh and bone hitting solid metal at high speeds, and then the squeak of industrial strength brushes coated with cleaning solutions gliding across the floor.

Clang. Crunch. Squeak. Clang. Crunch. Squeak.

The blue-eyed girl next to Dr. Douffman must have been focusing on the mechanical sound of it as well. She tapped her feet along with the rhythm while her eyes focused somewhere off in the distance.

I followed her gaze to a giant banner of Dr. Parkman that hung on the wall of the arena, his trademark slogan underneath it, "How will you live forever?" It was foolish, but the image of him suddenly made me feel guilty. I was spending more time ogling a girl than focusing on the experiment. Most people never got to see him in person, but Dr. Parkman was known for having little patience with unfocused scientists-in-training.

As if he was tuned into my thoughts, his voice suddenly blared from the loudspeakers built into the walls. "Remember Protocol #121, students! *Pain and progress go hand in hand!*"

Dr. Douffman nodded her head in agreement, waving the next student up to the jumping line. I wanted to remind both of them of Protocol #291: *Time wasted is irreversible.* It was clear to any of us that this experiment was a bust, but it was likely they would have debated that watching us fall thirty stories was hardly a waste of time.

Easy for them to say when it wasn't their bodies experiencing a three-hundred-foot fall.

Zeke went next and did a short dance before leaping off, eliciting a laugh from everyone and lightening the mood. I smiled with the rest of them, but then got caught up again in the white noise that the sight of the girl created between my ears.

Last summer we had done several experiments in zero-g and I always remembered how the lack of gravity made me forget I had a body. Looking at her felt similar in a lot of ways, I noted. It was as if I was just a floating consciousness with no attachment to the physical world.

I was so lost in my thoughts that I didn't hear Dr. Douffman's command for me to jump next. Tern, the good friend in a crisis that he is, thankfully grabbed my datapad and pushed me from behind, sending me tumbling through the air.

The fall only lasted a few seconds, but it was all I needed to form a hypothesis. The professors always spoke fondly of pivotal moments in research. These snap seconds when the data and experimenting pay off and the answer to a mystery suddenly reveals itself. The parts clicking into place.

Falling from the top of the makeshift building toward the quickly approaching blue gel provided enough clarity to help answer the question of why the sight of an unknown girl distracted me so.

It was love.

Then I hit the ground, a crunch filling my ears milliseconds before everything went black.

Then blue.

I woke up an hour later in a rejuvenation chamber, submerged in oxygen-rich water. My feet were still being re-grown, but everything else appeared normal. The scar on my shoulder from the terrible bug experiment was still intact. My crew cut was still slightly uneven at the top. Even my nails still needed to be trimmed. The nanomachines that were in my blood during the experiment meticulously recorded every detail of every cell and transmitted the data to the chamber, allowing me to be re-constructed from scratch, so to speak, to the state I'd been in $1/1,000,000$ of a second before the fatal landing. No harm, no foul.

Another victory for science.

On the other side of the glass an electronic banner of Dr. Parkman hung on the wall for me and my classmates to stare at while we waited to be fully re-grown. With his slicked back hair, he pointed his sharp index finger at us while the words, "Science Thanks You for Your Participation!" scrolled across the top over and over. There was also the occasional reminder of dinner specials scattered intermittently. Chicken and rice tonight, with a side of steamed asparagus and a slice of blueberry pie for dessert.

I didn't want to sound like a quark. I always liked hearing the thanks, even if it was just from a scrolling banner. Science itself thanks me for my pain and suffering. It was a reminder that I was a cog in a great machine, driving the whole human race forward. That would be my legacy. Granted, I could have done a better job being a useful cog on this one, paying more attention to the experiment rather than a girl. But this was certainly a beautiful girl. A girl that I hypothesized I loved.

I twirled in the water and leaned back, feeling the sinking sensation all around me as I sunk to the bottom of the chamber. My debriefing would follow once I was released. I managed, thus far, a perfect average on arena tests and didn't want to start making errors so close to midterms. But the girl kept making her way to the forefront of my mind. It was the blue of the water, reminding me of her eyes. A name would be a good place to start, I decided. First, her name. Then, a conversation.

A few minutes later, Zeke, fully re-grown, walked by my tank and banged his fat fists on the glass. I tried getting his attention to ask him about the girl, but he was too busy pulling his pants down and pressing his butt against the glass. My classmates around him thought it was extremely humorous and he took a bow before walking away, not noticing the bubbles flying out of my mouth or my attempts to wave him down with my hands. I let myself sink to the bottom again and just opted to watch my feet grow, wiggling each toe once they regained feeling. Zeke, that Neanderthal. I was going to shove his face into his dinner when I caught up with him in the mess hall.

After the reconstruction process was fully complete, Dr. Colonna came by to release me from the rejuvenation chamber, the water flooding out into the floor drains. I changed into some warm clothes before she took my vitals to make sure that the body just grown was actually me, and not some zombie that would go into organ failure in a few minutes.

"Start from the top again," she said and tapped her stylus against her datapad. I groaned involuntarily. We locked eyes for a second before she went back to her notes.

"In a rush today?" she asked.

I was fond of Dr. Colonna. She'd been a student not too long ago before earning a position with the Parkman Institute of Science and Solutions, so she remembered what it was like after a fatal experiment. The last thing most students wanted to do after experiencing physical death was to take a test, especially when there's a pending conversation with the potential girl of my dreams.

"Let's just say I have bigger goals in mind at the moment that don't necessarily promote the progress of PISS," I said.

She rolled her eyes and gave me a hard lemon candy to suck on. I promptly accepted her gift to help get the taste of oxygen water out of my mouth. "I hate it when students call this place that," she said. "And if you're serious about being asked to stay underground after you graduate, you should be mindful of who's around before you feel free to insult the Institute. If there's one thing Parkman looks for, it's loyalty."

"I know, I know. I'm confident in the details of my report, though. Can we just go through the basics? Please?"

She huffed but then I saw the hint of a smile. "Name?"

"Baltazar Harris."

"Today's date?"

"March 11th, 2167."

"What were you doing before you died?"

"I was a subject for Experiment #114165, testing Substance 37X's ability to soften the impact of a body in freefall."

"Result of experiment?"

"Uhhh . . . a conclusive failure. The subject was fatally injured, necessitating a cellular re-growth from the bottom up."

"The Parkman Institute of Science and Solutions thanks you for your participation in this experiment. Without its valued students, the Institute would be unable to help mankind rebuild society and expand its understanding of the known universe and blah blah blah, sign on the bottom. Watch for bleeding or any other sign that your brain is rejecting your reconstruction."

Now I was the one smiling. I scribbled my name near the big X and grabbed my things.

"Remember we're doing rounds soon," she reminded me. "Make sure your midterm experiment is up to snuff."

By that point, I was out the door, but I shouted back, "Don't worry, it's coming along great!" before making my way toward the mess hall. That comment was actually a fairly large lie because my AI project was coming along terribly. I was secretly tossing and turning with worry every night. However, I was a firm believer in keeping professors on a "need to know" basis. Right now, it was all about finding out the girl's name. Tonight I could schedule time to panic about my project.

I walked the glass halls, dodging the occasional mini-sweeper that shimmied by to ensure the floor was spotless at all times. Senior scientists in white lab coats moved back and forth, clogging my line of sight, but I was able to catch a glimpse of Tern walking with Ash ahead. I knew Tern had feelings for her and interrupting their conversation would qualify as a crotch-block, but Ash always knew the latest happenings on Level F. She would know who my mystery girl was, which was worth having to endure Tern whining about my interruption later.

I zigzagged through the crowd to catch up with them, bumping into Tern in the process and almost knocking him over.

"Hey, Balt," Ash said, her datapad pressed against her chest.

Tern rolled his eyes at the sight of me, apparently correctly deducing everything I was thinking in an instant. "Told you he would want to know."

"So you know who *she* is?" I asked, sounding more desperate than I'd hoped.

"I do," Ash replied, pausing and taking pleasure in watching me squirm.

"Sooooo . . . are you going to tell me?"

We reached the doors of the mess hall, the din of the students inside spilling out into the corridor. Tern shot me a sympathetic look and patted me on the shoulder before heading inside to secure us seats. I stayed by the doors with Ash, suddenly hot and sweaty despite the blowing air conditioning.

"You sure you want to know?" she asked.

"Of course . . . but I'm starting to suspect that I'm not going to like the answer."

Ash raised an eyebrow, as if she was about to deliver a crippling blow. "Zoe Culth. Our year. Transferred in from Level H."

Chemicals boiled over in my mind. Her name.

"Zoe, huh?"

"Yes, but before you get all excited, here's the wrench in your gears: her last testing group was H100C."

My head cocked back, fitting this jagged piece of information into the puzzle. "Wait, what? You mean . . ."

Ash slowly nodded. "Yep. She's the only survivor."

ZOE

"So, what do you think of the facility? Dr. Douffman told me she gave you the grand tour, as it were. I know it doesn't have the vegetation and animal habitats you are used to on Level H, but Level F has a reputation of excellence. More than seventy-five percent of our classes score "proficient" on their Parkman exams and we have over a five percent retention rate for junior professor positions."

I shifted in the plastic chair, causing the material to squeak. What was this guy's name again? I had met so many professors and scientists and degree-holding lemmings with datapads in the past few hours that they were all starting to blend together. Instead of making an effort to remember this one, I decided to just stare at the painting behind his desk. An ocean scene. I wouldn't know what to think if I saw that much water in real life.

I gnawed on my bottom lip before saying, "It's okay, I guess."

The doctor nodded, flipping through a file on his datapad that probably contained every last detail of my life. "Well, I've spoken to the board regarding your . . . ," he paused, adjusting his tie, ". . . special circumstances. They've gone to great care to make sure the transition is as easy as possible for you. You'll be enrolled in classes on this level to continue your studies. I know engineering is not your focus, but we felt having someone with your expertise could be helpful to many ongoing student projects here. However, instead of taking part in experiments in the arena, it's been decided that you'll come here during those time slots."

"Here?" I asked, my eyes drifting around the dark office.

"Yes."

"And what are we going to do *here?*"

"Just talk."

"About what?" I slumped, rubbing my eyes. How many days had it been since I slept?

The doctor cleared his throat again. "It was a terrible accident that occurred with your testing group. I'm sure things have felt difficult lately."

My gut reaction was to smack this stony microbe in the face and upend his desk. I know he thought he was being sensitive and nice to me, but every word that dribbled from his mouth made it that much harder to stay seated and not strangle him. Did he really think that, when I remembered seeing my best friend and classmates turned into charcoal, I said to myself, "Gee, this is difficult?" That was the problem with all of these lab coat-wearing scum: they thought that if they read about it in a case report, they understood it. As if life were that simple.

I scanned the rippling waves in the painting behind him again. I guessed there would be plenty of opportunities ahead to show him how wrong he was. No need to rock the boat just yet.

"I'm just tired is all," I replied curtly, biting my nails.

He nodded again. "I can imagine. I'll prescribe you some sleep aids. Just remember that anything you say in here remains between us. In my experience, students often feel hesitant to speak their mind to administration such as myself. As if Dr.

Parkman and the Institute is some form of 'big brother' watching everything the students say or do. But that simply isn't the case. You can trust me."

I nodded, lacking the energy to express my doubt about that. Like I would be imbalanced enough to trust any of them after what happened. After what Helena saw with her own eyes.

There was the standard portrait of Dr. Parkman and his slogan hanging on the wall alongside the ocean panting, looking as stoic as ever. His skin was pale and just as pristine as the hallways here, but his gaze fell heavily upon me. I found it hard to believe he wasn't watching us all, constantly.

How will I live forever?

Why did that have to be my goal when just living a normal life was hard enough?

"Dr. Douffman doesn't need to know what we talk about in here. Same goes for Drs. Herzman and Lebowitz . . ."

Now this guy was really pushing it. I took a breath and the room felt like it was closing in on me all of a sudden. Colder. I needed to get out. Immediately.

"I just want to head over to the dorms."

"You're not hungry? You've had a long day."

"I'm fine. I just want to set up my room and get some sleep."

He looked at me for a second before getting up to open the door. "Make sure you have a big breakfast tomorrow, Miss Culth. Your body needs the energy." He smiled and offered me his hand to shake, which I took reluctantly. Surprisingly, as dark and cold as his office felt, his hand was warm against mine.

Dr. Douffman was waiting outside to take me to the dorms. She had a scratchy voice that grated in my eardrums like claws scraping against glass, so of course, she was my main lab teacher and I would get to listen to her lecture for four hours a day. She started telling me about the projects they were working on in class: integrated robotics, advanced artificial intelligence construction, the usual refuse engineering students toyed with. I drifted in and out of the conversation, thanks to all the eyes watching me, as we walked through the halls, the walkway lights reflecting off everyone's spotless white pants as they strolled past.

It took me a second to figure out what it was about me that seemed to be getting everyone's attention. Then I realized mine were probably the only blue eyes any of them had seen in a while. It was just another reminder of how things were now. It was them and me. And this distance was only going to grow.

We rounded the halls until we got to the student dorms, the tall arches instantly looking familiar. The layout was a lot like the one in Level H: a common room at the entrance and stairways that led to several floors of sleeping quarters designated by class and sex. But that's where the similarities ended. Everything on this level just felt soulless and dead. The hallways were clean but sterile. The sliding doors didn't make that cheerful beep as they opened and shut. I looked down and caught a glimpse of my reflection in the floor, blurred from foot smudges. Nothing was going to feel like home again.

I registered my thumbprint and Dr. Douffman finally let me loose. I headed straight to my room, a ten-by-ten foot single on an all-female floor. I flew up the staircase and, after shutting the door, I lay on the soft foam bed and let the material shape itself to my body. It was almost like a hug. Almost. I closed my eyes and basked in the first silence in what felt like forever. Even the air seemed to stand still. Then I heard it. A quiet sound indeed, but I had been on edge for so long that my senses were heightened.

It was the sound of a refocusing camera. That soft glide as the lens clicks into place.

They were watching me.

Instead of trying to find it, I played along. I sat up and began looking through my bags, everything seemingly as I had packed it. But I knew better. I bet they spent hours going over every fiber of my clothes, examining and re-examining every particle. I slowly folded my things and put them into drawers, humming a song the whole time. I made sure to smile too, hoping they would see it. Maybe I was being overconfident, but I figured that if they wanted to get rid of me, they would have already done so. I was the only successful candidate left in Dr. Herzman and Lebowitz's experiment, and if I died, so did their breakthrough.

When I was younger, I used to read this book on my datapad that had a bunch of interesting facts about pre-war animals that weren't genetically archived. What was unique about it was all the pictures were hand drawn; lead lines filled in by pastels. I read it so many times I had it practically memorized. The illustrations weren't empty like everything was here. Those drawings were the invention of a real person, sketched to show us how we should remember real animals.

One part told about the Hognose snake and how when its predators drew near it would play dead, leaving its mouth gaping open and letting every inch of its body go limp. It would remain like this even while being prodded and tossed about, keeping up the act until its predator was sure it was safe to eat. It was at that moment, and only then, when it would spring to life and attack—at the very second its predator's guard was fully down.

Drs. Herzman and Lebowitz could feel comfortable. I would play dead. For now.

When I was done unpacking, I sat on the bed and listened to some music on my datapad, tracing the Hognose from memory like the artist in that book. I made it limp against a tree with the slightest hint of a glimmer in its eye. A spark. My finger glided along with howling music blaring through my headphones, feeling myself become so detached that I jumped at the sound of a knock on my door through the beats.

I pressed my thumb against the scanner on the lock, opening the metallic door. "Hello," a short girl greeted me. She was about my age with black frizzy hair and freckles stretching across her nose. "Your name is Zoe, correct?"

"Yeah," I responded. I didn't smile back, somewhat annoyed that so many people already knew who I was.

"I'm Cindee," she said, extending a hand, which I reluctantly took. "Some of us girls are going to view some torrents in the lounge if you wish to join us. That is, if you're not preoccupied with unpacking or anything of that nature. I mean, the torrents are just the ones PISS rents out, but they look pretty entertaining."

"PISS?" I asked.

"Yes," she laughed. "That's a nickname we call the Institute on this level."

"Seems about right." I wasn't in the mood to socialize with a bunch of girls I didn't know and who probably already knew my blood type and last quarter's grades, but I figured it wasn't like I would get any more privacy in my room. "Let me just grab a sweater."

Cindee nodded and, after I changed, I followed her to the carpeted lounge down the hall where four other girls were curled up on couches with snacks. Cerilla, Cinder, Cadza, and Cait. Yep, I was certain to remember these names.

"So how was it that you escaped the explosion in the arena?" Cadza asked the second I took a seat. "I mean, you can imagine how it seems rather suspicious?"

The girls pinioned me with hungry eyes and I wanted to crawl back into my room to escape their ambush. Cinder leaned in close. "What was the experiment for? All the reports are classified. Not that you *need* to tell us, but you can trust us."

"Definitely," Cait added, her hands folded on her lap.

I shrugged and stayed quiet, hoping they would just stop asking questions. It felt like the only escape was to close my eyes. There was no haven to be found from what happened, no matter which level they stuck me on. Cindee finally noticed my discomfort and changed the subject, the interrogation averted for the time being. The screen on the wall clicked on and I let the image bleed into my eyes.

The first torrent was from the early twenty-first century about some girl obsessed with clothes and struggling not to spend too much money. Pretty inane stuff, but even I loved watching how the world worked before the war. The city streets on the surface teemed with people, dogs, and birds, and a girl's most pressing concern was making sure she looked good. Not just living, but living well. Must have been great.

After that, we watched a short about a family on the surface after the war ended. The land was scorched and all they could do was wander the wasteland, scavenging anything they could find. But then they found one of the domes Dr. Parkman's grandfather was building where people were banding together to survive. All the Parkmans, whether it was the grandfather, father, or the pompous son who ran the Institute now, were always played by the most intellectual and charismatic actor they could find. Somehow, I doubted the real thing was the same up close. Call it my growing intuition to see through bullcrap.

In this torrent, Dr. Parkman Sr. gave a dramatic speech, laying out his plan to build laboratories underground so they could use the core's warmth for energy and begin science's quest to rebuild the world. The Institute would be his legacy, and it was our duty to pass it on. To contribute and find a way to "live forever," through what we create and add to the greater good.

The crowd watching clapped and cheered. One of the little kids standing near the front came by and grabbed his hand.

"You, little one," he said in a husky voice, "are the future."

The girls sobbed. I rolled my eyes.

We all knew the rest of the story. Because there's so much to be done on the surface to make it habitable again, the adults stay in the domes to work. The children are brought underground to live in the labs. To learn and grow, to be fulfilled by science. We will create and test the latest and greatest inventions until we turn eighteen, when we are either deemed intelligent enough to stay in the labs and continue contributing, or found to be not quite sharp enough and sent back to the surface to lend a hand in the ongoing struggle for survival (and to roast under the radiation clouds).

I didn't say anything during the torrents, biting my lip hard to make sure I kept it that way. I had heard these bedtime stories so many times I could recite the tales in my sleep. But now I saw them for what they really were.

Lies.

BALTAZAR

I had a naked dream that night, but it wasn't the sexy kind. I was in the chem lab, alone, working on my AI project. The scene appeared normal enough, but then Zoe entered, approaching me from behind while I was huddled over a workstation. She whispered something in my ear. Her voice was so soft though that I couldn't understand what she was saying, so I turned to face her. In doing so, I ended up spilling some jethro carbonate and was immediately engulfed in flames.

Directions for what to do in just such a predicament were spelled out on the wall, but Zoe was standing in the way, blocking my view. For some reason I didn't have the heart to say, "Pardon me, I'm currently engulfed in flames and you're blocking the emergency directions." I also didn't shout "ahhhhhhhhh!" I just stood there burning until, for some unexplainable reason, the fire just burned off my clothes and then stopped. There I stood, naked, and Zoe was gone. It got really cold and I just sat on the floor shivering.

Then I woke up.

No, there was nothing remotely sexy about this dream.

Needless to say, I wasn't feeling very energetic or engaged in class the following morning, and the rather dry lecture topic certainly wasn't helping. Dr. Douffman was droning on and on about the signs of radiation poisoning—something those who would be heading to the surface after graduating "should be sure to research." We had heard it all countless times.

"We wouldn't want you to become disfigured or mutated to the point where your legs swell up and you become relegated to activities that require you to remain sedentary all day," she explained, adjusting her thick glasses every few seconds because they kept sliding down her long nose when she spoke.

Tern vigorously shook his head in agreement while taking notes. Zeke, on the other hand, seemed to have realized his life's calling, raising his hands in the air in triumph.

I gave my eyes a hard rub and started scrolling through our textbook on my datapad, examining pictures of the irradiated surface. While the domes were safe and didn't appear *that* dilapidated, everyone living inside appeared haggard and worn out. Their populations, including the parents none of us could remember, had to work long hours under tough conditions just to survive. I examined their faces closely. None of them looked like me. They never did.

All communication between students and surface workers was forbidden because PISS felt emotional ties would be a distraction for both sides. Most felt the rule was rather harsh, but I actually agreed with it for the most part. None of us knew if our birth parents were alive or dead or even how our old friends who graduated were doing up there. Part of me didn't want to know, if I was being honest with myself. In the end, we all had a role to play. Personal feelings shouldn't get in the way with that.

I needed to remember that when thinking about Zoe.

"Just remember Protocol #307," I heard Dr. Douffman say when zoning back into her lecture, *"When in doubt . . ."*

"Vomit it out!" everyone chanted enthusiastically.

I couldn't argue with that either.

"And before we break for lab time to work on midterm projects, I would like each one of you to come up and briefly update the class on any progress or difficulties you're facing or may face in regards to your experiments. Remember, we're a scientific community here and it's important that we support and learn from one another. Why don't we start with . . ." she paused, her eyes scanning the room. "Zeke! Please step forward and address the class."

"I'd be happy to!" Zeke responded, and groans could be heard from the testing lab on the other side of the wall. "Aww, I promise it won't be that bad," he joked, and everyone laughed. I had to admit, what Zeke lacked in scientific prowess, he certainly made up for in showmanship.

"So, if you remember, I'm working on a food additive that will make the subject to which it's applied taste like bacon. Not just have bacon flavor though, but give off the same aroma, have the same texture, you know, really fulfill that bacon craving we all get from time to time."

More laughs came from my classmates. Tern and I just looked at each other smiling and shaking our heads. Zeke was certainly an unorthodox roommate.

"I see," Dr. Douffman said, seeming less entertained. "And you feel that this experiment will benefit mankind as a whole . . . how, exactly?"

Zeke craned his neck forward and squinted, as though she'd just asked why water was wet. "Well, mankind loves bacon, Dr. Douffman. And with the limited pig population remaining, we must do all we can to insure that we never lose bacon."

"You will live forever through bacon!" Cadza shouted from the back, and everyone clapped. Quite frankly, it was hard not to be inspired. Even I was suddenly craving bacon, ready to help Zeke lead the charge to a bacon-utopia.

Dr. Douffman, however, just closed her eyes for a brief moment and said, "Thank you, Zeke," once the ovation died down. "Baltazar, why don't we get an update from you next?"

My stomach churned. I disliked speaking in front of the class, let alone having to follow the one-man comedy act. Zeke winked at the digital photo of Dr. Parkman on the wall before heading back to his chair, patting me on the shoulder as we passed. The squeaks from my shoes against the linoleum floor echoed as I walked, my panic levels rising. My midterm project last year on hover shoes received gold honors and a group of scientists on Level Q were expanding on the concept for use in construction projects. Expectations were high for what I would produce this year, and I aimed to meet them at the very least. But for now, all I had was a ineffective robotic head that would say "you are great" in a monotone voice whenever I smacked the work table in frustration.

It couldn't even be objective.

Rather than being honest with everyone, I opted to devise a way to tactfully circumvent my lack of progress with my project. I took a breath, but the door to the class opened before I could say anything. Zoe walked in and all the oxygen fled my lungs, my brain sending sensations of electricity throughout my body. She seemed even more beautiful than yesterday and when she looked at me, I could barely remember my name let alone the finer details of my project.

"Ah, Zoe, welcome," Dr. Douffman greeted her. "Class, this is Zoe Culth. She's a promising transfer student from Level H. Zoe, you're just in time to hear about one of the most interesting midterm projects we have this year from one of our most promising students. Please take a seat."

"Yeah, Balt!" Zeke shouted from the back, and a few of my classmates cheered. But then the silence came and I could feel Zoe's blue eyes stare at me. My tongue lay lazily in my mouth and my throat felt parched.

I coughed.

More silence.

"I, uh . . ."

Major error.

"Well, why don't you start by reminding the class what your project is on?" Dr. Douffman offered, trying to assist.

I grimaced and ran my hands through my hair, trying to get my thoughts straight. But every time I felt ready to say something, I looked to Zoe and noticed how she crossed her legs as she sat. Or how soft the skin around her neck appeared. Or how chaotically perfect the wisps of her hair fell about her shoulders. My face twitched and I desperately tried piecing words together to make some sentences.

"I'm working on an AI."

Correction, one sentence.

More silence ensued. Tern was giving me a perplexed look

from the back of the classroom while Zeke was mimicking a choking victim.

Dr. Douffman cleared her throat. "And what is the purpose of this artificial intelligence?"

I looked to Zoe's beautiful blue eyes again. No one really knew what exactly happened to her class. PISS kept that sort of thing confidential. But students never died. Ever. It must have been horrible, whatever the circumstances were. She sat straight up against the chair. She had great posture. *What were the odds that she would end up in my class,* I wondered. Well, there were ten student levels, each with thirty-two classes, so one in three hundred and twenty. Pretty fortunate.

It was only then that I remembered that I was still standing in front of the class. And Dr. Douffman had asked me a question. About something.

Colossal error.

"Why don't you take a seat, Baltazar? I can see you're not feeling quite yourself today."

I nodded and awkwardly shifted toward my seat, my shoes squeaking again on the way back. I didn't dare look at Zoe this time, realizing how much of a malfunction I must have appeared with my initial impression. I looked to Tern to verify if the situation was as poor as I thought. He winked at me in an overly exaggerated manner, mouthing, "Nice job."

Solder it, Tern.

I kept my head down as Dr. Douffman began speaking on my behalf. "Well, *I* will let you know that Baltazar's project is one that all of you should take as an example of what kind of work we are hoping to see out of our students with their midterm projects. As you know, you are all currently living and learning in part of what the Parkman Institute of Science and Solutions calls the 'new labs.' State-of-the-art equipment, more classrooms, more robust testing arenas, etc. But a large portion of the staff, including myself, grew up and were educated in the 'old labs,' which have since been sealed off. Sixteen years ago, they became overrun by variant AIs left over from the Final War. Horrible machines whose sole purpose is to destroy and kill whatever life they come across."

Dr. Douffman's tone was grim and the room grew silent except for the sound of the occasional student shifting in their chair. Many of the older professors became wistful when they spoke of the old labs. Thousands of people had died, from what I'd researched, equaling almost seven percent of the remaining human population. The labs were sealed around the time I was born, so I didn't remember anything about them. The facility must have been impressive though, to make people take a moment to collect themselves when speaking of it. It was these types of responses that gave me the idea for my project.

"Many good scientists and security officials died to insure that this institute would survive here, including Dr. Parkman's father, the second in a line of proud scientists who conceived humanity's redemption. But Dr. Parkman's decision to seal the old labs gave us another chance to continue our work and ultimately heal the world with the power of science," she continued, her hand over her heart.

"Balt's experiment aims to help us regain some of this past. Using the talents and skills he has developed during his time here, Balt is hoping to create an AI that will enter the old labs once again. Once there, it will track the other AIs and learn of ways to eliminate them, hopefully obtaining valuable data that can be used to create a safer environment for all of us here. Perhaps, one day, it will even allow us to re-enter the old labs. This project is intelligent, it's ambitious, and most importantly, it benefits mankind. Always remember that *that* is our main goal here in the Parkman Institute of Science and Solutions. That is how you will live forever."

Zeke sent me a message on my datapad. *"Would bacon spray be useful in this epic endeavor?"*

A somber silence overcame the class as Dr. Douffman let us ponder the legacy of the old labs. I understood she meant the pause for reverence, but all I could consider was how disappointed all the professors would be once they saw how poorly my AI was turning out. I wondered if even Dr. Parkman himself knew about it. I didn't look up, but I could almost feel his picture on the wall watching me. Disappointed.

Hopefully he didn't even know about my project.

Mitchell Braverman went up next and updated us on his advanced piston configurations for drilling equipment. I feigned interest but was actually checking the schedule for upcoming experiments in the testing arena. Maybe there would be one that would allow me to throw myself in a blending apparatus. Between the pressures of getting my AI to work as intended and appearing like a complete malfunction in front of Zoe, it would be a welcome relief. Perhaps the Balt that would be reconstructed would not be as much of a disappointment.

ZOE

My first full day as a student on Level F was tolerable, but not much more than that. Cindee and Cadza were in my morning lecture which, aside from watching one short guy have a meltdown in front of everyone, was pretty uneventful. I spent most of the class finishing my drawing of the Hognose snake, ignoring the stares from my classmates. To them, I began to realize that I was more like another lab experiment than a classmate. A specimen to be studied and learned from.

Lab time was a bit better. I got to keep to myself without having to pretend to be solar and cheery for a change, working in a corner alone in peace. My midterm project was on trying to revive 21st century music. I was splicing some old servers for another project a few months ago when I stumbled across some fruit company's semi-intact database that had millions of tracks stored digitally. Most were corrupted and distorted, but I went through each one that still had some viability and tried cleaning them up, restoring them as best I could. Bit by bit, each one came to life like a seed buried in the dirt, slowly sprawling upward and showing its real colors.

Although my professors on Level H thought I was dwelling too much on nostalgia, a rosy way of looking at things past, they approved the project. Since no one on Level F told me otherwise,

I continued with my work. While the engineering flunkies spent their time messing with circuit boards and soldering irons, I fell into these snapshots of a time I hadn't known and never would. Armed with my headphones, I dove deep into the audio progressions and the world around me faded away. I knew the feeling wouldn't last, but it was nice while it did. The closest I could get to an escape from everything.

Whales used music as a form of communication, songs never exactly repeated within the same herd. One whale might borrow notes from another's song, but they always added their own interpretations when they sang, changing the rhythm and frequencies and ultimately creating something new. Scientists were never able to figure out why they did that, but I think that maybe it made the world around them seem less scary and easier to understand. Because they could add their own voices. I drew them once, swimming across murky waters, their songs to each other appearing like lights in the darkness. Maybe if I kept working on my project, the music would help me find my way too.

I worked without so much as looking at anyone else all the way until lunch. Cindee and Cadza waved me down when I got to the mess hall though and I felt obligated to sit with them. Thankfully, instead of probing for more information, they just gossiped about boys while I poked at my plate full of peas and potatoes.

"I hope they're not too disappointing," Cindee sighed, surveying the scene. "Our lot of males, I mean. Our apologies, Zoe. They're not exactly Parkman-esque, as you can see."

Cadza shrugged. "I disagree, I think Zeke's fairly pleasant. And humorous, too! We used to speak a lot in organic chemistry last semester and he could always make me smile."

"Not the brightest, though," Cindee retorted. She paused, giving me a chance to insert my thoughts, but I just shrugged. I really didn't care enough to comment and found myself paying more attention to what was going on around the mess hall. If the Institute was willing to go so far as to put a camera in my room, I wondered what they would do to keep an eye on me during lunch. It was probably safe, but I subtly crushed every piece of food on my plate with my fork to make sure there wasn't anything in it.

"And what occurred with Balt today?" Cadza laughed. "He appeared as if he was having an aneurysm during his project presentation!"

Cindee shook her head. "Maybe the pressure's starting to affect him. He's one of the few who has a chance of being asked to stay after graduation. Not that I'm scared of leaving for the surface, but I think everyone knows that until the radiation clears, being up there is going to . . ."

"Be completely unbearable?" Cadza offered and they laughed.

"At least we'll grow extra thumbs together."

I heard their words and smiled, but really, I was trying to think straight as all the pictures and torrents I'd seen over the years flashed in my head. The radiation on the surface. The dome cities. The Final War itself, maybe. Just how far did the implications of what Helena saw go?

"Are you testing this afternoon, Zoe?" Cadza asked. Her pink lip-gloss glimmered under the bright lights overhead.

"No. I've been assigned to meet with Doctor . . . I forget his name. I don't think I'm going back into the test arena for the foreseeable future."

"I can imagine having your class die in an experiment probably makes it seem less appealing," she noted matter-of-factly, like someone would note the date. "Was Paris Moldonovo in your class? I met him during an inter-level conference. I hope he wasn't killed."

I swallowed, thinking of the glimpse I caught of the doctors removing my classmates bodies from the arena. They were charred and their limbs were locked in awkward, impossible positions. I'd screamed and thrashed about so much when I saw them that I had to be sedated.

Mercifully, the bell rang just then and I headed to the psych wing to meet Dr. Grima (remembering to look at the name on the door this time) in his office, trying to flush Cadza's questions from my mind. Dr. Grima wasn't wearing a lab coat like all the others, reminding me he was a different kind of scientist—a mental one who was more interested in how you felt rather than what you contributed. The lights were brighter in his office this time, which put me a bit more at ease. Ever since the doctors' experiments had started, darkness and I weren't really running in the same pack.

"How are you today, Zoe?" he asked. Whenever he spoke, I noticed that his words rolled out methodically, like each was carefully planned.

"Okay, I guess."

"Are you enjoying your classes?"

"They're fine. We're just working on our midterm projects mostly."

He asked me all about my music restoration project and I

actually surprised myself by how much I said. I guess just talking about the notes and lyrics made me feel like myself again, the girl who lived before all this happened.

"There's this one great line from one of the songs I was able to restore that I think about a lot. It goes, 'With lovers and friends I still can recall, some are dead and some are living, in my life I've loved them all.'" I chewed on my nail, suddenly embarrassed and angry with myself for alluding to my old classmates. Dr. Grima seemed nice, but that didn't mean I could let my guard down.

"Powerful words," was all he said. He paused and I could tell that he was giving me the chance to continue. But I didn't. I swallowed hard and kept the feelings buried. There would be a time to let them out, but this wasn't it.

And he seemed to understand. I liked that.

We talked some more about classes and my future goals in school and I made something up about wanting to teach when I was sent to the surface or something like that. When it was time to go, I grabbed my bag and headed out. I wanted to go right back inside though when I found Drs. Herzman and Lebowitz waiting for me in the hall, their lab coats seeming a full shade whiter than everyone else's.

"Hello, Zoe," Dr. Herzman hissed. He smiled and I caught sight of his incisors catching on his lip.

Dr. Lebowitz adjusted her glasses and moved beside him, folding her mantis-like arms. "We've missed you on Level H and wanted to pay you a visit."

I didn't say anything and just concentrated on holding my ground. Thankfully, Dr. Grima appeared behind me and, as politely as a doctor could in front of his superiors, I guessed, asked to speak with them. His words didn't flow out as methodically this time. The doctors kept their eyes on me as they entered his small office and closed the door behind them. Part of me just wanted to run, but that would be pointless. Level H or Level F, there wasn't anywhere to hide. Instead, I put my ear to the door when the hallway cleared of traffic and tried to make out what I could.

Dr. Grima was saying something about "giving more time," but whatever it was, Dr. Herzman and Lebowitz weren't having any of it. I put two and two together, and my fears were only confirmed when they came back into the hallway and walked with me back to the dorms. Dr. Grima watched us as we left and I wanted nothing more than to head back inside his bright office and talk music again.

"Dr. Grima tells us that you've been making some progress," Dr. Herzman said. They both kept their eyes on me as if they wanted to make sure I wouldn't vanish under their noses.

"Yeah, my one hour spent with him really feels like it paid off," I responded, notably sarcastic. Dr. Lebowitz sighed like she was trying to hold herself back from ripping me to pieces.

"Nonetheless, you are feeling better, yes?"

"I guess so. As good as one could feel after watching all of their classmates incinerated. Sure."

We got to the entrance of the dorms and Dr. Herzman grabbed my arm, squeezing me with his bony fingers.

"That's good. Because we need to pick up where we left off," Dr. Lebowitz whispered. "*Project Wind* could be an unprecedented step for mankind. Dr. Parkman himself is very interested in its findings."

"It could change everything," Dr. Herzman reiterated.

"And now you're the only one left who's had success with the procedure."

I jerked my arm free and ducked inside, not looking back but feeling their stares as the automatic doors closed behind me. My walk turned into a jog and when I got to my room, I couldn't help but bury my face in my pillow. I wanted to scream until my lungs bled. With every passing second, the walls felt like they were closing in on me, forced by the miles of earth pushing down on them. My panic kept growing and growing until I started hyperventilating, the Institute crushing me from all sides.

I sat up and took a deep breath, doing my best to relax and think of anything beautiful. Tulips reaching for the lights above. A bird's song. After a minute or so, I was able to slow my heart rate down, but it didn't really help for long. My reality was still just that. Even outside of the testing arena, I was still their subject. Still their mound of flesh to prod. Helena and I were the only successful ones and they weren't going to stop until they figured out why.

I rubbed my right wrist, feeling the slight lump under the prosthetic skin I'd stolen from the lab on Level H before I left. It felt different to the touch, like rubber, but to the naked eye it was indistinguishable from normal skin. It was the perfect place to hide the proof of what Helena had seen. Her last gift before they took her away from me. It was also a reminder that I couldn't give up. That the rest of the truth was out there, waiting for me to see it for myself.

And that's when I realized what I had to do.

I had to escape.

BALTAZAR

While I always strive to remain calm and collected, I cannot deny the relief that comes from committing the occasional act of barbaric violence in a controlled setting. Case in point: annihilating an army of robots with laser Gatling guns.

A group of senior scientists approached my class that afternoon for volunteers to test experimental weaponry meant to aide those in the domed cities to defend themselves. On the surface, there were still AI left over from the war, packs of cannibalistic raiders, and other horrors that I could only imagine in my nightmares. They needed all the help they could get, and while armed combat wasn't something I normally excelled at, my hand was in the air before they could finish their request.

After being shot full of nanomachines by the med tech, Zeke, Tern, and I, along with a bunch of other boys from our class, ran through crater after crater in the testing arena, holding the trigger down as the barrels of the gun spun and let loose searing beams that cut through the machines. I ground my teeth as I fired away, not paying any mind to the oils and lubricants that splattered all over me.

Granted, aggression therapy technically went against Protocol #142 (*Ulterior motives undermine good science*), but sometimes we all need to step outside ourselves.

"And the Parkman's Most Effective Scientist award goes to
. . . Baltazar Harris with twelve confirmed kills!" Dr. Colonna
announced over the loudspeakers when it was all over. After a
bow, I blew away imaginary smoke from the end of my barrel in
triumph. If only Zoe could see me like this rather than having a
mental crash in front of our whole class.

"Ugh, you definitely stole some of my kills," Tern whined, his
gun almost dwarfing him as it hung from his shoulder. "I had all
of the ones that came around the left side! You probably just shot
them when they were down already." Then he stuck his tongue
out at me just in case his objection wasn't completely understood.

"Sounds like fighting words, Balt," Freedman said, winking
at me. "Will you take that? The nanomachines are still good
after all . . ."

Although more consequence-free fighting was tempting,
I opted not to shoot Tern down when Zeke snuck up behind
him and smacked him hard on his behind. Retaliation enough, I
deemed. "Let him enjoy the moment," Zeke suggested to Tern.
"He needed a testing arena rebound after the 'bug incident.'"

I shuddered at the recollection of the memory. Months ago,
I had been chosen for a bug repellent experiment that was being
developed to combat a new species of flesh-eating ants. Needless
to say, it didn't work and the creatures were free to feast once they
overcame the initial resistance the repellent produced. Hundreds
of them surrounded me and, given their minuscule size in relation
to mine, took hours to make any significant progress in consuming my flesh. Eventually the scientists in charge of the experiment
finally accepted that experiment's failure and evacuated me from
the testing room. I didn't need to be reconstructed, but I ended

up with a scar near my neck where the creatures concentrated their attack. Even now, I still couldn't look at an insect without cringing.

"Don't remind me," I said, shaking my head. Certainly, between the bug incident, my midterm troubles, and the "Zoe" situation, things had not been going my way the last few weeks. I had tried to make eye contact with her a few times during morning lecture and lab to try and gain a sense of what she thought of me, but she'd been busy drawing on her datapad the whole time and put on soundproof headphones during lab, never looking my way.

I knew that, statistically speaking, I faired a better chance of forming a relationship with her by just approaching her and striking a conversation, but I always lost my nerve whenever I thought about it. Need to get work done, I told myself as an excuse, rather than admitting I was spineless. My project's due date was not getting any farther away.

I got very little done on my project, of course. Anytime I attempted to focus, thoughts of Zoe kept forming, wondering what she was listening to on her headphones. What was she thinking?

Protocol #12: *It all starts with research and reflection.*

With my AI pushed aside, I spent the rest of the morning working on the text file I'd started when I first saw her in the arena, aptly labeled "Analysis of Feelings Toward Zoe Culth." Like any experiment, I deduced that if I kept dissecting my feelings toward her, this analysis would bring better understanding of the situation and, quite possibly, a sense of confidence. Maybe I could then gain an idea of what to say to her.

While progress was made, no breakthrough was found and I proceeded to lay waste to the aforementioned robots.

That, in the end, proved useful since the experience in the arena gave me an idea for what to do with my AI. After returning the experimental weapons and taking a shower to get the robot goop off, I reported to Dr. Colonna for my debriefing. I felt rather fortunate to be assigned to her because not only would she allow me to speed through the report, she was just the person to talk to about the "special permission" I would need.

She flashed a light in my eyes and read over my vitals, asking me the usual questions regarding the experiment. Since I didn't need to be reconstructed though, the process went by quickly.

"The nanomachines should deactivate in the next twenty minutes, so if you still feel like jumping off something tall, now's the time," she joked, hinting at a good mood. Nova.

"I'm content with staying alive, thanks. It's been awhile since I tested and came out in one piece."

"Statistically speaking, I suppose it has to happen once in a while," she said before looking back to her datapad. "Can you summarize the results of the experiment as you saw them, please?"

"Experiment #346112: Field Test of Molesan Gatling Laser against modified combat robots. Test equipment demonstrated great success, with the entire test group coming out alive except for one student. However, cause of death was due to tripping on an untied shoe lace and not due to any shortcoming of the test equipment."

"Those laces will get you every time."

"Protocol #21: *Success is found in the details*. Nonetheless, it was observed that the test equipment overheats after more than ten seconds of constant fire. This was already known, but other than that, no faults were observed at this time."

Dr. Colonna quickly recorded my results and smiled. "The Parkman Institute of Science and Solutions thanks you for your participation in this experiment. Without its valued students, blah blah blah, sign at the X."

Rather than rushing out like last time, I took on a serious demeanor after signing, folding my arms behind my back. "Dr. Colonna, I was hoping you would grant me a favor."

"If you want to take the laser to the dorms, the answer is no."

I couldn't help laughing at the thought. "While tempting, I had something else in mind. I've been doing a lot of thinking about my AI project and I feel I want to try a genetic implantation. That would require a temporary clearance level increase and access to the lab after hours."

She raised her eyebrows, which was expected, but indubitably a negative sign. "You know students aren't normally allowed that privilege."

I nodded emphatically, choosing my words carefully. "I know, but the more I dwell on my goals for this AI, the more it appears that it's going to need more intuition than I can program in such a short time. Plus, even with permission, it's not something I can accomplish during a normal lab period given the time required for the gene implantation process."

She didn't say anything, which led me to believe she was thinking it over. A positive sign.

"I would be extremely careful," I insisted. "Just in the genetics lab and out. No rummaging around."

She squinted, biting her bottom lip. Hesitation was another positive sign.

"I'll thank you in my Gold Honors acceptance speech?"

Then she sighed. Success.

"Just don't be foolish. Make sure to log in and out with everything you use. And if I hear that you and those friends of yours decided to grow some bull-chickens to fight or something, I won't hesitate to recommend you to the punitive board."

"You can trust me, Dr. Colonna. For sure."

Dr. Colonna made me a 72-hour keycard and I left the arena in high spirits. I shoveled dinner down as quickly as possible so I could get to the genetics lab early, experiencing a rejuvenating sense of confidence. But of course, given the universe's tendency to balance out, I bumped into Zoe on the way out. I emphasize *bumped*, both of us getting knocked down from the collision in the entrance way to the mess hall.

When I realized it was her, I experienced a miniature heart attack and helped her up as quickly as I could. "I'm *so* sorry! I didn't see you coming," I offered in a panic. I couldn't be sure, but it felt like all the blood vessels in my skin had burst.

"It's fine," she said, more to herself than to me. She didn't look me in the eye and entered the mess hall, disappearing into the crowd. I contemplated heading back to check out the laser gun at that point. With some effort, I could reach the trigger while sticking my face against the barrels.

Rather than opting for that messy self-termination though, I left and moved all of my equipment into the genetics lab. It was completely empty after hours since there were no classes in session. I turned on the lights inside and set up on one of the side worktables, putting the frames of the head together and mounting it onto a three-axis neck pivot. It was one of the first positive steps I had made in a while and it felt good to finally get something done. Perhaps, I considered, there was still reason to hope this project wouldn't be such a colossal disappointment after all.

With my protective goggles on, I did my best to keep my mind clear and work on the circuitry inside the AI head. By about midnight, I had the head functional to the point where it was able to fully process and hold a simple conversation, but so much more needed to be done. I could program computations to help it decide what the best course of action was in any given circumstance, but that would take weeks I didn't have before the project was due. I needed a shortcut.

My AI needed to be able to think on its own. I had never actually done a full genetic implantation, but had researched the process enough to understand how it worked. All it involved was fusing DNA into the CPU using the process the great Dr. Seagreaves invented years ago called "neuro-netting." The joining of man and machine. The man was a genius and one of my favorite scientists to read about. He pushed the field of engineering in such radical ways, making it clear that there is no limit to what can be done with mere metal. The AI would still be a machine, but it would grow its own sense of judgment. A personality almost. With a set series of genes making up its computing core, it would be able to make snap decisions and think on its feet while tracking and reporting on the variant AI in the old labs, maximizing its chances for success.

There were risks with this procedure though. Many genetically influenced AIs did appear "quirky" from the reports I'd read, sometimes doing a little *too* much thinking on their own. There were even cases where the AI would begin to question their programmed goals and pursue their own desires. It was risky, but my options were limited.

I cycled through the available genes for student use and decided on Smith, a genome with high potential in both logic and sense of cautiousness—two traits I figured would be useful. Once the genetic implant was packaged, I connected the AI head and sat back as the upload began, incorporating my algorithm for its mission and the existing databases in the Parkman Institute system so it would know the layout of the old labs. The process would take several hours, so I figured I would just forego sleep and sit with it the entire night. Tomorrow was a day off for students, so I could make up the REMs then.

With the upload in progress, I started working on a rough diagram for the body, but ended up dwelling on Zoe. Again. She had appeared annoyed with me when I bumped into her. If she didn't think I was a waste before, I certainly wasn't doing anything to dispute that notion. I knew I needed to forget about her and concentrate on the task at hand, but just the thought of her got me more excited than any experiment I'd ever done before. That had to mean something.

I opened up my text file dedicated to Zoe and started writing my thoughts as they came. Zoe wasn't the first girl I had feelings for, I reasoned. A year back, I had developed feelings for a girl named Molna who worked on a jumping pad with me for Physics lab. I used to sneak into her dorm after hours and we would kiss on her bed while her roommate was asleep. The whole thing was pretty nova, but I knew it was just an outlet for physical desire, nothing I would lose sleep over when it ended. Molna was nice, but she was just another girl.

I had read enough about hormones and pheromones to understand what caused attraction and supposed feelings of "love." It was chemical, like a drug. And like any drug, the effects would wear off, sooner or later. But one look from Zoe did more than any narcotic I'd ever been injected with. It knocked me off my feet while making my brain spin. It made everything else seem insignificant, even important things like my midterm project. She *changed* the way I saw things, and I felt like I needed to know everything about her. Besides her beauty, something unexplainable was pulling me toward her.

And like Protocol #1 states: *The core mission of the scientist is to not only figure out what, but why*.

I must have fallen asleep working on the Zoe file because the next thing I knew, Dr. Helgan was waking me up from my lounged position in my chair, an army of lab coats assembled behind her. They commented on how my snoring might be a sign of sleep apnea. Embarrassed, I shot to my feet and cleaned up my gear as fast as I could, grabbing the AI head and everything else in a haste. I was in such a rush that I didn't think to see if the genetic upload was complete until I found the AI staring up at me in my arms as I walked back toward the dorms.

It was about that time the terror set in.

"Don't worry, Baltazar," it said to me. "We'll figure out a way to gain Zoe's love and affection."

ZOE

The Institute was a blasted fortress.

On our one personal day of the week, I went to the student research lab early in the morning and started digging for anything that might give me an idea of how to escape the Institute. No doubt, they were monitoring what resources I was looking at, so I knew that I had to be smart. Every inquiry I entered into the databases had to appear innocent and not give away my true intentions.

I knew that the most direct route out would be using the surface lift, but that was basically like trying to get through a steel wall using osmosis. It was on Level A, where Dr. Parkman and the rest of the science board worked and lived. Level A was also the central hub for the security systems. It would be an impossible nut to crack. Other than graduates on their way to the surface and a few higher-ups, no one was given access to the lift. No one.

Aside from the lift, the Institute was shut off from the surface and completely self-sufficient. It generated power via geothermal energy from the Earth's core, used artificial light and greenhouses to grow food on Levels C and D, and there were enough natural metals generated from the mines to provide scientists with any raw materials they needed. If it weren't for the stubborn idea of not abandoning the surface, mankind could completely relocate underground and probably be better off.

Assuming all that surface stuff was true, of course.

The morning morphed into the afternoon and I continued searching through every available student database I could find without raising too many possible red flags. But no matter the source, the prospect of finding a safe way out besides the lift just didn't look promising. Bottom line: there were miles of earth between me and the surface, and I could dig for the rest of my life and not even come close. I started getting frustrated but whenever I felt like quitting, I thought of Drs. Herzman and Lebowitz eyeing me down like I was their next meal. That prospect kept me going. I would rather stare at the screen until I went blind than let them get their hands on me again.

"Hello, Zoe!" a voice called from behind me. I turned to see Cindee, her curly hair in pigtails today. "Doing some research for your midterm?"

"Yeah, sort of," I lied. "Not getting far, though."

"Well, maybe you should take a break then. The girls and I are going to cook dinner tonight on the floor and watch some torrents afterward. Would you like to join us?"

My instinct was to explain that hanging out with her pack felt more like an interrogation than an opportunity to relax. I knew Cindee was trying to be nice, but it was all in vain. I wasn't really looking for new friendships. Now, and maybe never again.

Then again, I thought, maybe they could provide me with

more information about this level. Something that would help me escape. "I have an appointment with Dr. Grima in a little bit, but I'll meet up with you after that."

"Nova!" she exclaimed. "Alright, we'll see you later then!"

I stayed at the terminals for another hour or so before heading to Dr. Grima's, my brain feeling fried from so much research. The last thing I wanted to do was talk about anything heavy so, of course, it didn't come as a surprise when Dr. Grima wanted to discuss the deaths of all my classmates.

"What is there to say?" I said, shrugging my shoulders.

Dr. Grima nodded and tapped his desk lightly. He let the issue slip by last time, but he seemed determined today to get something out of me. "Well, you must have some lingering feelings about everything that has happened. Do you feel lonely? Depressed? Angry?"

"Why would I feel angry?" I asked, probably a little too sarcastically. I looked into his eyes and he looked into mine. As nice and trusting as Dr. Grima came off, he was still one of *them*. And none of them could be trusted.

"What I meant was," he continued in his usual measured tone, "maybe you're feeling angry at yourself for not being with your class when it happened. A survivor's guilt. Or maybe angry with The Parkman Institute for letting it happen?" He cocked his head but kept looking right at me. It was so quiet in the office that I could hear my breathing get heavier.

The *Physarum polycephalum* mold could learn patterns of the conditions around it and adapt to survive. When anticipating hostile factors threatening its well-being, it would collect itself and harden for protection. It would see the danger coming before it even arrived. I drew it once, hiding among a pack of green moss, its skin as impenetrable as steel.

I looked to the corner of the room where Parkman's portrait hung. "Do you know how many mini-sweepers there are in this place?" I asked.

Dr. Grima shook his head. "Quite a few, I would assume."

"One thousand and twenty-four. One thousand and twenty-four small machines designed to clean the halls. An entire fleet of robots with only one job. One purpose."

"Right."

"We have food processors meant to recycle our food scraps. We have biodomes meant to recreate various environments for wildlife. We have gravity wells that give us the exact amount of gravity as the surface to keep our bodies prepared for when we return. We have safety measures for procedures, for precautions, and for rules. Something for everything."

After a pause, he replied, "I'm not sure I'm following."

"Nineteen of my classmates died, Dr. Grima. These were people that I had known since . . . forever. We weren't all close, but they were the closest thing I will ever have to a family."

There was another pause while I tried to stop my rambling. I bit my bottom lip. I needed to walk away from this conversation ASAP before I got myself in trouble.

"So . . . you're angry?" he asked again. His fingers were interwoven like a spider's web.

I took a deep breath. "I just know that, like all the machines down here, everything has and is done for a purpose. *Everything*." I paused in frustration. Why couldn't I keep my mouth shut? "And now if you would excuse me, I have plans this evening."

I left and took a shower before meeting the rest of the girls, opting just to stand in the hot water and let my muscles loosen up. I tried to shut off my brain and relax, but couldn't help but think of the water flowing through the pipes, being funneled from point A to point B through a massive maze of machinery. It all came from somewhere. There was a path through the chaos. I just needed to find it before Drs. Herzman and Lebowitz tested me to death.

Cindee divided up jobs for dinner. I was in charge of putting together the salad, which felt like the first time I was able to put my hands on anything green since leaving Level H. We had the new labs' most extensive garden area, and I used to spend some evenings helping the scientists there plant vegetation to keep the environment diverse. It wasn't the same, but just handling lettuce made me feel like that wasn't long ago. That it wasn't long ago that things didn't feel so bleak.

Dinner turned out pretty good and, after cleaning up, I dodged some questions about how I felt seeing my friends being "mutilated," their words not mine, and watched a torrent about some band trying to make it big in one of the Parkman domes. Dr. Parkman's father had discovered them and they ended up creating a national anthem for the new civilization "Rising above the Ashes." All brought to you by the Parkman Institute of Science and Solutions, of course.

The final scene showed the protagonists playing at the opening ceremony of the Institute, Dr. Parkman's father cutting the ribbon, and all the scientists and dome citizens cheering. Light from the sun streamed in through the thick dust clouds above for just a moment, the marble floors shining bright, before darkness returned and the fluorescents kicked in.

"I wonder if that lobby is still there," Cerilla thought aloud, popping a cookie into her mouth. "I mean, if the entrance to the old labs is still standing."

"I think I read that they closed that off too when they started finding the variant robots. It helped keep them contained on both ends so more couldn't find their way in. But thank goodness we have Balt on the case," Cait replied with a wink. "He'll take care of them, especially since we'd be first in the line of fire if they broke in."

"Of course," Cindee added. "The more I think about it, the more I actually feel bad for Balt. He won't admit it, but I saw him sweating over his AI during lab the other day. He has a long way to go before he's functional. I'm still holding out hope for him, but it looks like our *entire* class might end up getting shipped to the surface."

The conversation started snaking toward boys again, but I pulled them back, my mind stuck on the old labs. "What do you mean, 'first in the line of fire'?"

"Oh, I keep forgetting you're new to Level F!" Cindee exclaimed. "We're right next to the old labs, actually. Level F was the first level built in the new labs. It started off as just an annex to the old ones during Dr. Parkman's rise to scientific fame."

Cait nodded. "If you look around in the testing arena, you can see the old entrances. They're completely sealed up though, like we said, so we don't have to *really* worry about those robots breaking in or anything like that."

I shook my head, pretending to be relieved, but I was actually more excited than ever. "But the entrances are still there?"

"Yes," Cindee answered. "Maybe one day, if they can destroy all the rogue AIs, they'll open the tunnels up again and we'll be first in line to head back in."

I thought back over my brief time in the testing arena but couldn't remember seeing any doors, but they were there, I kept telling myself. I fought every impulse to keep myself from running to the terminals and looking them up, opting to just head back to my room. That kind of behavior would raise way too many flags, I reminded myself. But it was something. A possibility.

I lay in bed all night, thinking about it. The old labs were overrun but still there. *Right there.* A path to the surface. If I could just find a way inside, I had a chance. I just needed a way to navigate through them.

And I knew just the person to talk to about that.

BALTAZAR

"Well, you've outdone yourself this time, Balt," Zeke said behind me, his hands resting on my shoulders. He and Tern were attempting to console me, but there were no words that could dissipate the sensation of dread in my stomach.

Protocol #4: *Don't panic.*

"I'm screwed," I declared.

"You can't remove that directive or something like that?" Tern asked.

"No," I mumbled, my hands propping my head up on my desk in the lab. "Not unless I scrap the whole thing and start from scratch. With neural-netting, the directives are fused with the circuitry." I looked to see if Zoe was within an audible distance, but she was at her table with her headphones on, drawing on her datapad as usual. Regardless, as a precaution, I adjusted the voice volume on the AI's neck before rebooting it, watching the white lights behind the eyes grow brighter after a few seconds and blink at me.

"Morning, Smith," Zeke said, smiling. He still thought this error was humorous. He was such a malfunction.

Smith flexed the joints in his mouth. "It's actually past noon, so technically afternoon, Zeke. But yes, hello."

"Yeah, Zeke's not too quick, as you'll find out," Tern joked, which Zeke rewarded with a hard punch to the shoulder.

Smith looked at me and frowned. "What's wrong, Baltazar?"

"Smith, can you tell us your directives again?" Zeke asked for the thousandth time, and now I was the one delivering a punch before hiding my face in my hands.

"I suppose, although I'm not seeing the humor in it. Directive 1: Infiltrate and observe the variant AI found in old labs. Track their movements in an attempt to discern a definite pattern. Assess threat levels and possible solutions for deactivation. Report back with notable data."

There was a pause as I could detect Zeke and Tern trying to hold back their laughter. Malfunctions. Both of them.

"Directive 2: Help Baltazar Harris court and obtain the love of Zoe Culth."

"This is just too funny," Zeke said. "You created a blasted dating bot, you quark!"

Tern shook his head. "How did this happen?"

"I created this . . . irrelevant file about my feelings toward her. I must have saved it to the wrong folder. When I did the genome implantation, it was translated into code too and installed as a primary directive."

"Well, what did the file state exactly?" Zeke asked.

" Love is . . ." Smith began to recite.

"Don't answer that, Smith," I commanded, cutting Smith off.

"Too funny," Zeke kept saying.

"This isn't *that* bad," Tern offered. "It'll still track the variant AI like you wanted."

I huffed. "True, but it won't ever pass inspection. Once the professors learn that one of its primary directives is—well, you know—they'll scrap the whole thing. It's way too unpredictable to take seriously."

"Hmmm," Smith pondered. "Well, that's disappointing. I had so many great ideas regarding how to achieve my objectives. Speaking of which, you do realize you have a chemical stain on your shirt, right Balt? It isn't very flattering."

"I love this AI," Zeke announced. "He can be your personal love mentor."

"So screwed . . ." was all I could muster.

"Balt?"

We all turned to find Zoe standing behind us, her blue eyes locked on me. I shot up and sensed my forehead instantly grow hot. "Uh, hello, Zoe."

Protocol #4: *Don't panic.*

"Is that the AI?" she asked. "For your project?"

"I am," Smith announced from behind us, rolling slightly on my desk. "Pleasure to meet you, Zoe. Your eyes are quite breathtaking, if you don't mind me saying. Did you know that there are only three people in the entire facility with blue ocular pigments? Sadly, it appears to be a gene that has been hit harder since the Final War."

I did a quick survey of the lab for a hole in which to hide. No such luck.

"Flattering and informative," was all Zoe said, though. "Seems like you got yourself a winner there, Baltazar."

I just stood there like a defect before Tern elbowed me. "Uh, yeah. Balt's always been really skilled with engineering feats."

There was an awkward pause, which Smith tried interrupting

by coughing. That only proved to make the situation more awkward, since it was clear to everyone that he didn't breathe or possess lungs. "Looking forward to lunch in a bit?" the AI asked.

Zoe tilted her head. "Uh . . . sure. Actually, where do you guys usually sit?"

She wanted to know where we sit.

Why did she want to know where we sit?

I still was finding it difficult to say anything, so Zeke stepped in. "In the back corner. Under the giant Dr. Parkman banner. You're welcome to join us if you want."

She smiled, which made me smile.

"I think I might. I'm really interested in your project, Balt. If, you know, you wouldn't mind telling me all about it."

My lips made the motion to say something, but again my throat was dry and unable to force out any sound. Tern chimed in, "Of course he would love to tell you about his project . . . and what Smith's directives are."

"NO!" I blurted out. "I mean, uh, yer . . . yes," I didn't know what else to do, so I smiled again.

Zoe squinted her eyes. "Nova. Alright, well, see you then."

When she left, I turned back in my chair toward Smith, who didn't appear pleased. "Balt, next time try doing more than blurting out random sounds. Usually one has to be able to speak coherently in order to make someone fall in love with them."

"Listen to the robot, Balt," Zeke said, massaging my shoulders. "The window of opportunity has presented itself."

"I dislike you both . . . so much . . ." I said, trying to contain my rage.

Smith tried to give me some advice on what to speak about

during lunch, but I opted to just shut him down and return him to my bag. I watched the clock tick. Zoe left with a group of girls when the lab period ended and we followed from a safe distance to the mess hall. They were serving chicken curry, one of my favorites, but I just stared at my food when I got to my seat. The roiling mass of anxiety in my stomach contraindicated even the thought of eating.

"Feed the body," the prerecorded Dr. Parkman voice announced over the speakers, "feed the mind. Find your way to live forever."

"Female approaching, three o'clock," Tern noted with a mouth full. Zoe waved and sat down across from me next to Zeke. I suddenly became very aware of my posture and sat up, the chair making a notable squeak despite the din of the mess hall.

"So . . . how's your adjustment to Level F going? We engineers aren't too dull, are we?" Zeke asked.

"It's alright. I miss the vegetation and wildlife, but there are some interesting things here too. Your testing arena is nicer than ours. I heard that there are even entrances to the Old Lab in there, too. Pretty wild."

"Yes," Tern said. "They're all sealed though, so we don't have to worry about robots storming in and turning us to molecular dust or anything like that."

"Where are they exactly?" she asked casually.

Tern and Zeke looked at each other, trying to remember. I caught myself staring at Zoe and diverted my eyes toward my meal. I could barely glance at her without my cheeks turning red. She was thermal indeed.

"Near the strip, right?" Tern asked Zeke, who replied vaguely with a grunt. "Yes, there's a long tunnel on the north side of the arena. It's along there somewhere. Haven't been near it since I was assigned to test those rocket packs last year."

Zeke chuckled. "That was a messy one. They were still finding pieces of you weeks later."

"Speaking of which, I left my work table a mess in the lab. Zeke, will you head back with me to help clean up?"

"What? No way!" Zeke shot back. Tern grimaced at him after making an obvious motion toward me. I felt my face turn bright red and it still took Zeke a second to put the data together. "Oh, I mean, yeah. Sure . . . pal. See you, Balt. It was nice talking to you, Zoe."

Zoe waved to them and, before I knew it, we were alone—or as alone as it was possible to be in the crowded mess hall. She rotated a spoon in what looked like tomato soup and I watched her fingers moving adeptly.

"So what gave you the idea for the project?" she asked. She was so close I could see that her eyes were lighter than I originally thought. A more accurate description would be an aqua blue.

"I'm not sure exactly," I shrugged, attempting to compose myself as I felt my heart rate increase. "I believe it began with the concept of doing something which could benefit mankind, as they remind us often. I did some historical research and found that many pre-war conflicts were won due to a 'symbolic catalyst.' These were events, which in themselves, were not especially important in a literal sense, but acted as a motivating factor for others. When applying that concept to the Institute's current situation, it appeared that reclaiming the old labs, along with the elimination of a practical threat, could serve as a morale boost to everyone down here. It could be taken as an interpretation that we're conquering the past."

"That's pretty ambitious."

"Yes," I said, trying to fight back a smile. "I'm starting to believe it was a bit too ambitious."

She questioned me regarding every aspect of my project, from building and programming Smith to what PISS knew of the variant AI. I thought that a student from Level H would find the technical aspects rather boring, but she appeared to be legitimately interested in everything I had to say. Speaking about something I knew so well helped me build a sense of confidence and, soon, I worked up the courage to turn the microscope toward her. I couldn't waste this opportunity to find out more about her.

"So I notice you do a lot of drawing on your datapad during class," I stated. "May I see some of your drawings?"

Her head cocked back. "Really? You want to see them?"

"Of course," I said, nodding. "We don't see much artwork on this level. It's not exactly a hobby you see explored very often."

She presented her datapad and scrolled through some of the drawings she had done, the lines and colors instantly catching my eyes among the mute colors of the mess hall. They were all of animals, some that I recognized and others that I did not. I knew that the wonder of art was supposed to be in the emotional response it elicited and, looking at these pictures now, I felt nothing. However, my breath stirred as I listened to her talk about her work. The edges of her mouth curled into a smile as she spoke about it. In my case, it was the artist, not the art, that elicited all the emotion I needed.

"I dunno," she sighed, her confidence flagging as she

continued. "I'm sure they're not very good compared to what people created before the war, but I like drawing."

"Why do you think that?"

She looked down to the table, and I could tell the gears were turning in her mind. "I think . . . sometimes the world just isn't as beautiful as it is in my mind. And I want to create something that shows how I see it."

A quote from my organic chemistry book popped into my mind. "The world is full of magic things, patiently waiting for our senses to grow sharper."

She seemed to understand the thought, nodding slowly. "I guess it's up to us to find those things."

"Our responsibility," I added. "It's how we can 'live forever.'"

We spoke until it was time for the afternoon testing sessions. She showed me more of her drawings and I showed her some schematics I had created for Smith—the closest thing I had to art. When the bell rang, I offered to walk with her to her appointment with a Dr. Grima, but she declined. I could tell she was pleased that I offered, though. I believed that she had enjoyed our conversation too. She waved to me as we departed, and this time I hoped that I wouldn't have to get reconstructed later in the arena. I didn't want to risk losing any bit of my time with her in the transition.

ZOE

Instead of his usual probing questions, Dr. Grima asked me to play him some of the music I was restoring for my project. I pulled up what I had on my datapad and streamed it to his speakers. He would comment here or there, but mostly he just sat back in his chair, his arms folded and thumbs feeling the material of his tweed jacket as he listened. I tucked my knees to my chest and listened to the words, escaping inside them for a bit.

"I like this one a lot," I said after I played him a restored track I called "Pocket of Secrets." It was full of electronic beats accompanied by a female singer, her voice sounding upbeat and cheerful as she sung. The actual lyrics told another story though. To the world, she appeared just like a normal girl, but inside she was anything but. She had a "pocket of secrets" that she dared not let anyone know.

I could relate.

"Interesting song" Dr. Grima mused, twirling a pen in one hand. "Do you think a lot of people do that? Act one way but feel something completely different on the inside?"

I shrugged, trying not to give anything away. "I think everyone has secrets. And sometimes, you just need to put on a show for others to keep them."

"A necessary part of life, sometimes."

"For some more than others."

Shut up, Zoe.

I switched tracks and we stayed like that, listening to music in his bright office. Dr. Grima didn't ask me how I felt or how I was coping or anything like that. We just sat and listened until time was up and he reminded me of our appointment tomorrow.

I nodded and smiled, doing my best to keep the tune in my head all the way back to the dorms. Today wasn't such a bad day, I though. Talking to Balt was definitely a smart move. He was the classic advanced Institute student, overly logical with everything and sounding like a walking datapad. The AI he'd created would be perfect for getting through the old labs. Although it wasn't finished, it could lead me along and notify me of variants close by, giving me a chance to hide. It wasn't the perfect plan, but it was looking like the best shot I had.

I realized there was something more to Balt though, the more I thought about him. I liked the way he looked at me. Cindee was nice enough, but I knew I was still the "other" in the eyes of her and her friends, this thing from Level H they were trying to understand. During my conversation with Balt, I didn't get that sense. His curiosity felt more rooted in *who* I was. It helped me remember that *Project Wind* wasn't who I was. That the last few weeks didn't have to define me. It was a warm feeling that made me feel rooted to myself again. Maybe, if things were different, he could help me blossom again.

But things weren't different.

I headed back to the dorms and felt the world crash around me at the sight of the ghouls Herzman and Lebowitz waiting near the entrance, their eyes growing wide at the sight of me. They looked paler than usual, too. Maybe it was a sign that they had finally found a way to rid themselves of the last bit of humanity left in them. A bad sign for me. I felt frozen in place and they didn't waste any time swooping in for the kill.

I took a deep breath.

The dead-leaf katydid could adapt itself, from its color to its posture, in order to hide from predators. It could perfectly mimic its environment. It did such an excellent job camouflaging itself that scientists found it nearly impossible to accurately determine the size of its population. It was almost as if they were made of glass, almost invisible until the light shone the right way.

"Good afternoon, Zoe," Dr. Herzman hissed. "How was your session with Dr. Grima?"

I stayed frozen in place, barely daring to breathe. If I tried hard enough, maybe I could be almost invisible too.

"Not productive then, I take it," Dr. Lebowitz surmised and took my wrist, feeling my pulse. Her hand was ice cold. I pulled my arm away but still didn't look at them. "Nonetheless, we were hoping you would give us some time this evening and help us with an experiment."

The way the word *experiment* rolled off her tongue sent chills down my spine. I started feeling like I was visible again and exposed, so I shut my eyes. "I have a lot of work to do."

"Oh, don't worry about that. Your professor is Dr. Douffman?" Dr. Herzman asked.

I nodded ever so slightly.

"Yes, don't worry. We'll send her a message that you helped us with a very important project. You do know what we're referring to, yes?"

I did know. I could never forget.

"*Project Wind* will change everything, Zoe," Dr. Lebowitz said. She put her arm around me and they started leading me away from the dorm. I wanted to run and scream until my voice cracked, but there was nowhere to go. The harder I fought, the tighter they would squeeze. "With Helena gone," she reminded me, "you are the only one with whom we have had any success. We know this isn't easy, but we need you to be brave."

"For mankind," Dr. Herzman said.

Dr. Lebowitz repeated the words, as if they were meant to put me in a trance. As if it made anything and everything they did to me okay.

They led me to the other side of Level F, taking a faculty lift further underground. They didn't say where they were taking me, but did they have to? I knew where this trip ended. I felt like my hands were shaking so I buried them in my pockets. I didn't want to give them the satisfaction of knowing I was scared.

With a ding, the lift opened on Level H. Home. Although it hadn't been long, the white halls seemed darker than I remembered. More grim. We passed the Grand Gardens, the largest green habitat in the Institute that stretched as far as the eye could see. All my life I had wandered its paths with hopes of getting lost amid the trees, but now I couldn't even register them. I was focused on the chamber behind the black wall of the testing arena. A place where the air was cold and smelled of chemicals.

Drs. Herzman and Lebowitz swiped their ID cards to get past two security guards and I was back in their lab, the walls covered with glowing green monitors standing at the ready. They pointed to a window and I looked through the glass, surveying a dark spherical room.

"The secret lies inside you, my dear," Dr. Lebowitz explained. "We've gone through the data forwards and backward and, besides your eye pigment, there's nothing clearly different in your genes from the rest of your class. Therefore, we believe that the answer must lie in something even deeper. Inside your very being."

I closed my eyes again and just listened to the sound of my breath. The air in my lungs going in and out. Out and in, like every other person did. Dr. Herzman began to explain what the sphere did, but I just blocked it out. I didn't want to know. With a wrinkled hand, he led me inside and shut the door behind me with a thud.

The room was so cold that I could see my breath in the thin air, the only light coming from a small window that showed the lab through which I entered. I approached and watched them fiddle with consoles, standing suddenly upright. They were speaking to someone, but the walls were so thick no sound made it to my ears.

And then I saw him.

It was a little surreal at first. I'd seen the face so many times, I would recognize it anywhere. Anyone would. But even with him standing there, staring right at me, I didn't believe it. It felt like I was seeing a figment of my imagination. Something too grand to be real. He never broke eye contact with me as he said something to Dr. Herzman, who turned a knob on his console.

Then it came like a wall of fire.

A surge ran through my body, making my face and hands

twitch. I could feel my hair fraying. For a second, I could even smell it burn. I hunched over in a desperate attempt to catch my breath, but then it happened again. The second wave pushed me down to my knees and I was so weak I couldn't even scream.

The waves kept coming faster and faster and soon it was almost like all the atoms in my body were being pulled apart, dissected one by one. I lost sense of everything. My mind unfolded itself and soon I didn't know who I was anymore. Why I was here and where here was. I didn't know if I was real and this was all a nightmare, or if the nightmare was truth and I was just part of it, a phantom of someone else's worst nightmare.

My mouth tried desperately to form the words to beg them to stop, but my voice was gone, almost like it never existed. I couldn't see him, but I could feel his stare through the blur of light shining down on me as the waves of fire kept coming. Still watching. Always watching.

I don't remember the waves stopping. Or them picking me up and taking me back to Level F. Or them leaving me in front of the dorms. I just stood there like a zombie staring at the front doors of my dorm building. Hours passed and only one thought crawled through my hallow head.

If there was anything left inside me, it would soon be gone.

BALTAZAR

"Well done, Balt. Well done, indeed," Smith congratulated from his spot on my dresser. "I knew you could make some progress with Zoe if you could just start speaking coherently." Zeke, Tern, and I were all crammed inside the communal bathroom between our rooms, our elbows bumping into each other as we scrubbed our teeth.

"Thank you, Smith."

"Now, do you think you'll be able to ride this wave of confidence and build me a body anytime soon?"

I spat a wad of toothpaste into the sink. "Right. I still need to do that, don't I?"

"Not that I'm complaining or anything. It's just fine rolling around like an egg on your dresser all afternoon. However, there is a remote chance my IQ of two hundred and fifty might be better served in other means."

Zeke waved his fist through the air. "My sarcasm detector is blowing up right now."

Tern finished rinsing out his mouth. "I'll lend you a hand on our next personal day to finish him up if you want, Balt."

I smiled. Sometimes my friends weren't complete malfunctions. "Thanks, Tern. Did you take note of that, Zeke? That's evidence of true friendship."

"Oh, please. I had your back at lunch!"

"Yeah," Tern laughed. "Although I wonder if you would have actually helped me clean my workstation if circumstances were different."

"Tern, why ask yourself questions to which you already know the answer?"

I walked over to Smith and played a drum roll next to him, causing him to wobble. "I'll have a body for you very soon, Smith. Although you'll most likely be decommissioned once Dr. Douffman discovers that one of your main directives is to win the affection of a female. But at least you won't be forced to roll into the scrapper."

"Forever the optimist," Smith answered.

I began to dress for bed, but noticed that the data disk on AI tendencies I borrowed from Ash a few days ago was still on my desk. It wasn't a priority, but I was feeling too full of energy to sleep just yet. I decided to return it.

Noticing me put on my slippers, Zeke asked me to bring him a snack from the dispenser, preferably one that was high in sodium.

"And a chocolate bar!" Tern yelled as I shut the door behind me. Normally I would deny their requests for "junk food" at such an hour on the grounds of looking out for their physical well-being, but my success with Zoe had me in such a mood that I thought I would even get something for myself. Something sweet perhaps.

I headed up two floors and stopped when I caught a glimpse of someone sitting on the landing above me. Whoever it was didn't say anything, but was curled into a ball in the corner. Their back was against the metal wall and had their head down, hidden in their hands. I didn't say anything and proceeded onward to Ash's room to slip the disk under her door, but paused on the way back for a more thorough observation.

The white hair was enough.

Zoe didn't appear to be crying, but from her posture I could tell something had happened. Something bad. Her shoulders were slumped and she resembled a collapsed mass more than a person. It was odd seeing her like that. For the first time, she was not larger than life to my eyes. I approached her slowly but she didn't say anything, or even seem to register I was there.

"Zoe?" I called out. She didn't flinch.

I waited a few seconds before repeating her name softly, but again received no response. Then, biting my bottom lip, I took a seat adjacent to her, noticing now that she was twitching ever so slightly.

"Are you okay?"

She still didn't say anything. Her pale hand was perched on her knee and I took it in mine, trying to read her pulse. Her skin was ice cold. She pulled it away as if my touch was uncomfortable and finally looked at me. A sensation like electricity sparked through my chest at the sight of her, so close to me. But there was something different about her now, I realized. It was as if a light behind her aqua blue eyes had faded.

"Is everything alright?" I asked.

She just stared at me, not blinking. Not breathing. It was scary, actually. It was almost as if she was a replica of a person, not flesh and blood. Finally, she took a breath. "Balt?"

"Yes," I tried saying but realized nothing came out of my mouth, as if her breath took mine. I swallowed hard and it felt like a bunch of gears tore down my throat. "Are you okay?"

Her lips moved, but then she stopped herself, closing her eyes. She took my hand and I helped her to her feet. When we stood, she looked around, appearing as if she didn't know where she was.

"Would you like my help getting to your room? Would you like me to get one of the professors?"

At the mention of the word "professor," she shook her head violently. "No!" she coughed forcefully. "No, none of them."

"Okay, okay," I assured her. "How can I help you?"

She looked at me again and squinted, like she was examining me. "I can't go . . ." she started to say before putting her head down, rubbing her temples. "Just take me to your room."

My first thought was: Protocol #791: *any student found in another's room at night shall be issued a citation.*

The second: Screw it.

"Uh, yes," I stammered, "sure. Definitely." I slowly led her down the stairs. She took every one gingerly, as though she were testing out the surface of each to insure she wouldn't go straight through one. Thankfully, we didn't encounter anyone in the halls, but I stopped in front of my room before heading inside. "Just give me a moment."

She leaned against the wall, nodding with her palms against the white glass. In one swift motion, I headed inside the room, looking around frantically and shutting the door behind me.

"No snacks?" Tern asked.

"I need you to sleep in Zeke's room tonight."

All tucked into bed, my roommate looked up from his dat-apad. "What?"

I motioned behind me. "Zoe's outside."

"Wh-what?" he repeated and suddenly Zeke poked his head from his room opposite the bathroom.

"Wait? What?" Zeke asked in a poor attempt at a whisper. "You man-beast!"

I shook my head. "No, it's not like that. Something's wrong."

"Yeah, something's wrong," Zeke responded, dancing into our room. "You aren't in bed with her yet! Boom!"

"But Zeke doesn't even have a second bed," Tern rationalized.

"We can cuddle," Zeke answered, the thought clearly making Tern nauseous.

Smith, still on top of my dresser, asked. "Is it safe to say Directive 2 will be accomplished shortly?"

"No!" In frustration, I hit Smith's power switch at the base of his neck and then knelt in front of Tern. "In all seriousness, I will owe you for this."

Tern thought for a second and huffed before dragging a pillow and sheet with him through the bathroom. Zeke sung, "Balt's gonna transfer some fluids!" and made one last inquiry on the status of his snack before I shut and locked the door. It was quiet then and I opened the entrance again, finding Zoe right where I'd left her.

"Sorry, come in," I said. She did so without looking at me.

My room wasn't a complete scrap yard, but I was suddenly embarrassed by the clothes on the floor and various pieces of school equipment scattered about. Zoe didn't appear to take notice though. She just stood in the middle of the room and only moved when she caught a glimpse of herself in my wall mirror. Inch by inch, she moved closer, eventually reaching out her hand to touch the glass.

"Do you want to tell me what happened?" I asked quietly.

She continued to stare at herself in the mirror, dragging her fingers ever so slightly over the glass. "Is this . . . real?"

I didn't say anything at first. I didn't know what to say, quite honestly. Besides, I was trying to think of a plausible explanation of her behavior. Maybe she'd had to test this afternoon and was experiencing a side effect of a drug. Or maybe whatever had happened on Level H was starting to really sink in. I ran my hands over my head, feeling the sensation of the short hairs bend against my skin. "Yes, this is real. You're in the dorms."

Zoe blinked several times before sitting in the middle of the floor. She tucked her knees to her chest and rocked slightly. "Your room is kind of messy." Her voice was still soft, but it was the first thing that began to resemble the Zoe I knew.

"Yes," I grinned. "I'm sorry about that."

"It's fine. I'm not the neatest person myself."

I debated whether to ask her if she wanted to talk about what happened again, but instead I just sat across from her, our toes touching ever so slightly. She grabbed one of mine in between hers and squeezed. "Ouch," I laughed.

A slight smile curled onto her lips, but she still didn't look at me. "Sorry." She wiped her eyes and I saw a tear fall onto her hand before she quickly covered it up.

We were silent for a bit and I struggled with what to say. I thought of the emotional toll the past few weeks must have caused her. No one used the word "family" in the Institute, but it was an unspoken understanding that our classmates were probably the closest thing we would ever have to that sort of relationship. What was there to say to a girl who'd lost her whole family? Thoughts of losing Zeke and Tern felt foreign, almost impossible. I couldn't remember a time when we weren't together. If I did lose them, would I be struggling to grasp what was real too?

"Do you want to listen to some music?" I asked, thinking of her sitting in the lab with her headphones on. "I have some pre-war tracks. Not much."

She didn't look at me but she said, "Sure."

I rose and pulled up the files on my datapad, electronic tones pouring out of my speakers as a male singer slowly sang about a failed relationship. No matter how hard he tried, he couldn't escape his past.

"I know this song," she said, her head rising up. She looked at me and I thought I was going to melt. "It's good."

"Yes," I concurred. "I don't know who sang it, but I enjoy it."

"The Broken Robots. Or, at least that's what I call them. I recovered a few things from them. A lot of their songs have these deep bass sounds like they're broken robots trying to reboot themselves."

I nodded, the bass notes filling my ears. We didn't say anything at first, just listening to the music. Soon I walked back over to her again so we were sitting face to face with our toes touching.

"Do you ever get the desire to escape?" she asked, her gaze directed toward our feet.

I sighed, the checklist of all the things I needed to get done forever imbued on the back of my mind. "Of course, especially when responsibilities and expectations appear to build up. I think it's natural."

"No, I mean *really* escape. Like not just this place, but from people too. Forever. Find some corner of this world where no one can get to you, no one can ever hurt you, ever make you feel anything . . . just exist numbly in this space that is yours." She appeared to dwell on that thought before shaking her head.

I wasn't sure how to respond. The song kept building and I reached for her hands, holding them up and pressing hers against mine like we were on opposite sides of a wall. She looked at me and I looked at her. I wanted to say I was sorry for happened to her. I was sorry for whatever was still happening to her. I wanted to say that I was willing to do whatever I could to help her and make some of that pain go away. I wanted to tell her that the future was promising and as beautiful as the art she created and things were going to get better.

Instead we just sat like that until the music ended. But in many ways, I felt like she knew what I was thinking.

After a few more moments, Zoe crawled into my bed and picked up the empty digital picture frame sitting on my night-stand, checking to make sure it was on. I gulped. How to explain this without seeming like a quark?

"It reminds me of my parents," I explained after she held it up to me. "Reminds me that I came from somewhere, that there's life outside the Institute and what we are doing here is ultimately for them." I thought of them working under the dome, picturing their outlines as they worked tirelessly. I hoped, just for a second, that they thought of the boy they gave up. The boy who had never met them, but who would never forget them. "I know Dr. Parkman wants us to live forever through our work. It's the ultimate goal. I just . . . think that family is important too. Being part of one and continuing it is another way to live forever."

She didn't say anything, just nodded and put the frame gently back where she found it. I stood still, debating what to do next. My first instinct was to get in right beside her in my bed, drape my arm around her and hold her close. But I wasn't sure that's what she wanted or was here for. In the end, I lay down in Tern's bed and just watched her sleep before my own eyes felt too heavy to stay awake, the night passing by in a dreamless flash.

My alarm sounded in the morning and I walked over to the beeping wall clock, rubbing the sleep out of my eyes. When I looked over, I saw that she was gone, my invisible parents watching her empty pillow. There wasn't a note or any sign that she had ever been here. For a second, I wondered whether the whole experience was just a dream. I showered and changed, deflecting questions from my roommates until I had my bag in my hand, ready to depart for the day's lecture and classes. It was only then that I realized I was missing one key item.

The top of my dresser was bare.

Smith was gone.

ZOE

After scurrying back to my room, I hurriedly typed a message about feeling ill to Dr. Douffman. She responded promptly with, "I'm sorry to hear that. Drs. Herzman and Lebowitz said you helped them with a project and might be feeling a little bit out of it today. I've attached your assignments for now. Make sure you head to the medical wing if your symptoms linger."

I focused on the phrase "a little bit out of it" and wanted to find those two monsters and claw their faces off, hurt them as much as I could before guards dragged me away, thrashing and screaming. But true revenge was surviving. Escaping. I had to remember that.

I took a break from my violent fantasy and sat in the tub with the shower running, staring at the tiled wall and hoping this would be the one place I could have some semblance of privacy, where I wouldn't feel the eyes of Dr. Parkman watching me.

The events of the last twelve hours felt like a blur. I still couldn't remember exactly what happened on Level H. I remembered the doctors and feeling afraid. And the room. That dark, cold spherical room. I couldn't fully figure out how I ended up in Balt's room, though. Was *he* part of it? No, he seemed too innocent for that. I remembered the empty picture frame that sat near his bed. A reminder that there was more beyond these walls.

He definitely had the right idea.

Stealing his AI probably wasn't the best way to thank him for taking me in last night. Just thinking of him waking up to find his midterm project gone made my stomach clench under the guilt, but this was survival of the fittest. If I was going to get out of here, I had to be willing to do anything.

I turned up the temperature of the water and emerged from the shower after the steam fogged all the mirrors and, hopefully, any cameras that were watching. After wrapping a towel around myself, I pulled my dripping wet hair into a ponytail and took the AI head out of my bag. I quickly connected it to my datapad to monitor his coding and make sure it wasn't sending a warning signal out or anything like that. Thankfully, the initial boot looked clean. The AI was completely autonomous, without any needed connection to the Parkman database or anything else that might let it be tracked. When the boot finished, its white eyes glowed and widened at the sight of me.

"Oh, um . . . hello, Zoe," it said.

"Hi. I'm sorry. I don't remember your name. Sam?"

"Smith," it corrected. "Is it polite to ask why you're half naked with me in a sauna?" The lens in its eyes zoomed in and out, trying to adjust to the fog.

My instinct was to lie. Tell it that Balt wanted me to take it to the old labs to complete his project. That it was for the good of PISS, or mankind, or some garbage like that. But if Balt was half as good at programming as people said he was, Smith would be smart enough to see through my ruse. And if it indeed had a genome implantation, empathy was probably my best shot to get it on my side.

"I need your help, Smith," I whispered. "I need to get to the surface, and the old labs seem like the only possible way to get there undetected. You know the layout and can track any variant AI in proximity, right?"

Smith blinked several times. I could tell the implications of what I was saying needed some time to process. "Um," it stuttered softly. "Well, yes. Within a fifty meter area, but that isn't much when you compare it to how fast they can travel. Not to mention the conditions of the old labs are most likely deplorable by this point. They will not be easy to traverse, especially for me 'sans' body. May I ask *why* you need to get to the surface?"

I felt the muscles in my neck twitch as the vague memory of the dark metal room resurfaced again. And a pair of eyes, watching.

"Because I'm in danger. There are scientists here who are torturing me and I'm not going to let them continue."

"Well, if you feel that is the case, you can go to the advisory board or . . ." it began to suggest, but I cut it off, shaking my head.

"There are no other options, Smith. They killed my class-mates and they won't stop until they get what they want from me so they can finish *Project Wind*. This is the only way. You help me do this, and you'll get to track the AIs there like you're programmed to do. Win-win for both of us."

"*Project Wind*," it repeated, computing. "I don't have a re-cord of anything by that name. What is it?"

Another twitch. My wall grew higher.

"If I told you that, you really would think I was crazy."

"As opposed to now," it joked, but turned off its smile when it saw my stony expression. Smith's eyes drifted downward, thinking. Then they looked right to left, surveying the floor. "Well, it's not like I have a choice in the matter, now do I?"

I smiled. "Not exactly. No."

"Well, coming with you will allow me to complete one of my directives so, sure. Why not? When do we go?"

"Tonight."

"Tonight . . . as in later this very day?"

I nodded, the prospect of leaving feeling suddenly exciting, liberating.

"Oh. Oh dear. Are we prepared?"

"I just need to grab some supplies and find a way to get through the doors in the back of the testing arena."

"Hmmm," Smith answered, processing what needed to be done. "That won't be easy. Not only is that concrete double enforced, it's magnetically sealed. It will take quite an impact to break through it, if that's what you're planning. And the journey through the labs won't be short with eight levels between the entrance and the surface exit. You might need supplies for several days."

"I'll take care of it," I said, trying to hide how nervous its logic was making me. But I couldn't wait any longer. I wouldn't. "I'm going to shut you off now. I'll see you when we're ready to go."

I reached for the power switch, but Smith shouted, "Wait, wait, hold on a second!"

"What? We don't have any time to waste."

Smith's eyes looked around, as if it was having trouble finding the words. "I think it . . . would be in your best interest to . . . consult Balt on this."

"What?" I asked, confused. "Balt's probably going to call security on me the second classes end. Why would he help me?"

Again, Smith looked around. I don't think even it knew the answer to my protests, which made me instantly suspicious. "It's . . . worth asking, no? He's resourceful and . . . smart, and I really do believe . . ."

I shook my head and just hit the power button, my patience officially spent. I slid Smith back into my bag with my datapad and turned on the overhead fan to get rid of the steam, pretending that I had just gotten out of the shower when the air cleared. I wiped the mirror and began to dry my hair, thinking hard as I stared into my reflection. A chill ran down my spine and I shivered. I looked paler than usual, the blue in my eyes a shade darker. Rather than dwelling on it, I finished drying off and changed. I had to stay focused.

Getting supplies wouldn't be too bad. Cinder was doing her midterm project on travel supplies, trying to condense more elaborate meals into small pills by reverse engineering and making adjustments to the nutrient pills in Parkman's popular "Wasteland Survival Kit." There were boxes upon boxes of those pills sitting at her workstation in the lab. They tasted like garbage, but they were easy to pack and would keep me alive for weeks.

The sealed doors to the old labs felt like the higher mountain to climb. I needed to know exactly what I was working with, I decided. I needed to survey the area.

When I was ready, I walked over to the observation deck, a glass hallway that hung above the massive testing arena where people could watch us be guinea pigs for an afternoon. I didn't see my class—my *new* class, that is—but there was another group down there testing some sort of variation of the experimental gel cushion I'd seen when I first got to Level F. It still didn't look like the scientists were getting anywhere, though. One by one, the kids jumped off the makeshift building and plummeted toward the ground.

For a second, I contemplated whether just jumping without nanomachines would be the better choice. Even if I got inside the old labs, the odds of making it through to the surface were minute. Microscopic.

If only I could just follow in Helena's shoes. Figure out how she did it.

I rubbed my right wrist and felt the foreign object still under the skin. Thankfully, in that dark room, the scanner the doctors used on me didn't detect the object. Or maybe it did, but they didn't consider it noteworthy. That second possibility was almost funny to think about. I thought back to the day Helena gave it to me and how it changed everything. After the countless injections and exposure to rays, which contained who knows what, we stood in those pristine white rooms that were so bright they almost blinded me. I remembered thinking how tired I was and how I just wanted to be back in my room, sleeping under my covers, smelling my sheets and thinking about absolutely nothing. It was all so vivid in my mind. And then it happened. I was . . .

"Zoe?" a voice interrupted.

I turned quickly, thrusting my hand into my pocket, hoping no one had seen me rubbing my wrist.

Dr. Grima stood before me. It was bizarre seeing him outside his office, like part of my brain just assumed that that was the only place he existed. He approached me in his usual jacket with elbow patches and leaned on the railing beside me, gazing out at the testing arena.

"Didn't go to lecture today?" he asked, watching the students jump and cringing when they made impact.

"No," I said, trying to sound sick. "I'm not feeling very well today. And I was starting to feel . . . uncomfortable in my room, so I decided on a walk."

He nodded, apparently buying my story. "Is there any particular reason you think you're not feeling well?"

I looked to him but he just kept looking out at the arena. If Dr. Douffman knew, he probably knew what happened, too. But he wanted me to say it. And I couldn't. Saying it made it more real, somehow. And I didn't want it to be real.

"No reason."

We stayed like that for a bit and I saw the tunnel where the boys said the old lab entrance was. It was toward the far side of the arena, wide and tall enough for a tram to pass through. Sneaking down to it without being noticed would be one thing, but doing any work on the door without anyone seeing me was something else entirely. The odds felt like they kept on building. I closed my eyes, trying to keep my wall up as high as I needed it to be without letting my worry pour out like a river.

"Have you ever read anything about the bar-tailed godwit?"

Dr. Grima's question caught me off guard and it took me a second to answer. "That was a bird, right?"

"Yes," he said, "quite an extraordinary one at that."

"What made it so extraordinary?"

Still watching the kids fall, he began, "It was the true king of the Pacific Ocean, a body of water that stretches thousands of miles and separates two continents."

"Is that what the picture you have above your desk is of?" I asked.

He smiled. "It is. Hopefully I'll be able to see it one day. But the bar-tailed godwit had not only seen it, but was recorded to have flown over it without ever once stopping for rest or food."

I cocked my head back. "How is that possible?"

Dr. Grima rolled his hand into a fist and gently tapped the glass. "Sheer determination, I suppose. The unrelenting desire to keep going."

I thought about his words for a while, picturing the bird with its wings outstretched, flying high above an endless blue sea. How tired it must have gotten. How many times it thought that it just needed to turn around or simply give up and plummet.

"I think it serves as a lesson for all of us, really," he went on. "Greatness is sometimes defined by simple determination, that strength to keep going when a task seems too difficult or impossible."

I felt a sweat build up on my forehead. Did he know that I was trying to escape? How could he? I was so careful. Did they all know?

Then Dr. Grima turned to me. "Don't give up, even when there might be others who are making things . . . harder for you. If you want it badly enough, you can do anything. Overcome *anyone*. Do you understand me?" He waited for me to nod to show that I understood, which I did after a few seconds. "You don't have to come by today if you're not feeling well. Rest. I'll see you tomorrow."

He waved as he left and I waved back. I stayed watching the arena for a while, taking some mental notes before moving to the lab when I knew my class was heading to the arena and wouldn't be there. I told the security personnel monitoring the hall I needed something from my worktable but grabbed as many of the nutrient pills from Cinder's desk that I could fit in my bag when they weren't looking. Of all the dangers that lay ahead, as long as I had these pills, starvation and dehydration wouldn't be one.

But no matter how hard I tried, I couldn't think of a way to get through the old lab seal, short of stealing some explosives from the testing arena supply room and setting them off. It seemed hopeless, but I told myself that if a bird could fly across the ocean like Dr. Grima said, I could break through a door and climb to the surface. I wanted it badly enough.

I headed back to my room, planning on grabbing Smith and making my way for the arena. The supply room inside contained tons of things used in experiments. There had to be something there I could use. But I stopped at the end of the hall on my floor when I caught sight of Balt standing outside my door. He didn't look too happy.

BALTAZAR

"Hello," I greeted Zoe, doing my best to sound casual although I was feeling anything but. "How are you? I mean, how are you feeling?"

She squinted, fidgeting with her bag. "Fine."

A silence settled over us and I shifted my stance, suddenly hyper aware of my hands and unsure of where to put them. I had rehearsed this conversation over and over in my head throughout the day. Now that the time had actually come to confront Zoe, my gears had stalled. Conflicting emotions battled within my head, but I did my best to ignore them. I was here for my AI. No need to over analyze anything else.

"You haven't seen Smith around, have you?" I asked, as if the answer wasn't obvious. I pictured him rolling off my dresser during the night with a clank, rotating his way out of my room and tumbling down the hallway in search of freedom. A truly unlikely scenario.

Zoe kept a straight face, looking me right in the eye the whole time. "No."

This was not going as I envisioned. Why wouldn't she just admit she took him? All the evidence indicated it. She spent all of lunch questioning me about Smith, down to the finest detail.

Then she asked to spend the night and suddenly, he was missing. My attraction to her may have clouded much of my judgment, but I wasn't a quark.

I swallowed, unsure of what to say next. I could feel my blood pressure rise, my heart increasing its pace. I wanted to be strong, assertive. But the words which finally found their way out of my mouth weren't reflective of that.

"Well, if you see him, can you let me know?"

Hypothesis: The subject, me, is a spineless worm.

"Sure," she said tersely, shifting her stance. "Is that all? I have a lot of work to catch up on."

Her gaze felt like a battering piston. "Yes, uh, sorry. Have a good evening."

I started walking down the hall in the opposite direction of the stairway I needed. I was so frazzled though that I didn't even realize it until I came to the lounge. Still, I wouldn't turn around. I didn't want her to see how crushed I was. I turned the corner to the lounge and moved out of view, leaning against the glass wall until I heard her door close. Then I rewarded myself by smacking my head against the glass, a great bong sound ringing throughout the floor.

Evidence to support hypothesis: subject cannot confront a girl he is attracted to despite the fact he knows she stole from him.

I replayed our lunch together, focusing more on the other implication her theft had. She wasn't interested in me. It was data acquisition, nothing more. I recalled the sensation of our toes touching, a possible precursor to more physical interaction. But it was nothing of the sort. Defense breaking. I tried tempering the sensations of anger building within me, but it cut my ability to think rationally. I had never felt this out of sorts before. I hated it.

"Argh!" I groaned. I bonked my head against the wall again, this time a lot harder. From the throbbing pain that resulted, I knew I'd overdone it.

After rubbing my forehead, I took a second to collect myself and made my way back to her room. I knocked hard on her door, a determined scowl on my face.

Variable: The subject returns to girl he is attracted to and is prepared to confront her with his evidence.

Zoe opened the door. "Balt," she greeted.

I pointed my finger at her as if I was prepared for a heat beam to fire out. But the edge on my words was softened. I believe it was look of her eyes. "I think that . . . um, you're not telling me the truth. Possibly."

Zoe squinted again behind the cracked door. "Possibly?"

Conclusion: Hypothesis confirmed. Only the smallest fractions of a spine have been detected.

I could feel my face running hot, my heart beating into overdrive. I ran my hands through my hair trying to regain a sense of balance. It was only then, face to face with her, that I began to consider the other part of the equation. Why *would* she take Smith? Or, better yet, why would she need Smith and have to lie about it to me?

"If you require Smith for something, that's fine. I hope he helps," I began to ramble. "While not finished, he's more than capable. It's just, I know you have him and would rather you just be honest with me on that point. You sought me out to ask about him, you asked to spend the night and were in the perfect position to take him. It's just . . . I greatly enjoyed my time with you and . . . it doesn't feel good to be lied to. If that's all you wanted from me fine, but please grant me more respect than this."

The moment my lips stopped moving I felt simultaneously relieved and devastated. I must have appeared like a broken android, spinning my gears. But I held my ground. I wanted the truth.

She looked at me and sighed, covering her eyes with one of her hands like she was tired. After a second, she began shaking her head as if she were furiously trying to tell herself 'no, no, no,' but instead she said, "I do have it. I'm sorry."

"Oh," was all I could muster at first. I got what I wanted, but it didn't stop this sinking feeling in my stomach. Coming clean didn't appear to have a positive effect on her either, the two of us just standing there, unsure of what to do next. Finally I asked, "Why did you take him?"

Then she looked at me with a steely stare. I felt exposed, naked, like in my dream. I could see her jaw tense up but she never broke her stare. Suddenly, as badly as I wanted to know what was going on, I was no longer certain I was ready for the answer.

"Can I trust you?"

I swallowed. "Yes. Yes, you can."

"You have a higher security level clearance, right?"

I felt in my pocket and pulled out the keycard Dr. Colonna had made me the day I completed the genome implantation, checking the expiration date on the back to make sure it was still good. "Yes, how did you know?"

"You just strike me as the type that would have been given one to do extra work or something."

I know I should have been insulted by that, but she was right. Clearly.

"I'm sorry," she said. "That didn't sound as rude in my head."

"It's fine. It's was an accurate presumption."

She looked up and down the hallway before turning back to me, giving me one last squinting stare. Dropping her voice to a bare whisper, she said, "Meet me in the bio lab in about fifteen minutes. Leave the door cracked and make sure no one sees you go in." Then she shut the door, leaving the silence of the hall to fill my ears. I wasted no time heading down to the labs, both excited and terrified about our secret and highly illicit meeting. It was foolish, but I couldn't help but think that maybe she wasn't *not* interested in me after all. It appeared there was just more going on than I thought.

I quickened my pace, going as fast as I could without being in an obvious hurry to anyone who passed by.

When I rounded the corner near the bio lab, I stopped in front of the door and listened for footsteps, waiting until it was quiet before swiping my clearance card and sliding inside, leaving the door cracked as Zoe had instructed me to do. Once inside, I turned on the lights and paced about the room, hypothesizing what Zoe was going to tell me. Was she working on a project that would need an AI? Maybe something with her midterm? Then why the secrecy?

Time crawled by, and by the time Zoe walked in, I was half expecting that I worn a furrow in the floor from my pacing. Before I could say anything, she put her finger to her lips. She closed the door behind her and turned off the lights, leaving the lab completely dark. I could hear the sound of her shoes squeaking against the spotless floor, drawing nearer until I felt her hand grab my arm. She pulled me under one of the work desks. Unable to see, I misjudged its height and smacked my head against the top while going under. "Aagh!" I groaned. At this rate, I was going to develop a concussion.

Zoe turned on her datapad and the soft blue light illuminated her face. "Are you okay?"

"Yes," I said, rubbing my head. "I think I've just taken too many knocks to the head today."

She pulled Smith out of her bag and turned him on, the white lights of his eyes glowing. He blinked several times before registering us, adjusting to the darkness.

"Balt!" he exclaimed before Zoe shushed him. "Oh right, sorry, sorry, sorry. All secrecy and whatnot. I'm glad you consulted Balt, though. I knew he would help. Are we all ready?"

"Consulted me about what?" I whispered. Zoe reached her arm over the desk and grabbed what looked like a small electron microscope, plopping the device down in between us. She then closed her eyes for a second, taking a deep breath. "What I'm about to tell you stays between us. No one else can know. Not Zeke or Tern, and especially not anyone with the Institute. Do I have your word on that? Both of you?"

Somewhere in the darkness, I had the sudden sensation that someone was watching us. I turned and saw nothing, wondering if it was the eyes of the Dr. Parkman's picture hanging on the wall, trying to monitor us through the black. But it was just a picture, I reassured myself.

Smith and I glanced at each other before looking back at her.

"Yes," I conceded. What choice did I have, really? My curiosity was piqued too much to walk away now.

"Certainly," Smith concurred.

She swallowed and began scratching her wrist, her nails digging into her skin. Her motions were so forceful that I reached over to stop her before she hurt herself.

"It's prosthetic," she explained. "I hid it under here to keep it a secret."

"Hid what?" I asked.

She pulled away a layer of fake skin, revealing her wrist intact underneath and placing the object that had been hidden there in the palm of my hand. I examined it closely, tilting it back and forth in an effort to see better.

"What? What is it?" Smith asked impatiently.

I held the small strip in between my fingers in front of them. It was so delicate and thin I was nervous that I was going to drop it.

"Is that—" Smith began before Zoe cut him off.

"A blade of grass," she said.

ZOE

Smith began scanning the grass, emitting small lasers from its eyes that ran over the small strand in Balt's fingers. My heart beat faster just looking at it. Still, I couldn't help but worry I was making a mistake. That the more people I got involved, the more likely word would get out. Or that more people would get hurt. But I didn't have a choice. Balt wouldn't let me swipe his midterm project without a legitimate reason, and there was nothing more legitimate than the truth.

Rather than being blown away by the blade of glass, the two of them just turned to me, and Balt placed it gingerly back into my hand. "I'm not sure I understand," he stammered, sounding somewhat dejected.

"It's just grass," Smith concurred.

"There are fields of vegetation like this on Level H, no?" Balt went on.

"Plus it's pretty much dead," added Smith.

I shook my head. "You two aren't getting it." Slipping the blade under the slide of the electron microscope, I turned the device on for Balt. While he adjusted the objectives, I hooked up my datapad so he could see the file entry on it.

Smith rolled its eyes. "No offense, Balt, but shouldn't we be letting the superior intelligence here take a look?"

"Just a second," he replied, focusing in on the blade. His eyes never blinked and I could tell the gears in his brain were turning at max speeds. I was starting to see why everyone said he was such a star student. He had a level of focus that was uncanny, like he was able to tap into a part of himself specifically designed for problem solving. I could almost feel it when he figured it out. "This wasn't grown here."

"What? Come now, let me examine it," Smith clamored. I removed the slide, letting the AI scan it once again. "Hmmm, fine texture. Durable," Smith determined. Its eyes turned a shade of blue as it zoomed in. "Ah, I see now, Balt. Artificial light wouldn't produce this kind of cellular growth. Or these pronounced vacuoles. Probably requires a lot of water to thrive fully. Species: Smooth Cordgrass, which according to my database—"

"Is extinct," Balt finished, reading the information I'd pulled up on my datapad. "Eradicated during the Final War."

"Odd," Smith concluded.

Balt turned to me. I could see a sense of uneasiness settling over him. "Where did you get this?"

"From my best friend, Helena," I explained.

"Where did *she* get it?"

"The surface." As the word left my lips, I could feel a flutter in my chest. I had seen the grazing fields on Level H countless times, but the thought of a field full of this grass up above, wild and pristine, was almost too much to comprehend. An endless sea of green, with an ocean of blue above.

"That can't be," Balt began, moving his hands about as he spoke. "The fallout from the war created dust clouds that blocked out the sun. The rain's acidic. There's no way something like this could have grown on the surface."

"Not unless Parkman is lying to us." There. I'd said it. It was out there. And it felt equally exhilarating and terrifying.

A palpable silence ensued that was broken only when Smith let out a low whistle. "That's quite an accusation, Zoe."

"Think about it. We've been in this underground lab our entire lives. Everything we learn, everything we believe, comes from Parkman. How do we really *know* what's happening up there?" I spoke confidently but Balt just kept shaking his head.

"That doesn't make sense. Why would we be down here if the surface were fully habitable again? What does Parkman have to gain by lying to us?"

I was startled to hear a suggestion come from Smith. "Autonomy?"

"What?" Balt shot back.

Smith rolled its eyes. "Well, it makes sense when you think about it. Experimenting 101: no regulation. The more freedom, the better. And where is there more freedom to do whatever you like than a facility hidden underground?"

The suggestion seemed like a thorn in Balt's mind, forcing him to rub his temples. He squashed the seed before it could be planted, continuing to shake his head. "But we're not hidden. What about the surviving cities? Our . . . parents? Wouldn't they try to get word to us down here if they knew we were being lied to?"

"You know the policy on communication with the surface, Balt," I reminded him.

"I know, I know," he replied. "Protocol #504: *Contact with the surface creates longing and is best avoided*. But why would ex-students lie to us, too? After turning eighteen and heading up, why wouldn't they try to get word to us that we were being lied to?"

"Maybe, if they're not all dead, they're in on it," I interjected.

My words dug the thorns deeper, but he needed to see what felt so clear to me.

"Look, Balt. I don't have all the answers. But I know what Helena said she saw was real. I know that this blade of grass came from the surface and that means things up there are not what they are telling us. They *murdered* her—and the rest of my class—to keep it a secret," I revealed, the words instantly feeling heavy in the air. Like acknowledging the truth had killed them all over again.

"I was chosen at random for a drug test, they said," I recounted, my lungs seeming to fill with water as I went on. "They injected me with something and the next thing I knew, I had been asleep for hours and there had been an 'accident' in the testing arena. The first nanomachine malfunction in the Institute's history." I shook my head to vent some of my anger. "Bullcrap. They knew Helena had seen something she shouldn't have and killed her and anyone she might have told. But they still needed me to continue their experiment."

"This *Project Wind* you speak of?" Smith offered.

I nodded. "You saw what they can do to me, Balt, last night," I said, looking into his eyes. "It's like living in a nightmare. I *won't* let them get their hands on me again. I need to get out of here. Through the old labs. That's why I need Smith. I just don't have a choice."

I knew it was an unfair position to put him in, dumping all of this on him. Unlike me, he still had everything to lose. He still had a future. If the Institute realized he knew I was trying to escape, who knew what they would do to him? He didn't even know me. I was just some girl who transferred into his class.

He had a million reasons to say no.

"Okay," he concluded quietly, biting his bottom lip. "I'll help you."

At first, I didn't know what to say. What does anyone say when you wish for the moon and someone brings it to your doorstep? My ears burned hot, and for an instant, I wondered if one of the gravity wells was malfunctioning because I suddenly felt so light with relief that I could have floated to the surface. I reached for his hand and took it in mine. "Balt, you will *never* know how much this means to me."

He took a deep breath and glanced at Smith before looking back at me. I had never been one to pay attention to eyes, but I noticed then that Balt's were a light brown. A soft color. Like earth. The kind that might sprout grass. "So . . . when do you want to go?" he asked.

"As soon as possible. I have supplies all ready to go. I just need to find a way through the sealed doors in the arena."

"I could probably use a body if you can spare a moment," Smith mentioned, and Balt smiled at the request.

"Sorry, Smith. It appears that you'll have to rely on your superior IQ for this endeavor."

"Drat."

Balt ran a hand through his hair, something I was beginning to notice he did when he felt overwhelmed. "Let's just take the night. I'll see what I can come up with and hopefully we can figure out a way during tomorrow's testing session to get you through the doors. Is that acceptable?"

"Yeah," I answered, smiling in spite of myself. "That's acceptable." I felt like I should thank him somehow. Hug him, shake his hand, or something for not turning me in and agreeing to help me. But I couldn't bring myself to do anything other than offer a simple "thanks," before packing my bag. I shut Smith down and gave it back to Balt for the night, figuring it might come in handy. We snuck out of the lab and walked back to the dorms in silence, separating at the staircase in between our floors.

"Balt," I called to him before he got too far away, feeling this whirlwind inside me finding its way out. "I just want you to know that . . . I did approach you the other day to learn about your AI. But I also enjoyed talking to you."

The muscles in his long arms flexed as he held onto the railing and I caught him grinning. It looked like he wanted to say something else, but he simply shook his head. "I'll meet with you over breakfast first thing in the morning."

When I got back onto my floor, I entered my room and crawled into bed, burying myself in my covers. In the darkness, the excitement was too much to allow me to get any sleep. I just kept thinking of smelling air fresher than I'd ever breathed, of seeing the wild world above with my eyes instead of my mind.

Of not being afraid anymore.

BALTAZAR

My perception of the previous night was that it was somehow simultaneously the shortest and longest one of my life. When I returned to my room, I turned my desk so the light from my datapad wouldn't wake Tern. At first, I sat just staring at the screen, agonizing over everything that had occurred and the task ahead. Protocol #15 stated: *The more you know going into an experiment, the greater your chances of success.* All I could do was berate myself for not asking Zoe more questions. How did her friend get to the surface in the first place? What was *Project Wind?* How could she be so certain that PISS had killed her classmates? But then I kept arriving at the same thought.

What if she was right? That blade of grass couldn't have been grown underground. That seemed clear enough. But did that mean there really was a conspiracy?

I still wasn't sure, but Zoe was. That much was certain. She was going to attempt an escape with or without me. And she needed my help.

So I got to work.

I started by reviewing the following day's schedule, which instantly offered several possibilities. Our class was scheduled to complete a problem analysis in the testing arena, giving us free access to the supply room for our solutions. That would make it easy to get our hands on the right tools to create a distraction.

There would also be a phase cannon testing in the tunnel where the entrance to the old labs was. I thought the electrical discharge of the beam might be enough to strip the magnetic seal of the door temporarily, but it was an extremely dangerous device. Being within five feet of the beam would turn most organic material to dust, including any girl trying to escape the Institute.

I popped some painkillers to combat a throbbing headache and did my best to focus, trying to take stock all of the tools we had at our disposal. There were only so many possible combinations of solutions and I used Smith to determine the probability of success of each one, taking into consideration the endless variables that could occur: human error with the phase cannon, random supply inspection by testing arena personnel, even the chances of spontaneous lab implosion from ground tremors. The numbers didn't look good, no matter how we sliced it. The night passed in the blur of schematics and statistics and, with our resources exhausted, the best Smith and I could do was come up with a plan that had a five point seven percent success rate—basically a one-in-twenty chance that I would be able to get Zoe through the door safely. They weren't encouraging odds, but they were greater than zero, and sometimes that's enough.

I rubbed my eyes and leaned back into my chair, my gaze settling on the empty picture frame by my bed. I followed the lines around the blank space , like the walls to an endless maze. Maybe my father was like this, I wondered. A fool for girls in need. Or maybe I was in this predicament because of my mother. Maybe she was overly curious and couldn't go on until she understood everything around her.

I turned the blank picture around and crawled into bed, letting the questions tumble over and over each other in my mind until I fell asleep. Then, roughly ten minutes later, my alarm went off and I stumbled into the shower. After intentionally dawdling so Zeke and Tern would head the mess hall without me, I met with Zoe at a back table. We did our best to remain inconspicuous, speaking in hushed tones. She moved sluggishly, hints of dark circles under her blue eyes. I watched her pull a belt from her bag and she showed me a separate strap of carbon fiber she'd attached to it.

"I worked on this last night," she explained. "I figure I can strap Smith into it and then tie it around myself. That way it can sit on my shoulder and see everything I see, and I'll have both my hands free."

"Good design," I said, examining her work. It wasn't the most efficient stitching I'd seen, but it would suffice, given the circumstances. Even though I had just spent the entire night coming up with a plan, it wasn't until the belt was in my hand that everything began to feel real. In a few hours, we would attempt to do something never done in the history of the Institute.

"Any luck finding a way through the door?"

I took a sip of coffee, wincing at the bitterness. "I have something, but I'm not sure you're going to like it."

"A plan is a plan, Balt. The best thing I could think of is just grabbing as many explosives as I could and setting them off. Tell me what you've got."

I opened my bag and retrieved my datapad, guiding her

through the rough outline I'd come up with less than an hour before. She leaned over, inspecting every note I had scribbled down. I couldn't help but notice the skin where her neck met her shoulder. It shuddered ever so slightly with her breath. In only a few hours, I thought, she might be gone. Forever.

"The key is the phase cannon being tested in the tunnel," I explained, getting back on task. "It's perfect, actually. When phased particles move through the air, they absorb the electromagnetic energy around the beam, ripping away the electrons they come in proximity to."

Zoe's eyes grew wide. "So that will eliminate the magnetic seal on the door! Nova! Balt, this is great!"

I squinted. "Not exactly. I read the experiment report and checked the dimensions of the tunnel. The door isn't close enough to the beam to strip the seal."

"So what do I do?"

"Well, the angle of the beam can be altered with some hacking that Smith can initiate wirelessly. It won't take much. Maybe just a couple of degrees to get it close enough. That would provide you a window."

She looked at me, our noses practically touching as we hovered over my datapad. "How big of a window?"

I swallowed hard. "According to the report, the cannon takes twelve minutes to cool down between bursts. So we will have twelve minutes to get down the three-hundred foot tunnel and get you through."

"Wait, what? What do you mean *we*?"

"Well," I explained, tracing my finger over the tunnel diagram to zoom in on the door, the dimensions of everything around it becoming visible. "The concrete of the door is double-reinforced. Any blast that would create a big enough hole to get you through would need to be so big that you, me, and basically everyone in the testing arena would be killed."

"So, force isn't going to work. Then what?"

I double tapped the top corner of the screen, pulling the next diagram up. "Have you ever heard of a 'matter mover'?"

Zoe thought for a second before tilting her head. "Sounds vaguely familiar. It's an experiment that originated on Level M, right? Construction?"

"Yes," I said, pulling up the diagram. "It's a device that creates rays that rearrange atoms so that the user can manipulate one material and, theoretically, mold it into any shape they wish. So for our situation, we can compress materials together and make a hole."

"But I thought it basically . . . didn't work."

"It *sorta* works."

"Sorta?"

"Sorta. Not a precise term, I know. The reports indicate the device had a success rate hovering around forty percent. The most common issue cited was that users had to keep changing the angle of the beams every few seconds to maintain the shape or the device ends up just producing some fancy lights. I can manipulate the beams, maintain a hole, and return the matter back to its original form after you're through."

Zoe shook her head. "And then get out in time before the cannon goes off again? That seems pretty risky."

"It's the only plan that has a legitimate chance of working,"

I explained. "Plus, there's one prototype in the supply room of the testing arena, under access level blue."

Zoe squinted. "I can't get access to blue level equipment though, Balt."

"I can. My upgraded clearance is still active until tonight."

She shook her head. "It won't take them long to figure out how I got through, Balt. They'll easily trace it back to you. And then—"

"It's okay," I protested, feeling the heat rise from my collar. Was it really okay?

Zoe looked to me, watching me squirm in my seat. She was giving me the chance to back out, but I had made my decision. I wanted to help her. I would deal with the consequences afterward.

She grabbed my hand and whispered, "Thank you."

I nodded, her contact and thanks feeling more fulfilling than any honor I ever received for a project. "Don't thank me yet. There's still one other piece of the puzzle: the distraction."

"What do you have in mind?"

I looked toward the back corner where Zeke had a stack of pancakes covering his face like a mask. Tern sat across from him, shaking his head.

"I don't want them in danger too, Balt."

"We don't have to tell them anything," I explained. "I'm just going to ensure that their supply selection for the problem analysis has some . . . distracting results. That's all."

"Balt—" she began, but I cut her off.

"I thought this through. Trust me. Just worry about what you're going to do once you get on the other side of the door."

She didn't say anything else, staying silent until we decided to move back to our normal tables. We had to pretend that today was just an average testing day. I laughed at Zeke's jokes and went over supposed plans for Smith's body with Tern. When I could, I would watch Zoe sitting a few tables away, trying to see if she appeared as tense as I felt, but whenever I saw her, she appeared calm. Relaxed. She chewed her food and nodded when her friends spoke, never betraying the anxiety she must have been feeling. I realized then that this was just what she did. What was going on in her mind was her own. She didn't let her thoughts or feelings show like I did.

It almost made me jealous.

I got quiet and poked at my eggs with my fork, my appetite evaporating under levels of stress that made my worries over my midterm project seem like fond childhood memories. When the bell rang, my class slowly made its way to our lecture room with Dr. Douffman, a chill running down my spine the whole time. Class started as normal, but I couldn't concentrate on our lesson regarding subatomic particles. I was more focused on all the countless things that could go wrong, but then another grim scenario appeared in my head.

What if we succeeded?

What if Zoe got through alive and everything she said was true? Not only would I never see her again, but I'd be left to the mercy of an institute that was built upon lies? I figured I would face some stiff consequences but, if Zoe turned out to be correct, I had no concept of what they would do. Would they kill me? Make it look like an accident like H100C?

I realized that the decisions I made over the next few hours would drastically alter the rest of my life. Up until now, I had always thought I knew what I wanted that life to be. I was certain about so many things. Now, I couldn't help but question everything.

ZOE

During lecture, rather than worrying about the ten thousand things that could—and probably would—go wrong with the escape plan, I thought about Helena. Towering Helena with rosy cheeks and brownish hair, the color of a Dogwood's bark.

She'd been my best friend for as long as I could remember. We were sort of the black sheep of our group, never quite fitting in with the rest of our class. While they were off measuring mercury levels in the soil, we were running around the tree lines, making crowns out of broken vines and branches and playing queens of the forest. They were always polite to us, but it was always us and them, even as we got older. They were the serious scientists, and we were the dreamers who spent their afternoons hiding in the gardens, drawing on their datapads.

I was thankful that, whenever I thought of her now, I didn't picture a charred corpse. Now, when she came to mind, I imagined her in a grassy field instead. The sun would be shining and she'd take off her shoes to feel the grass under her feet. I bet she felt absolutely free for the first time in her life and, rather than just enjoying the trip while it lasted, she'd reached down and pulled up one of the blades of grass to bring back for me. The only way she could share that moment.

When Helena had handed the blade of grass to me after going

to the surface, she seemed just as light as the small green plant. She sighed as she spoke and her eyes were so wide, like they were open for the first time. She wanted me to see it, too. She placed the blade in my palm and wrapped my fingers around it. I remember her hands being warm, baked by the sun.

"Keep this hidden," she said, never a trace of fear in voice, even though she must have realized how dangerous her newfound knowledge was. "We were right. There *is* more than this."

And that was the last thing she ever said to me.

As the minutes ticked away, I grew more scared but more confident. This was what I needed to do. I ran my hand over my bag and felt my datapad among the many packets of nutrition pills. I felt like the bar-tailed godwit, sitting on the shore and preparing to take flight. There was a storm ahead, but I knew I just had to spread my wings and go, go and never look back.

The bell to signal the end of lecture sounded like an explosion to my eardrums and I tensed up at the sound, turning to see Balt packing up. His face was about ten shades whiter than usual and he kept fumbling with his datapad, trying to get it back in his bag.

"You're all thumbs today, Balt," I heard Tern comment.

Zeke patted him on the back. "Guess his all-night study session used up all of his manual dexterity," he joked and Balt did his best to seem annoyed but it was clear he was distracted. He looked to me and, as he passed to get to the door, I gave him a slight nod. It was time.

I separated from everyone and headed to Dr. Grima's office, prepared to seem mentally stable and ask permission to join my class in the testing arena today. To at least observe and take notes. I contemplated just skipping the appointment but didn't want to risk him notifying anyone that I had gone AWOL, especially after our talk yesterday. This whole plan was time-sensitive and the slightest setback could screw everything up.

When I opened the door to his office, I saw Dr. Grima at his desk, but there was someone sitting in my seat. The man stood and turned at my entrance, his presence instantly filled whole room. I got one look at him before my skin grew hot and my knees buckled. It felt like a wall of flames had just knocked me sideways. Like I was suddenly back in the doctors' dark testing chamber.

It all came back clear as day. I remembered his eyes, watching as I was torn apart.

"Dear girl, are you alright?" Dr. Parkman asked. When I caught my breath, I saw that I had dropped my bag, my datapad and meal pills spilling out on the floor. I fell to my knees, desperately trying to pick them up.

"I'm fine," I stammered, doing my best to conceal the ripping pain suddenly gnawing through my stomach. "I'm just . . . startled to see you, Sir."

Dr. Parkman smiled to Dr. Grima, who had rounded his desk and handed me a few of the meal pill packs that landed near his feet. Their label reflected in the light above and I worried my cover was blown, our plan foiled before it even began.

Dr. Parkman took one packet from Dr. Grima, smirking after a moment's examination. "A big fan of these, are you?"

He offered them to me and I slowly placed them back in my bag, the pain in my stomach intensifying the closer I got to him. "Yes, sir," was all I could manage. I tried looking him in the eye again, but the wave of fire returned, and it took every ounce of my strength not to keel over.

Dr. Parkman let out a snide laugh. "Can't blame you. A fine breakthrough, even if I do say so myself. I developed the basic formula when I was about your age. My third gold honor during my time as a student."

"Zoe, why don't you take a seat?" Dr. Grima offered, eyeing the beads of sweat sliding down my forehead. I did as he suggested and Dr. Parkman stood across from me, his hands tucked under his armpits. "Dr. Parkman just wanted to stop by and see how you were doing."

The walls felt like they were closing in. I didn't dare make eye contact with him again.

"Dr. Grima tells me you've been making some progress," Dr. Parkman said, his voice slicing through my brain. "That's good to hear. We want our best and brightest out there on the front lines for science, of course."

I looked at Dr. Grima, trying to block everything else out. "Yes."

Dr. Grima cleared his throat. "Well, I think Zoe is a very resourceful young scientist who is handling her situation with the utmost fortitude."

Dr. Parkman patted my shoulder and his touch felt like fangs digging into my skin. I cringed and bit my lip to keep from screaming in agony. "I can tell. Drs. Herzman and Lebowitz have said the same. It makes me very proud. I've lived my life with the goal of 'living forever,' like my father and his father before me. I have accomplished that through my work but, in many ways, I see you and the rest of the Institute's students as another way I have succeeded in that regard. I see you all as the children I was never able to have, descendants of the Parkman legacy."

There was a silence and I could feel him staring at me, his gaze devouring every inch of my body. Another wave of fire struck and I couldn't help but gasp. I was surprised flames didn't shoot out of my mouth.

"I was hoping to head into the arena today," I managed. "To take notes. Would that be okay?"

While ants could speak to each other by rubbing the ridges on their body, they could also communicate with each other chemically. By releasing chemicals from various glands, they could notify each other of danger ahead. They spoke volumes without making a sound.

I kept silent, but said everything I needed to Dr. Grima. He stared into my eyes and I knew he understood.

"Excellent," he said after a second. "Then I think you should go."

Dr. Parkman continued to stare at me. Through me. I fought the pain and finally looked him in the eye, trying my best to appear unafraid. His lips parted into a smile but it didn't make him appear any less frightening. He turned back to Dr. Grima, commenting, "Can't fight the scientific spirit."

"I shall see you tomorrow, then," Dr. Grima offered, giving me his blessing to go.

I adjusted my backpack. "Goodbye. Thank you, Dr. Grima. Dr. Parkman," My words came out heavier than I'd wanted but I made for the door without further hesitation.

"Before you go, Zoe. I was hoping you could lend us your services once more this evening, since you're feeling better," Dr. Parkman said as I had my hand on the door. "Drs. Herzman and Lebowitz have some suggestions on how to proceed, and I'm very interested to see what they can uncover."

Terror filled my lungs to the point where I felt like I could drown. Visions of his eyes through the window of the dark room came flooding back and the ripping sensation began again.

"I've already notified the lift technician," he continued. "After dinner, we will be expecting you on Level H."

I nodded as if I understood, but I was down the hallway before they could say anything more. My feet moved as swiftly as a gazelle's and I kept my eyes forward, feeling the pain leave my body with every step I took away from him. There was absolutely no going back now. I would throw myself in front of that phase beam before I would allow that monster to speak to me ever again.

I took a deep breath when I signed in for the testing arena, passing through the double doors and feeling the metal underneath my feet change to loose gravel. The floor rotated materials depending on the tests being conducted. Whatever the problem analysis was, it apparently required a ground with some give.

Hundreds of feet above, fluorescent bulbs glowed like stars and I slowly walked toward the middle of the arena. My classmates were sitting on the ground in a circle with their datapads out as they listened to Dr. Douffman. She stopped her speech when she noticed my arrival and nodded in my direction. "Glad to see you're joining us today, Zoe. Why don't you join Cindee's group? Even if you don't feel up for it, you can just take notes. We're just about to go over the assignment for today."

I sat with the girls and did my best to appear calm, but inside I was trying my hardest just to keep it together. My eyes were glued to the mouth of the tunnel where a bunch of scientists were working on the phase cannon. The machine was massive, easily twenty or thirty feet long, with a complicated tornado of wires making up its core. They spilled into a long cylindrical tube and the whole contraption gave off the faintest blue glow. From the look of it, I had some time before it started firing, but not much.

Then my eyes caught sight of Balt. It was cool in the arena but he was sweating bullets, wiping his forehead with his sleeve every few seconds. I was sure he was going to back out, but he turned his datapad so I could see it over his shoulder. It simply had the number thirty on it.

Thirty minutes until the cannon started firing, I realized.

So it was settled. In thirty minutes, I would either be leaving the arena proudly through the old labs, or as dust through a mini sweeper.

BALTAZAR

Dr. Douffman reviewed our problem analysis, challenging us to create something that would gather raw material in a padded container and then launch it five hundred feet in a in any direction safely, presumably for use to gather resources in difficult-to-reach locations on the surface. As I listened, or tried to pretend listening, one thing was certain: I would have made a terrible spy.

"You know, people usually shower *before* putting their clothes on," Zeke whispered into my ear.

I ran a moist sleeve over my forehead for what seemed the ten-thousandth time, every inch of my skin feeling like it was boiling. "You're not hot?" I asked, as if I couldn't understand why everyone else wasn't dripping with sweat.

Dr. Douffman cleared her throat in my direction, catching my comment to Zeke and doing her best to tell me to solder up with her eyes.

"Sorry," I offered. She clearly wasn't feeling sympathetic to my excessive perspiration.

"As I was saying," she continued, "make sure to document everything your team theorizes and does. I cannot stress that enough. If the mechanism you devise does not launch your ball the sufficient distance on your first attempt, it will be easier to draw on what you have already discussed rather than starting from scratch. The arena supply room is open to your disposal. And, of course, if you need help with anything or further information, please don't hesitate to ask. You have three hours beginning . . ." she said before looking down to her datapad, ". . . now."

"Wooo, go team, go!" Zeke cheered as our class rose to their feet. He and our other team member, Freedman, started going through some complicated handshake.

"You okay?" Tern asked, taking a spot next to me. "I haven't seen you sweat this much since that time you got a C in Organic Chemistry."

I watched Zoe walk with her group toward the supply room, but she kept to the side, subtly waving me over with her hand.

"Yeah, um," I said before my brain completely failed me and I forgot what Tern had just asked. I felt like I was walking on paper-thin glass and the slightest misstep would send me plummeting. "Just give me a second. I need to tell Zoe something."

He nodded in acknowledgement but I could tell Tern was starting to suspect something, and that got me even more nervous. Perhaps assuming I could trick him into creating a distraction was an oversight. I certainly didn't calculate how my inability to remain calm would affect our chances.

I jogged over to Zoe and walked with her, the two of us keeping our heads down and trying to seem as nonchalant as possible. "I have Smith in my bag and am going to get him to adjust the phase cannon remotely," I said, trying not to sound apprehensive.

"Okay," she said, chewing on one of her nails.

"Just be ready to go on the signal."

"We have a signal?" she asked, confused.

"We don't, do we? Just keep an eye on me. When things get misty in here, be ready to move."

She nodded and touched my elbow, pushing the fabric against my moist skin. "You can still back out of this," she said softly. "I won't be mad. You can say that I stole your keycard and took the matter mover. I can try to figure it out myself."

I bit my bottom lip, my last chance to escape this situation in front of me. But I had sealed my fate the day prior, when she asked if she could trust me. She could. She could trust me with anything.

"We're in this together," I told her.

Zoe squeezed my hand before turning to catch up with the rest of her project team. I looked over to see if Dr. Douffman was watching, but she was speaking to the scientists working on the phase cannon, her back turned. I quickly switched Smith on and left him face-up in my open bag near where our group was scheduled to work.

"Is it time?" he asked.

"Yes."

"Ohhhhh, this is exciting," he whispered eagerly.

I bent down on one knee and slowly tilted the bag so he could see the cannon. "I need you to adjust the angle of the beam. Just like we planned."

Smith smiled, almost giddily. "Certainly. That phase cannon is a Q series. We're practically cousins."

"Good. Alright, we'll come for you when it's time."

I started to walk away, but Smith called me back. "Balt, you aren't going to just leave her, are you?"

"What do you mean?" I stammered.

"Well, even if you are able to get us into the old labs, the danger will have only begun. Zoe is brave and I certainly have the intellect, but your inclusion in the party will definitely increase our chances. Not to mention that Directive 2 will be almost impossible to achieve . . ."

"Smith! Just . . . focus on the beam."

I walked to the supply room, my stomach turning into a tangled ball of live wires. The possibility of following her *had* crossed my mind, but it seemed like too much of a risk. I couldn't make a decision like that so rashly.

I found Zeke, Tern, and Freedman shopping around for parts in the supply room. Tern was busy writing notes on his datapad while Zeke and Freedman took turns shouting out unhelpful suggestions on where to start.

"So where are we at?" I asked when I rejoined them.

Zeke let out a war cry and took a steel pipe from a stack near the wall. Freedman armed himself as well and the two began hacking at each other, swinging the pipes like swords.

Tern rolled his eyes. "At the very bottom, as usual," he replied. He turned his datapad toward me and went through the rough sketch of a launcher prototype he had drawn up, his pristine handwriting uniform on the sides. "If we're going to launch the ball the required distance, we're going to need quite a bit of 'oomph,' to say the least. I say we make those two monkeys build us a basic catapult, and you and I will work on an engine. I was thinking something hydraulic. We can probably piece one together in about an hour and have the ball across the line with time to spare."

I smiled, picturing the design come together in my head. It was the most normal I'd felt in the last twenty-four hours. "Sounds good."

"Are you all right?" Tern asked again in a low voice. I didn't want to lie to him but knew I couldn't tell him the plan. Once it was discovered what I did, he would be questioned. The less he knew, the less likely he would be punished.

"You trust me, correct?"

He cocked an eyebrow. "Yes, why?"

I nodded toward Zeke, who was now trying to balance the pipe vertically on his palm. He took his eyes off it for a second and it crashed onto his head, the steel thudding against his skull. He and Freedman had to hold their stomachs to prevent themselves from falling over in laughter.

"We can't kill him, if that's what you're thinking," Tern commented.

"Not a bad idea, but no," I said. "I was considering something . . . comical for this."

"Comical? Like what?"

"Remember when we used to set off those radiant sparklers in the hallways when we were younger?"

"Yes," he grinned. "I still have no idea how we didn't get caught."

"Right," I laughed. "Why not relive the old days for a little while?"

"The days before we were serious scientists?"

Zeke tried balancing the pipe again with the same result.

"Well, some of us."

Tern looked at Zeke, smiling. "Alright. Nova. What do you want to do? Nothing too crazy, right?"

"Right. Just a 'little oversight.'"

A bead of sweat trickled down my nose. I felt guilty for tricking Tern, but he would understand. At least, that's what I told myself to feel better about it.

We went over to the chemical closet and I retrieved a liter of petricite and five cubes of super-cooled ice, making sure they didn't come into contact as I packed them away in the containers Dr. Douffman provided us. Tern grinned, instantly putting my idea together, and thought for a second before saying, "I like it. Some harmless fun. The phase cannon scientists are going to be pissed, though, when the entire arena fills up with fog."

I shrugged, "It will clear in minutes. No big deal. Technically it could be the superconductors in our machine, so we can explain that we were using them for the engine and it slipped."

"I don't know what you did with my friend Balt," Tern answered, "but I like this new one. Let's steal Zeke's pants in the confusion."

"What's that?" Zeke asked, overhearing.

"Nothing," we responded in unison.

With the rest of my team collecting the necessary equipment, I walked over to the higher clearance equipment room and checked out the matter mover, the box-like device small enough to fit in my pocket. The button configuration was slightly different from the one I'd read about on my datapad but, after a few seconds of examining it, I had a good idea of how it worked.

If it worked, that is.

With my signature electronically filed in the log book, I took a deep breath before heading out. Soon, there would be no turning back. Protocol #20 stated: *Always consider the consequences of your actions.* I didn't want to at the moment and I knew that was a bad sign.

By the time I reentered the testing arena, Zeke and Freedman were busy setting up the frame for our catapult while Tern arranged the petricite and ice among the other parts for the engine, flashing me a smile when he spotted my approach. I did my best to appear calm, but my heart was beating so fast I thought it was going to burst out of my chest.

I watched Zoe from afar as she worked with her group, shooting me glances every few seconds. The hairs on the back of my neck stood on end and I thought, at first, that it was just nerves. Then my ears heard the faint hum emanating from the phase cannon. A blue light erupted from the cannon's barrel and made the walls of the side tunnel glow.

I quickly set the timer on my datapad and watched the seconds tick away, one by one. I looked to her one last time and it struck me then that this would be the last time I ever saw her, the last time she would be in front of me, the last time I might feel something that I could describe with a term as illogical as "love" for someone. I knew I was being a quark, but at the beginning of the biggest decision in my life—that's what occupied my mind, not the fact that I was risking my grades, my reputation and standing with the Institute, or my life itself.

But how I was risking losing her.

I walked over to retrieve my bag where Smith lay tucked inside. At my approach, he whispered, "Nice guy, that phase cannon."

"Did you do it?"

"Was there any doubt? The next shot will take off the magnetic stripping. It's now or never." His tone was calm. Confident. I tucked him back inside the bag and brought it over to my friends, waiting until there were about ninety seconds before the next shot to pick up the petricite and ice.

"This is going to be hilarious," Tern said.

"Yeah," I replied, not looking at him. "Thanks, Tern. For everything. Tell Zeke too."

"What do you mean?"

I clenched my teeth, dropping the cubes and letting gravity do the rest.

The air around us instantly began to grow damp and foggy. It felt refreshing against my sweaty skin, quite honestly, and spread even faster than I thought it would. Soon the fog had gotten so thick that I couldn't see more than a few feet ahead of me and I felt alone in the arena, losing all sense of direction.

The rest of my class started yelling. I could hear Dr. Douffman instructing us to stay calm and still, but I started to move through the fog in Zoe's general direction. Her outstretched hand grabbed arm after a few seconds and she dragged me in the direction of the tunnel, going so fast I almost tripped over my own feet. A blue light flashed through the fog and I could feel the hair on the back of my neck stand up again. The cannon had fired. We had exactly twelve minutes.

While I was having trouble getting my bearings, it felt like Zoe had a nose for the tunnel. We found the entrance before I knew it, and the two of us began running at full speed toward the end. The fog had not yet begun to spread down the long tunnel, so after a few feet we emerged from the mist, the yellow lights on the walls shining down on us.

"I can't believe we're really doing this!" I called out, but Zoe didn't answer, her eyes feverishly scanning the walls for the doors to the old lab. There was a moment of panic when we reached the end and we couldn't find them, but then I caught a glimpse of a warning sign hidden in the shadow of a support strut on the side reading: "LAB ENTRANCE: CONTAMINATED. NO ENTRY PERMITTED."

"This is it! This is it!" Zoe shouted to me, running her hands over the concrete. The doors were about twice the size of standard doors and a slightly different shade of concrete than the wall. "Smith, time?"

"Ten minutes, eleven seconds," Smith called from my open bag.

"We're gonna do this!" Zoe yelled. She turned to me and I pulled the matter mover from my pocket, feeling the smooth surface of the box between my fingers. I pointed the lenses of the beams toward the doors and took a deep breath before hitting the trigger.

"Here goes nothing."

The lights flickered red and green against the concrete, moving about like two circular gears. They moved about, but there was no visible effect on the concrete. With each passing second, my knees felt more and more like they were going to buckle and I could see the first real sign of worry from Zoe, the color draining from her lips.

"Oh no . . ." she began to say but then I felt the box grow heavier in my hand. I moved my wrists about and began to feel the weight of the concrete bend with my motion, like it was suddenly a thick liquid and the beams of light were spoons. I inched closer and sped up my twirling, churning the concrete with such speed that it eventually began to part, a hole appearing in the door, darkness appearing on the other side.

"Yes! It worked! I knew it would work!" I shouted, relief washing over me as I tried to keep the hole stable. "Zoe, I—" I began to say, turning to her. But she wasn't there.

"Zoe?" I called again.

"Where . . ." Smith shouted, "where is she?"

The fog crept in slowly and my wrists began to ache from twirling the beams, the weight of the concrete tearing at my muscles.

"Zoe?" I shouted, panicked, but only my echo could be heard. "I didn't see her go through!"

"Nine minutes, thirty seconds," Smith counted.

Every muscle in my body tensed, my brain barely able to contain a thought. Where is she? Did she change her mind? Did someone grab her? The matter mover hissed and I thought about stopping to look for her. But from the sparking sounds the small box was emanating, it was likely that if I closed the hole, I wouldn't be able to open it again.

"Nine minutes, Balt," Smith called, a worry in his voice now as well. "What do we do?"

I couldn't see the phase cannon, but felt the barrel pointed right at me somewhere within the fog. Our plan was quickly falling apart and I reminded myself that the odds of this working were slim in the first place. A long shot. But we were so close.

"We still have time," I replied, my voice dry. I promised her

I would help. I promised I would buy her a window. I closed my eyes, concentrating on making the same motion with the beams to keep the hole open. "We'll wait as long as we can."

Dammit, Zoe. Where did you go?

ZOE

This isn't happening.

This isn't happening.

But no matter how many times I said the phrase, when I opened my eyes, I found myself in the dark spherical room on Level H, the frigid air gnawing on my skin.

Somehow I'd done it again.

And at the worst possible time.

I wanted to stop and think but the only thing my brain could focus on was Smith's voice counting down. I had ten minutes to get back to the testing arena on Level F or I was dead, one way or another.

Frantically, I ran to the door of the sphere but stopped myself before tugging on the handle, making sure to check what lay outside through the small window. I caught a glimpse of Dr. Lebowitz through the glass, her back turned while she worked on something at a dissecting station. Her elbows rocked back and forth with a hacking motion at something, almost in rhythm with the seconds passing. The fluorescent light above her reflected off a bone saw to her left, bright red blood spattered on the blade.

I gulped and tried to survey the rest of the area. Dr. Herzman was probably close by, but it didn't look like anyone had noticed me yet. I could sneak out and get to the lift. I could still make it.

"Nine minutes and thirty seconds," Smith's voice whispered in my mind.

I slowly pulled the hatch back and was able to open it without making Dr. Lebowitz turn around. With my eyes locked on the exit, I crawled on all fours, the sterile floor bruising my skin as I went. Dr. Herzman emerged from a side room and I quickly ducked under the long worktable in the middle of the lab, tucking my legs under and waiting in fear of him calling out my name. But the next few seconds passed in silence. He hadn't seen me. I watched his legs walk past from under the table and wanted to stay put until a path was clear to the door. But the clock kept ticking. There was no time for waiting.

I followed the length of the table, trying not to bump into any of the chair legs pushed underneath, but it got harder the closer to the exit I got. When I was just a few feet away and the table ended, I had no choice but to make a break for it and run. Run and never look back. I took a quick look behind me to make sure Dr. Herzman was still moving the other way and emerged from under the table, opening the exit door to find none other than Dr. Parkman on the other side, his hands folded behind him.

We locked eyes and I felt my knees go weak, the sensation of burning moving through my body. I was crumbling before him, paralyzed by his gaze.

"Zoe, I'm glad to see you have joined us," he said and I gasped, the fire ripping me apart. But with a fleeting flash of strength, I was able to push him aside, continuing on my mad dash toward freedom. His shouts for security filled the halls but I kept going, letting my fear propel me forward. I felt stronger every step further I got from him. If I could make it to the lift, I told myself, I had a chance. I still had a chance to get out.

Seven minutes, thirty seconds.

I darted through the halls, bumping into students and professors alike in my frantic gallop. I could hear the commotion building behind me, but I kept my eyes ahead, finding the lift at the end of the large hall that led to the dorms. I hopped over a table of students playing a card game, knocking over their drinks with my feet. When I stumbled into the lift, I hit the button for Level F as the scrawny lift operator began to berate me. "This isn't an elevator, miss! Do you have clearance? What's your name?"

Thankfully, he didn't choose to stop the lift before yelling at me and the doors closed, the compartment making its ponderous ascent. I delivered a swift kick to his knee, forcing him down. Nimbly, I moved behind him and pulled his arm behind his back, twisting it awkwardly until I could feel the bone bending unnaturally under the pressure. He groaned like a wounded animal, but I just kept my eyes on the level indicator above, inching past G and slowly moving toward F.

A drop of blood ran down my nose and onto my lips, a copper taste filling my mouth. Must have been from my trip. It happened the first time, too. I let the blood continue to run down my chin, keeping my grip on the lift operator's arm until the doors opened onto Level F. With the chime, I let him go and began running with everything I had toward the testing arena.

Five minutes.

The usual white lights in the hall began to flash red. Security was on the way, and it wouldn't be long before they would start sweeping the floor for me, Tasers in hand. My mind grew numb with dread. I stood out like a sore thumb, running about the level with a bloody nose. I wouldn't be hard to find. And even if I made it back to the testing arena, I worried Balt had bailed when I'd disappeared. Without him and the matter mover, there would be nothing to greet me there but a concrete wall. But it was my only hope. I wouldn't lie down and submit without trying.

The Alaskan malamute could cover over a thousand miles in a matter of days. It would run despite heavy blizzard conditions, with temperatures reaching as low as forty below zero and winds up to sixty miles an hour. I drew them once, the pack appearing like a dark blur across the frozen tundra.

I ran until my lungs felt like they were going to collapse on themselves like a dead star.

And then I kept running.

When I rounded the psych wing and reached the hallway that led to the testing arena, I could hear the shouts of security officers growing louder and louder somewhere ahead of me. They were heading in my direction and would cut me off before I got to the arena. Before I could come up with an alternate route, a door opened in the hallway and I felt an arm yank me inside a room.

I tripped and nearly fell but landed on a desk, my body pushing its contents clumsily to the floor upon impact. I turned to see that the owner of the arm was none other than Dr. Grima and before I could say anything, he put a finger to his lips. I obeyed, the shouts growing louder outside. Frozen in place, I listened to my heartbeat until the barrage of the security officers' boots outside grew to a cacophonous climax and then lessened with every passing second.

"Zoe, they're calling your name over the intercoms," he informed me. "What happened? What are you doing?"

I just wiped away the blood on my face with a sleeve before pushing him aside and dashing out the door again. That wasn't how I wanted to say goodbye to Dr. Grima, especially after he'd proved that I could trust him after all. But there just wasn't any time for goodbyes. Not for anyone.

I turned the corner and burst through the doors of the testing arena. The fog had mostly cleared and I found my class assembled in the center, Dr. Douffman taking a head count. She called out to me to assemble with the rest of the class, but I just kept my legs churning. The tunnel was within sight.

Three minutes.

The scientists on the phase cannon began to scream about the next shot being only minutes away as I passed them, but I continued to bolt down the tunnel, ignoring them like all the others. I kept my eyes glued to the side where I'd left Balt in front of the door and felt a wave of relief when I found him in the same spot, still twirling the beams in a circle to maintain the hole. Smith was the first to spot me and shouted from the bag, "There she is! There she is!"

Balt turned to look and the distraction interrupted his motion, the crunch sound of the concrete reforming filling my ears. The hole was now just a little wider than my arm by the time he got control of it again.

"Where did you go?!" he asked, focusing on the beams once

more. "I heard our class calling out our names, and all the alarms. I—are you hurt?"

"You did great!" I said, gasping for air. Not having time to explain my bloody nose, I grabbed Smith and buried it within my bag, tossing it over my shoulder. I wanted to kiss Balt for not abandoning the plan, but didn't want to interrupt his motion, the hole growing slowly again. He had saved my life. I hoped he knew that.

"Smith, time?" I asked.

"One minute, fifty seconds!" it responded. "Best hurry!"

Balt looked at me and I could tell that there was more he wanted to ask me. More that he wanted to tell me. But instead, I flung my bag through the hole and followed once I thought it would be big enough to let me pass. The concrete was jagged and scraped my skin as I scurried through, leaving behind a small trail of blood from the cuts that disappeared with the motion of the concrete. I just ground my teeth through the pain, refusing to stop so close to freedom.

When I reached the darkness on the other side, I fell a few feet before my body smacked hard onto another concrete surface. Only then did I opt to just lie on the floor and let myself bask in relief. This was it. I'd made it!

The path ahead was pitch black and, when I got to my feet, I turned back to look to Balt on the other side. To take one last look at the boy who was willing to risk everything for me. "Run, Balt!" I shouted, worried he wouldn't make it out of the tunnel before the blast came. But he just stood there, watching me.

"What are you doing? Go!" I screamed.

I saw him look down the tunnel once before looking back at me. Then, without another word, he pulled up hard on the beams and the concrete split in half, a long tear appearing in the wall. He grabbed his bag and began to shimmy through, the hole he'd made closing in on him fast. Instinctively, I dropped my bag and ran to him, grabbing his hand and pulling him through. He shouted in agony but made it through in one piece, his body falling on top of mine. He tried to stand but I could see one of his feet was awkwardly bent, his brown left shoe now torn and stained with blood. The wall had fully sealed behind us, leaving us in complete darkness.

I fumbled in the dark for my bag to retrieve Smith, my efforts accompanied by Balt's grunts of pain. The lights from its eyes were enough to illuminate the direction it faced, so I tied the belt I had made for it around me and put the AI in its place on my left shoulder. I then reached out to Balt and tried to help him up. Any weight he put on the foot made him groan deeply, so I wrapped his arm around my shoulder, letting him put his weight on me. Why had he done this? Why had he followed me? In the darkness, things suddenly felt more complicated. This wasn't how I'd hoped this would go.

My mind raced. It was only a matter of time before the authorities realized where we went, so I wanted to be as far away from the door as I could. While the variant AI lurking in the shadows were enough to worry about, I was sure Dr. Parkman would want to come after me, especially after they put together how I got to Level H unnoticed. But it would be harder now with

Balt here, injured. Still, I couldn't just leave him behind to be captured. Could I?

With Smith lighting the way for us, we began our way down the tunnel toward the old labs, unsure of what lay ahead.

BALTAZAR

Zoe dragged me down the dark tunnel as best she could. Grinding my teeth, I did my best not to complain, but even the passing air made the nerve endings in my foot explode in pain. The muscles in my wounded leg ached from keeping my foot elevated and I could feel droplets of sweat running down my neck even though it was so cold we could see our breath.

Just a bit farther, I kept telling myself. Just another minute. One more minute. Finally, my vision began to blur. I would pass out if I didn't rest. "Can we . . ." I started to say, the effort to speak more laborious than I'd expected, "stop . . . for a second?"

Zoe didn't say anything at first. She took another step before leading me toward the side of the tunnel, letting me use the wall to lower myself slowly to the ground. When I was finally sitting, Smith looked at Zoe and the light from his eyes illuminated her face. Her mouth and chin were stained a dark red like she had just bitten into some sort of fruit. She must have noticed me staring because she pulled a rag from her bag to clean up the best she could. I thought about making a joke, but the pain kept surging up my body.

"Why did you do this, Balt?" she asked, standing over me and using Smith's lights to examine my foot. "Why did you follow me?" She sounded more confused than anything, perhaps on the verge of frustrated.

Smith turned to her from his spot on her shoulder. "I don't mean to interrupt, but I think you could be a bit more grateful, Zoe. We would never have made it through the door without Balt's help."

"This isn't a game, Smith. We've no idea what's out there, and the last thing I need is to—"

She stopped herself before she could say more, but the damage was done. I looked to her but couldn't see her eyes through the darkness.

"You can say it," I mumbled. This was all wrong, I thought. This was not how I'd imagined this would play out when I decided to crawl through that hole. It wasn't that I expected to be Zoe's knight in shining lab coat. I followed because I wanted to help her and find the truth out for myself. Now, I was a liability that decreased her chances for success rather than increased them. I shivered in the cold and my foot began to grow numb, a very bad sign.

Zoe shook her head. "I didn't mean that. I'm sorry . . . it's just . . ." She turned to look down the tunnel, Smith's lights dimly illuminating about ten meters. Beyond that, there was no telling how far the tunnel ran. "I was prepared to throw my life away for this. Now, with you here, it . . . complicates things."

The gravel near the wall scraped against my skin and I suddenly became hyper aware of how different this place was. These weren't the glass corridors of the new labs. There wouldn't be a mess hall filled with food waiting for us, or a warm bed to climb into at night. If we died, there would be no nanomachines and rejuvenation chambers to bring us back.

After a sigh, Zoe turned back to me, kneeling toward my foot. "Let's take a look at this."

"Allow me," Smith said and the lights from his eyes turned green, a laser scanning my foot through the bloody tatters of my shoe. After a few seconds, he redirected his sight to the wall near my head, illustrating the results of his scan. My foot looked like a smashed beaker under the skin, little x's appearing in all the spots it was broken.

"Not looking good, Balt," Smith diagnosed. "You have multiple compound fractures and are still losing blood. We need to get it immobilized and have you start a regimen of penicillin to prevent an infection from forming."

"I don't suppose you have any in your bag?" I asked, and Zoe shook her head. My jaw tightened. "I suppose we started out on the wrong foot," I joked before letting out a fit of coughs, the shaking making my foot throb painfully. Zoe took my hand and caressed it with her thumb.

"Smith, where do we go?" she asked.

Smith's eyes turned a lighter shade of blue, and soon a 3D hologram of the old labs appeared floating between us. The layout was basically a series of large rectangular floors stacked atop each other, each level comprising of countless rooms and hallways. Smith hummed and eventually a small red dot appeared in one of the side tunnels toward the bottom. "Here we are."

Zoe ran her fingers through the hologram, counting each floor above us. I watched her lips move as she went. ". . . Six, seven, eight," she counted aloud. "We have eight levels to get to the surface."

"And thankfully only one to reach the medical wing," Smith added, highlighting a section on the other side of the labs above us. "According to the Institute's records, this place was abandoned in a bit of a rush, so it's possible there are supplies left behind there we could use to patch you up, Balt. See? Everything is going to be fine."

I nodded but was more focused on trying to figure out the scale of the hologram. It didn't look far, but a few inches on the map was a much longer walk in reality. The tunnel we were in seemed to go on forever and it was no bigger than an inch on the hologram.

"Then that's the plan," Zoe determined, standing tall again. "We grab some medical supplies on our way, and then keep heading up. We should get moving."

She extended her hand toward me but I didn't take it. Instead I ran my hands through my hair and felt the sweat moisten them before tucking them under my armpits. I was unsure if it was the pain, the cold, or the disorder everything was in around me, but I felt completely out of sorts. I needed to straighten something out, for my own peace of mind, if we were going to continue. "You asked me before we started this if you could trust me," I said. "I hope you see that you can."

"Balt, of course . . ."

"But *I* need to know I can trust *you*. Starting with what happened in the tunnel."

Zoe shifted her stance, rubbing the back of her neck with her hand. It looked like she was going to try and just brush off the question, so I shook my head again. "I need to know we're . . . together on this. No secrets."

"Between *any* of us," Smith added, making sure we included him.

Slowly, she sat down beside me, looking downward and tracing her fingers over the cement floor. "I told you that my class was chosen for this experiment called *Project Wind*. After we signed confidentiality agreements, they told us that the purpose of the experiment was to alter certain genes and areas of the brain responsible for perception using waves and genetic implantations in order to see whether a human being could . . ."

She stopped and so I asked, "Could what?"

Then she looked at me and I could make out her blue eyes in the darkness again.

"Teleport."

My head shot back. I wanted to laugh but there was nothing about her expression that led me to believe she was joking. "Wait, are you serious?" It then hit me like a thousand-pound counterweight. She didn't just wander off in the tunnel. She'd teleported somewhere else.

Smith glanced back and forth between us. "Remarkable! I would give my right ocular processor to get a glance at that computation."

"How many times have you done it?" I asked. "Teleport, I mean."

She shook her head, as if it hurt to remember. "Twice. The first time was in the lab on Level H when the project was just starting out. They told me to stand there and after a while I got so tired, I started daydreaming about being back in bed. Being comfortable under the sheets. Then I started feeling lightheaded and suddenly . . . I was there. In my bed."

"Just like that?" Smith asked.

"Just like that."

"What about back in the tunnel? What were you thinking then?" I prompted.

She wiped her eyes and I could almost feel how tired talking about it was making her. But I needed to know. "I was just thinking how great it will feel when I never have to worry about being back in the Level H labs again." Then she let out this awkward laugh. "I just wish I could figure out how to do it. I can't just do it on command, no matter how hard I try. Helena was the only other student in my class with whom the experiment was any success. That's how she was able to get to the surface. If only I could just figure it out and follow . . . we wouldn't be here"

"What do you feel when it happens?" I asked, my curiosity piqued.

She looked back to the concrete, feeling the surface with her hand. "It's like you stop existing. Like you're there and then . . . you just fade away. I don't know how it happens, but clearly it doesn't have the greatest effect on me," she explained, wiping droplets of drying blood around her nose.

"Well then," I decided, "we'll make sure you stay right here with us in this rundown ruin of a lab full of robots that want to murder us."

She smiled and I felt a bit warmer. "Why did you do it?" she asked me suddenly. "Decide to come with me, I mean."

Smith rolled his eyes but I just shook my head, as if I needed to think about it for a second. This wasn't really the time for declarations of love, so I just said, "I just knew I wouldn't be able to forget what you said. I would always be wondering if you were right about PISS. I just realized I needed to see the truth for myself, too." I thought of the empty picture frame in my room for a second, wondering if, sometime soon, I would be able to finally fill it in. Assuming, of course, that we made it to the surface alive.

We sat for another minute or so until I felt ready to move again. Zoe wrapped my arm around her shoulders and we continued on, Smith's ocular beams lighting the way. I didn't know what lay ahead, but as long as we stayed together, I told myself, I would be fine. I needed the truth, but I needed her, too.

ZOE

As we walked, my teeth chattered so hard that I began to think they might break. I wasn't prepared for this cold. In fact, I wasn't prepared for a lot of things. Balt was doing his best to gut it out, but his face was so pale I wondered if he would even make it to the medical wing. I knew I wasn't strong enough to carry him if he passed out.

We stopped at a broken section of wall and were able to create a crude crutch out of some piping. It helped, but his strength was quickly fading. Together we trudged forward slowly but steadily until, after what felt like hours, we came to a light at the end of the dark tunnel. The concrete gave way to a partially collapsed wall and, after some wiggling through the rubble, we found ourselves in a massive room. It looked like the remains of an old testing arena. Above, hundreds of fluorescent lights still buzzed and shined.

"Out of one testing arena and into another," Balt commented, staring upward. His voice was notably weaker. I felt Smith send out scans from my shoulder as we moved, directing us toward a door on the far side. The floor was covered with loose dirt and each step we took left footprints in the seemingly unblemished soil.

Further along, we came to a large hole in the center of the arena, plunging a few feet deep into the dirt. There were remnants of some sort of green material on the sides, rubbery and organic by the looks of it. Around the edges, small tracks about the size of our hands led out from the hole in all directions. I knelt down near one and let Smith examine it.

"Hmm," the AI thought aloud, a blue light from its eyes running over the tracks. "It appears to be some sort of insect. Hexapedal from the looks of it, with quite an advanced tarsus section."

Balt slowly trudged to our spot with his crutch and squinted at the tracks, watching me pick up one of the slivers of green stuff. I felt it with my fingers. "This seems pretty fresh."

"Agreed," Smith concurred.

"I studied a fair amount of bugs on Level H, but nothing that seems to match this. Might be something genetically engineered for an arena test." I felt under my nose to make sure I wasn't still bleeding. "So besides killer robots, we might have to watch out for giant insects too. Perfect."

"Incredible how they found a way to survive and thrive in here," Smith remarked from my shoulder. I know it was just being curious, but its proximity to my ear was starting to get on my nerves. It was almost like it was a voice inside my head—an overly informed voice making a point to illustrate all the things that could kill us.

We turned to Balt who didn't say anything, looking even paler. "Are you alright, Balt?" Smith asked.

He shook his head, his hands trembling ever so slightly. "Yes, it's just . . . I really don't like bugs." He scratched under his collar and I noticed then a scar near the base of his neck, brown against his pale skin.

I ran my foot over the tracks in front of us to erase them, hopefully easing his worry. "Let's keep moving. The door is up ahead. Do you need a hand?" I asked Balt, watching his labored breath. I offered to help him move, but he waved off my offer. I still slowed my pace so that he could keep up and, when we got to the door, I wiped the dust from the glass to get a peek of the hallway beyond to make sure there were no surprises waiting on the other side. Under the flickering lights, everything seemed clear, so I pushed the heavy door forward, the three of us continuing to tread down corridors long abandoned.

We hit an intersection further down and did a quick map check to figure out which way to continue going. Although it was a long shot, we decided we would try out the main lift that connected all the floors.

"Who knows," Smith suggested, "maybe it's still operational and we'll be able to ride it all the way to the surface!"

"Somehow I doubt our luck is that strong," I argued.

Balt shrugged, leaning against the wall, his face covered in sweat. "The lights . . . are still working," he said faintly. "That means there are still operational systems. How long exactly has this place been abandoned, Smith?"

Smith made a clicking sound. "According to Institute records, sixteen years, eight months, and twelve days."

"It doesn't matter," I said. "Let's just get there."

I caught a glimpse of Smith giving me a weird look and helped Balt get moving again, his breath getting heavier and coming out in heaves.

I didn't mean to be such a downer, arguing at every turn and squashing any hints of optimism they still held to. Even I realized, if there was one thing we needed to hang on to, it was hope. But everything felt jarring, like this place was trying to claw into my head. From the piercing cold, which made my bloodstained shirt feel like a rock, to Smith's voice cutting through my eardrums, to Balt's increasingly dire situation, none of this was going the way I hoped. It felt like it was only a matter of time before the bottom dropped out from beneath me.

The hallway we reached was pitch black, so we took our time with it, making sure Smith's lights illuminated every step. We made it about halfway down before Smith's voice halted us, its eye lights turning red.

"Shhhhh," he whispered. "Don't move."

We froze as instructed and I looked back to Balt's face, watching him as we listened. There was a crackling sound in the distance, like a wire sparking. We stood still as death for what felt like an hour and I was ready to dismiss Smith's warning after a few seconds, but then I heard it above us. A series of thuds. The sounds came from further down the hallway and when whatever it was got right above us, its weight was so heavy that it made the ceiling tiles shake violently. Even after it passed and its steps faded into the distance, none of us moved or made a sound.

A bead of sweat dripped down Balt's nose and he waited for my signal to move again, which I hesitated to give. Variant AI. If we bumped into one, the only option was to run. Run and hide. That wouldn't be easy with Balt wounded.

Smith whispered directions and we followed, Balt trailing

a few feet behind, trying his best not to groan in pain. Ruined hallway followed ruined hallway, and eventually we came to another set of glass double doors without incident, pushing them aside to reveal the lift entrance. We didn't get far though, stuck in our tracks at the sight that met our eyes.

"Well . . . feces," Balt concluded.

Feces was right.

The lift of the old labs wasn't like the one in our labs. Rather than just an unusually wide elevator, safely contained within reinforced walls, this lift sat in the middle of a massive gap in the lab ceiling. It was actually made up of a whole series of smaller lifts, connected to a singular spire that ran through the center of the entire facility like a spine. Various walkways connected the shaft across the open area so you could see every level above or below you as you walked, just by looking around. It must have been a sight to see before, but now it was the epitome of devastation.

Most of the walkways that led to the central lift bank had been destroyed, leaving the shaft inaccessible across the enormous pit. I looked up but there weren't enough functioning lights to see more than two or three levels above us. Below, it wasn't much better. The gap appeared so deep I wouldn't have been surprised if it led all the way to the core of the Earth.

"So much for that idea," Smith muttered.

"Maybe not," I said, pointing to our side. There were the thin remains of a walkway that reached across the massive opening. At one point, part of another walkway above it had collapsed. Together, the wreckage created a rough-looking ramp that lead to the floor above. It didn't look very sturdy, but it wasn't very long, probably only six or seven meters. For an able-bodied person, it wouldn't be a challenging climb.

Balt, though, was no able-bodied person.

Smith shook back and forth on my shoulder. "Under normal circumstances, I would say sure. But this isn't an experiment in the testing arena. There are no nanomachines to bring you two back if you fall a hundred stories to the ground."

"Are there any staircases nearby, Smith?" Balt asked, leaning on his pipe crutch.

After a few seconds, Smith pulled up the hologram again, highlighting the closest one, on the other side of the level. "We would need to double back and head around the gap."

"And hope we don't bump into one of those machines in the process," I added.

Balt nodded. "Or one of those . . . creatures that made the tracks in the testing arena."

Smith still wasn't convinced, rolling its eyes. "This isn't a race, people. It's longer, yes, but a better option than trusting that scrap of metal to hold our collective weight. And with Balt's foot, that isn't an easy climb."

I looked over the wreckage again, inspecting the way the metal had fallen. There were more than enough rivets in it for Balt to use his hands. He could do it. And I'd rather fall to my death than get torn apart by those variant AI.

"I say we try it," I concluded. I hated putting Balt in that spot, but the cold was eating me. I wanted to get out of here as quickly as possible.

Balt looked over the edge again before inspecting the ramp and grimaced, the sight clearly not appealing to him. His lips were crusting in the cold. I didn't want to admit to myself that I was forcing him to go, but when he looked to me, I gave him the slightest nod. I wanted him to try. Again, Balt trusted me.

"I can do it," he whispered. "Let's go."

Smith sighed. "Alright. But for the record, this is a terrible idea."

I was the first to step out on the walkway, the metal feeling surprisingly sturdy and solid beneath my feet. The further along we went though, the narrower it became, the darkness becoming more visible below us. "Watch your feet," I reminded Balt, but he shook his head.

"That makes me look at the fall."

I kicked a loose piece of metal out of our way and watched as it went tumbling down the gap, spinning into the darkness and never making a sound again. I gulped and just kept going on ahead, hoping Balt didn't notice that there was seemingly no bottom below us. The walkway opened up a bit when we got to the ramp. I gave the fallen piece of walkway a push but the series of twisted metal tiles never budged. It felt as sturdy as the concrete in the tunnel.

Bending my knee, I planted my foot in a hole of one of the collapsed beams and pulled myself upward, grabbing on some frayed copper wiring to steady myself. I planned each spot two moves ahead and slowly scaled the ramp, Smith turning about to check on Balt.

"One step at a time, Balt," Smith encouraged.

I looked back and caught a glimpse of him huffing. He was moving a lot slower, making sure not to put any weight on his foot, but he was coming along. Each pull made him shake and

I decided when I got to the top, I would look for something to lower down that he could grab on to. Maybe the added support would help. But in my stomach was this growing sense of dread, worrying that I was pushing him too hard.

With the summit within sight, I grabbed hold of a thin metal strut, using it to pull myself up. I put my foot within another hole in the ramp to continue my motion, but froze when I felt the ramp shudder as my weight shifted. Some loose pieces of concrete gave way and tumbled down, smashing against the walls of the level below on their way down into the darkness.

I waited until the wave of white-hot fear spread through my body before calling out to Balt. "Balt, are you . . ."

But before I could finish my sentence, the entire ramp shook and the metal strut I was holding came loose. I fell amid the wreckage and hit my back hard on something, twisting in the air as I went. My hands flailed about and found a grip on another strut, my fingers going white as they held on and a sharp pain lashing against my back. I looked about and realized then that the entire ramp had collapsed and was now dangling above the abyss below, Balt somewhere below me unseen.

If he hadn't already fallen off.

BALTAZAR

With a jolt, the metal beneath my feet gave way. I fell back and caught sight of the darkness below, sliding toward it for a few terrifying seconds with increasing velocity. Before I fell off the crumbling structure completely, my crutch caught on something during my tumble. My shoulder exploded in pain, but my fingers held tight, leaving me suspended in air with my legs dangling over empty darkness.

My breath quickened and drowned out everything else. Dirt and dust fell into my eyes, making them burn. Discomfort and strain continued to dig into my shoulder as the momentum of the fall rocked me back and forth, but I didn't lose my grip. I still had a chance.

In an effort to stop the motion, I threw my other hand up and gained a hold of my crutch. The extra support helped stabilize my sway, but I could feel the strain building within my muscles, my grip growing weaker by the second. I frantically looked about for something else to help me ascend the ramp, but there was nothing within reach. I was left with nothing to do but calculate what would give first, the tensile strength of my crutch under the pressure of the crumbling ramp or my muscles under my weakened physical strength.

My brain ran the numbers for both equations and, even with the most generous of estimates, both equaled I was screwed.

"Balt!" I finally heard over my breathing, my mind coming back from the equations. It was Zoe's voice, quickly followed by Smith's.

"Are you okay?"

I took a deep breath and felt the pain in my shoulders spread to my chest. I didn't have enough breath to respond though, just hanging on was draining enough. I swayed about and tried unsuccessfully to pull myself up again, getting my elbows bent to about a forty-five degree angle before my strength gave out. I closed my eyes, feeling gravity pull me down, too exhausted to try again. I just wanted to stop the pain and let go. I wanted to be out of this cold lab forever. But then I heard her voice again.

"Balt?"

I opened my eyes and caught sight of a new piece of frayed metal above me that had slipped out from under a piece of rubble. Gathering as much air into my wheezing lungs as I could, I swayed with the momentum of the wreckage once more, waiting until the optimum point in my motion before letting go of the crutch with one hand and making a swipe at a plate above me. My fingers caught the sharp edge and I was able to throw my elbow over the flat piece of metal, the added leverage enough to ease the pain in my arms temporarily. I caught my breath for a second before letting go of the crutch with my other arm and making for the next higher piece, grunting as I went. My muscles throbbed with such pain that I thought they might burst like balloons, but

I was able to muster just enough strength to climb onto a flat metal beam, saving myself temporarily from the threat of falling.

"I can hear him!" I could hear Smith shout. "He didn't fall off! Balt, are you hurt?"

I lay still for several seconds, giving my limbs some rest before slowly making my way on my stomach along the metal beam. There were odd indentations along the structure's side that I used to maintain my balance and keep myself from falling again. Absentmindedly though, I planted my bad foot on a piece of concrete and I could literally feel bone shards grinding together and poking against my skin, a blinding pain shooting up my leg. I let out a scream, my entire body throbbing while I wiped some dirt out of my eyes.

Protocol #121: *Pain and progress go hand in hand.*

Inch by inch, I moved up the strut until I caught sight of Zoe and Smith on top of what remained of the ramp. Zoe lay belly down on a metal beam that stuck out from the floor of the level above, Smith watching from her shoulder. I could also see then that the ramp holding me up was actually nothing more than a mere series of metal rods caught on broken concrete, chips of the latter breaking apart more and more with each sway of the wreckage.

My mind retreated again to math, estimating how long it would take for the force applied by the weight of the ramp to break the concrete, computing the metric tons of force standard concrete could take before giving way; meanwhile my arms kept pulling me up, crawling closer and closer to Zoe's face watching me from above. I was only a few feet away from her when the ramp creaked violently again. Falling a few feet back down, I caught my arm on another beam, wrenching my humerus nearly out of the socket. My strength was gone and all I could do was feebly raise my hand up to Zoe in my daze, hoping that she could reach it.

She regained her balance on the beam above and stared at me. It might have been myself losing consciousness, but I lost sense of time. That moment, staring at her eye to eye, seemed to last forever. It was as if the entire scene was cryogenically frozen. Slowly, she slid back off the beam out of my view and I just closed my eyes, conceding the struggle and waiting to fall.

In the darkness of my mind, I lost myself in the rocking motion of the wreckage and dwelled on the thought of my mother, of all people. I always pictured her with long black hair and soft skin. I'm not really sure why. I wondered if she held me just once before she turned me over to Parkman. Did we have a moment where I was safe in her gently rocking arms? Was she sad to let me go? Or did she feel relieved of the burden of another person to take care of?

Something hit me on the forehead, snapping me out of my reverie. Through blurry and burning eyes, I found a rope of twisted wires sitting on my chest. I coiled it around my arms as best I could and held it close to my stomach, almost like an umbilical cord. Slowly, I was hauled upward, the pain from my wounds and foot intensifying. *I must be dying*, I thought. I had experienced the sensation of my body shutting down enough times in the testing arena to recognize it. This was it.

My last thoughts were of Zoe, hoping she would be able to

make it to the surface. That would make this worth it, I thought. Then everything went black.

Then blue.

When I awoke, I was submerged in water, or some other kind of clear fluid, with a tube running down my throat. By pure reflex, I shot up through the surface, my head breaking the surface of the liquid like a missile. I pulled at the tube in my throat, feeling the plastic slide and initiate my gag reflex. When it was finally out, I began coughing so hard that I thought my lungs would burst. It took me several seconds to regain my breath, and only then did I begin to observe my surroundings.

I was floating in some sort of cylinder—a beat-up rejuvenation chamber from the look of it, the glass in front cracked but still holding together. Around me was a poorly lit lab with equipment strewn about, broken bits of ceiling littering the floor. On a table across from me, I caught sight of a bone saw, bright red with blood. My shattered foot still felt numb and when I examined it through the murky water, I saw that that leg was gone from the knee down. Amputated.

"That was a close call, Balt."

The voice startled me and I moved back in horror as two metal clamps grabbed the sides of the tube. A spider-like machine slowly made its way into my view, Smith's head mounted incongruously on the top, his white eyes a welcome sight.

"I'm glad to see you, Smith," I answered, relief washing over me. "For a second, I thought you were a variant AI."

He rocked his head from side to side. "Knowing our luck, I wouldn't be surprised if one came across our path now, with you short a limb."

I blew my nose hard to clear it of water. "So what happened?"

"Shock," he informed me. "You passed out while we dragged you up what was left of the ramp. Or while Zoe dragged you, that is. I just cheered her on. I told you two that path was a stupid idea. But no! Why listen to the AI with meta-intelligence?"

"Point taken."

"We were able to get you on a gurney and roll you over here, but infection had spread so far that there was nothing we could have done but amputate. So Zoe hooked me up to this medical chassis and I went to work. Thankfully, this rejuvenation chamber had enough juice left in it to grow back your leg. You should be good to go in another fifteen minutes or so."

I closed my eyes and focused on my leg, a burning sensation tingling my skin as the nanomachines in the water slowly rebuilt the cells. "Where's Zoe?"

Smith motioned toward the door. "There's a bathroom down the hall. She went in there to clean up a bit." He was silent for a second, inching closer to the tube. "I think we need to talk about her."

I floated closer to his face. "What do you mean? Is she okay?"

"Oh, she's fine. Safe and sound. But, it's just . . . well, how much do you remember before you blacked out?"

I scratched my head, trying to remember the ramp. The images were there, but most of it felt foggy, like it happened in a dream almost. "I remember falling. And the cord coming down."

"Do you remember when she was ready to let you fall?"

A thud-like sensation hit my stomach. "What? No."

"I don't want to be accusatory, but I know what I saw. Before you fell the second time, you were close to the top. You raised your hand to her and, if she really wanted to, she could have reached you."

"She wouldn't have let me fall if she could have avoided it."

Smith looked to the ceiling. "Look, I'm not saying that we should abandon Directive 2 or anything like that . . ."

I covered his mouth with my hand, looking back to the door to make sure she wasn't there. "C'mon, Smith. Not nova."

"I'm just saying. The three of us are in this together, but *you* are my creator. I'm trying to look out for *you*. I can't help her fall in love with you if you're dead."

"You must have miscalculated, Smith," I insisted. "Zoe wouldn't do that. Most likely, the circumstances made her scared and she hesitated. It wasn't exactly the easiest of situations to be in."

Smith inched closer in again and checked the door by peering over one of his robotic legs. "All I'm saying is that Zoe is a survivor, first and foremost. That much is clear. You may be willing to risk it all for her, but I know what I saw. She's not going to risk getting to the surface safely for you. Just make sure you remember that."

We didn't say anything after that and I thought about Zoe as I floated in the water, waiting for my leg to fully reconstruct. The truth was I did remember what Smith was referring to. I reached out my hand and she'd just stared back, indecision filling her eyes. But I wasn't going to condemn her for that. I didn't know what was going on in her mind.

When I was finally able to wiggle my toes, I pulled myself out of the rejuvenation chamber and Smith handed me a towel and a fresh pair of clothes to change into. The air was ice cold so I dried and changed as quickly as I could, welcoming the clean shirt and pants that felt ten times warmer. I breathed into my hands to restore some feeling back into them, but stopped when a loud scream reverberated down the hall. Zoe.

I didn't hesitate to run to her.

ZOE

As hard as I scrubbed, I couldn't get the blood and dirt off my skin. But I still felt filthy, so I kept scrubbing. I rubbed the ratty soap I'd found against my skin so hard that I was turning red, the blood vessels underneath the surface breaking. It felt like the filth would always be on me, like I was tainted with the dirt of the old labs, never to be fully clean again.

My eyes teared up under the shower, but the streams of water pouring from the rusted showerhead hid them. The boiler was still working so I did my best to move and give all of my frozen limbs some time under the hot water before it ran out. The relief was only temporary though because the air was so cold that the second a part of me wasn't under the water, the chill attacked my wet skin, freezing me once again. Eventually I just gave up and turned off the shower, drying off as quickly as I could and putting on the fresh pair of clothes Smith and I had discovered in a locker. The shirt was too small and the sleeves only made it to my forearms, but it was dry. A new skin to inhabit.

After tossing my old clothes into a corner, I walked to the only sink that wasn't broken and filled my hands with cold water to help me swallow a meal pill. It tasted extremely bitter and made me wince going down, but I could feel my stomach filling in seconds, vital nutrients making their way into my bloodstream. I felt better, but not well. Still filthy and cold.

In my head, I repeated the words to one of the songs I had restored for my midterm. A girl, accompanied by beautifully resonant piano notes flowing smoothly like the fins of a stingray, sang it. But as wonderful as the sound of the instrument was, the girl's tone sounded fractured and on the verge of breaking. She repeated over and over to herself that everything was going to be alright, but the tone of her voice indicated she really believed quite the opposite. I mouthed hollow encouragements and stared at myself in the mirror across from me, a grime slowly consuming it from the edges. Dark patches had formed under my eyes and my skin was a ghastly white. I grabbed at my hair, locking eyes with this person that looked back. Her eyes were black. Lifeless.

Like the girl in the song, I kept telling myself that things were going to be okay. That the worst was behind us.

But saying and believing were two very different things. I thought back to Balt, when he'd fallen on the collapsed ramp. The ramp I suggested we climb. After he fell, he'd reached a tremulous hand toward me and begged me with his eyes to help him. But I just lay there on the beam above, not moving. It was just a moment, but telling enough for me. The first thought that came was how it would be easier to go on without him. I wouldn't have to get more attached to him and be filled with worry.

When you cared about people, it was only a matter of time before you lost them. That was a lesson the Institute had never prepared me for. Helena was my best friend, and the void she left was so big that part of me wondered if I had simply become the void, the emptiness, and incapable of being filled anymore.

If it wasn't for Smith shouting in my ear to grab that wire rope, I wondered if I would have let him fall after all. Even after everything he'd done for me.

I blinked in the mirror, but I swore my eyes never closed.

I ran my fingers through my wet hair and tightened as I went, pulling so hard that I could feel the strands being ripped from my scalp. I hated the girl I was looking at, this dark girl with empty eyes. I grabbed a shard of glass from one of the many broken mirrors in the room and began to hack away, cutting clumps of filthy hair. My scalp burned as I went, but I didn't stop until the floor was littered, leaving my head lighter. Cleaner.

There was still so far to go. And I worried that even if we did make it to the surface, who would be the girl who emerged from the darkness? What was the price I had to pay to get out of here?

It was only for a second, but in the mirror, I saw faint bands of light, flashes of Dr. Parkman standing behind me, smiling. Pain instantly pricked my skin and I screamed, whirling to face him. But when I turned, no one was there.

I was breathing so hard that I thought I would swallow my tongue. And no matter how many times I told myself that things would be okay, I didn't believe it. Somewhere deep inside, I knew how this would end.

Balt came hurrying in a moment later, limp free. He had on a new shirt that fit him closely, giving me a look at the outlines of his arm muscles under his sleeves. I was surprised to see him for some reason, and he mimicked my shock, his head cocking back at the sight of me.

"Are you alright?" he asked.

I'm so sorry, Balt.

"Yeah," I answered, rubbing my eyes. "I thought I . . . it's nothing."

He walked closer and smirked. "Got tired of the hair?"

I ran my hand over what was left on my head, the short strands feeling wet and uneven. "I just wanted to be free of it."

"Looks pretty thermal."

Unbidden, a smile broke on my face. "Thanks." I looked down to his leg, feeling it with my foot. "Guess the rejuvenation chamber helped?"

He gave a little hop, rotating his ankle on the injured foot. "Feels as good as new, actually. If you need me to kick anything, I'll be ready."

I laughed, imagining us running into a ten-ton robot and Balt's kick resulting in a loud thud. "Let's hope it doesn't come to that."

We were quiet then, and the guilt of my thoughts consumed me again. I couldn't look him in the eyes and, sensing something was bothering me, he took my hands in his. I watched his breath beneath his shirt. After a few moments, I couldn't help looking up into his eyes, and then suddenly I was lost—caught in those soft, brown eyes. I realized I was changing. Slowly. Helena's death, the doctors' torture, and the glacial cold of this place were getting inside my brain and, if I was going to survive, I had to shut them and everything else out in my life. But when I looked at Balt, I felt like the girl that had lived before everything had gone wrong, that I was still the girl who drew and got lost within herself walking among the wooded paths of Level H. That was how he saw me.

So I took a step forward and kissed him. He was rigid at first, not expecting it. But as the seconds passed, his lips glided over mine and he held my hips in his hands. I rested my forearms on his shoulders and did my best to let go, to forget this cold, dark lab and Dr. Parkman, and just remember, if only for a few seconds, who I was.

Then I realized how much trouble I really was in. If I let this continue, the void that Balt would leave might be even greater. And surely then there would be nothing left of me.

I pulled away, flustered. "This is . . . we can't do this." His eyes were glazed and I wasn't sure he heard me. "Let's just get moving again," I suggested and exited the bathroom as quickly as I could, leaving him standing there—probably feeling extremely confused. I wanted to just run back and kiss him again, but I knew I was doing the right thing. This trip was a bomb ready to go off, and the shrapnel would be too much if I let myself get more attached to him. Better not make it any harder on myself.

I headed back to the operating room with the rejuvenation chamber and Balt slowly followed. We found Smith flailing about; the medical chassis was attached to the wall and was limited to how far it could move. "Oh, thank goodness. We thought you had been attacked or something."

"I just got spooked," I explained. "I'm sorry." I shuddered from the cold and took a deep breath, doing my best to forget the glimpse of Dr. Parkman that had crept back into my mind. I must be more tired than I thought.

"What happened to your hair?" Smith asked, but Balt answered for me.

"It's the latest style for old lab excavations. Don't you know anything, Smith?"

His joke was enough to disarm Smith, but I could detect the

hurt hidden in his voice. I had made things worse, as always, but he wasn't going to cast me aside. I just hoped that he didn't do anything ridiculous like risk his life to save me again.

"Well, if we're all in high spirits again, I suggest we get going. The quicker we get moving, the sooner we can leave this awful place behind us for good," Smith suggested and pulled up the map of the labs. We traced our point and decided to head for the closest staircase now that the lifts were out of the question. The nearest one wasn't too far away and, with any luck, we could use them to get up a few floors.

We had to detach Smith from the medical chassis, much to its chagrin. Balt mounted it back on the strap I'd made and offered it to me, but I declined. "I think it fits you better. A boy and his robot."

Balt and Smith looked at each other, shrugging after a second. "I suppose you're with me. I'll try not to make the trip too rocky for you."

Smith rolled its eyes after a few steps. "I literally don't think your shoulder could be any more unstable. Thankfully, I don't need to eat, or else I'd be puking my robotic guts out by now."

After making one last pass through the room for any useful supplies we could carry, we set off. Using his eyes, Smith lit the way as we moved through the first few dark hallways, traveling as quietly as we could. When we found the staircase, it took our combined strength to push the door open enough to squeeze through. Once on the other side, we saw why: a pile of rubble had fallen on the other side, blocking the door's swing. The stairs leading up were clear and we were able to make it up another level. Unfortunately, that's as far as the stairs would take us.

"Better than nothing," Balt declared, staring at the tons of jagged metal that filled the stairs going up. "One down, seven to go."

"You don't think we could try clearing it or something?" I asked.

"It would take quite a bit of time," Smith answered. "And the possibility of a cave-in as we went would be something to worry about."

This time I didn't argue. I wanted us to be safe. We exited the staircase, leaving the medical level behind us and entered the education and testing level. Progress. We checked the map again and started moving toward the next closest stairwell, coming across an old classroom that still had power. Lines of chairs were bolted to the ground on both sides of the small room and there was a desk in the corner. I walked behind it and checked the drawers for anything useful but, other than a disassembled datapad, it was completely empty.

A large painting of Dr. Parkman Jr., the current Dr. Parkman's father, hung on the wall, his hands on his hips. He looked huskier than his son, but they had essentially the same face. Pale, aged skin and slicked-back black hair. The image of Dr. Parkman standing behind me in the bathroom flashed in my mind and I felt a chill run up my spine. Even here, he was still watching us.

"This is interesting," Balt said, waving me over. I emerged from behind the desk and found him kneeling on the floor, a floor tile removed near him. Under it, there appeared to be a circuit center and, after fooling with some of the wires, the lights in the room began to flicker.

"Ahhh, don't do that," I warned.

He squinted. "Sorry. But this could be helpful. Smith, I would like to connect you. Can you initiate the virtual interface?"

"I'll certainly give it a try," the AI answered and after it was attached, it projected a large holographic cube with it eyes, each section of the cube's surface pulsating a different color. Balt began to move his fingers about it, dismantling the cube piece by piece and moving the smaller components inside each section around. He had his patented Balt concentration in full force and, after a few seconds, I could hear little clicks emerging from the hallway ahead, the lights turning on.

"Great job, Balt," I said, looking down the well-lit path ahead. "We'll be able to see everything ahead of us."

He nodded but didn't look at me, still focused on the cube. "Just give me a few minutes. I still see a few systems I can reinitiate. Who knows, maybe I can even find a way to get the lift running again."

I nodded but turned my attention back to the lit hallway, catching something moving at the end of it. I inched closer and, without warning, I caught a glimpse of a blur of light moving past the end of the hall. My shoulders jumped. I wanted to ask Balt or Smith if they'd seen it, but they were too focused on the cube.

I swallowed hard. "I'm just gonna go check something out," I said.

"Wait, what?" Balt answered, breaking his concentration to look at me.

Smith squinted in my direction. "Are you sure that's a good idea?"

It wasn't. Not at all. But between this and my glimpse of Dr. Parkman in the bathroom, I knew *something* was happening, and if it was all in my head, I didn't want the others to know I was seeing things.

"It'll be okay," I reassured them. "I won't be far."

I started walking down the hallway, looking back a few times to make sure they weren't following me. I gave my eyes a rub and concentrated on my breathing, wondering what I wanted more. Did I want to find something at the end of the hall? Or did I want to be losing my mind?

BALTAZAR

"I don't like this, Balt," Smith reminded me for what seemed like the ten-thousandth time. It's not that I disagreed. I didn't wish to separate with Zoe in this dangerous place either, especially since it was clear something was bothering her. But what was I supposed to do? Tie her up and carry her to the surface?

Distracted, one of my fingers slipped and accidently touched a live circuit. I flailed my hand through the air, but it did little to assuage the burning sensation throbbing in my nerves. "Ahhhhhh, son of a butane torch!"

"Oh. Sorry," Smith said bashfully. "You should be concentrating."

I sat back on my rear and sucked on my finger, the circuit cube hovering before me. Smith was right, but I just couldn't focus. Not after that kiss. Protocol #76: *Expectations should be tempered because the outcome often never meets the desired threshold.* Those few seconds did more than meet my expectations. Kissing Zoe created within me sensations that I would have to spend lifetimes studying linguistics in hopes of accurately describing. Awe? Bliss?

She said it was a mistake but I wasn't sure why. How could anything that felt so right be a mistake?

"Zoe said she would return shortly," I said, trying to get back on task. "We'll just work on getting as many systems running as we can and then get moving again when she returns. Protocol #19: *worry about the problems in front of you, first and foremost.*"

"You're still reciting Parkman protocols?"

I looked to the oil painting of Dr. Parkman's father above us. He was the man who'd taken his own father's concept for a scientific refuge and turned it into what it was today, expanding the lab and scope of the projects being conducted. Our Dr. Parkman was given a lot of the credit for PISS, but really, it was his father that deserved his portrait in every room. Or, at least I thought he did. If what I thought I knew about him was true.

"The protocols are still good advice," I argued. "Regardless of whether everything else PISS told us is a lie. Can you assist me with this system on the bottom here?" I asked, hoping to change the subject. "The one that's flashing green."

Smith made the holographic cube larger, the section in question turning to face me. "What do you think it is? More lights?" he asked.

I squinted, tracing the sub-circuits emerging from it with my eyes. "I don't believe so. There's a video signal embedded in it. Many of them are fried, but there are a few still . . ." I trailed off as I focused on shifting the power lines without shocking myself again. I slowed down my breathing to steady my hands, removing the broken lines so I could concentrate on what was still viable. Then, in a flash, a series of boxes appeared before me. Most of them were just blank, but a few showed video feeds from various parts of the labs.

"It's a security network," I realized after examining the screens, pulling up the still active cameras to get a better look.

"This is helpful. We could use these to possibly find a safe route to the next level."

"Or get a lead on something that might murder us," Smith suggested.

"That too."

My eyes scanned the feeds one by one, taking in everything I could before switching to the next. Most of what they showed was pretty unremarkable: a dark empty hallway, a broken-down lab, a pile of rubble. But in the corner of my eye, I caught something move and highlighted it, attempting to take control of the camera. The camera trembled as it turned but I was able to find the object as I paned left.

It was Zoe, staring at a wall.

"Oh, it's just Zoe," Smith stated, before zooming in closer. "What is she doing?"

The camera was continually flickering in and out, the image quality shoddy at best, but it was definitely her. I felt bad spying on her, but at least it reassured me that she was safe.

At least physically, that is.

For over a minute, she stared at the blank wall, the surface completely devoid of any features. She ran her fingers across it ever so slightly as if she wanted to touch it, but was afraid something was going to emerge from it and bite her. It reminded me of the night she stole Smith. When I found her in the stairway then, everything around her appeared strange to her eyes.

Suddenly, in the feed, her head turned like she heard something, even though the camera wasn't picking up any sound. She started moving down the hall, turning the corner and forcing me to switch feeds to continue following her.

The closest I could get was a shot from a hallway watching two thick security doors on busted hinges. Zoe walked past them slowly and I eased the camera lower to see into the room. It appeared to be a small lab overlooking something through a wall made entirely of glass. She stopped before the glass wall to look out. Whatever she saw though, it was out of my line of sight.

"Looks like she found something," Smith said. "Should we try to get another angle?"

I shook my head, turning off the feed. "Negative. If she finds anything of worth, she'll inform us when she gets back."

"You're not concerned that she just lopped off all her hair and is going for strolls through an infested lab, feeling walls?"

"That was rather bizarre, wasn't it?"

"It's a little more than bizarre, Balt. It's troubling. What if she's . . . you know . . . starting to become unhinged?"

The notion seemed illogical to me, like a faulty equation. "Unlikely," I argued. "You said it yourself, she's a survivor. She's tougher than that. We'll ask her about it when she gets back. I'm sure it'll make sense then."

Smith rolled his eyes, dropping the issue. We continued to work on the circuit, but Zoe stuck in the back of my mind. Even after allegedly being ready to leave me to die, her kiss confirmed for me that the feelings I had for her were more than some chemical attraction. I was indeed on the verge of discovering something great in my pursuit of her. The thought of her kiss filled my chest with warmth, my breath suddenly even more visible in the cold.

It was then that I started to worry that, when it came to her, maybe I'd lost the ability to remain objective. Perhaps, no matter how dire our situation became, I wouldn't be able to make logical choices when it came to her. If she *was* cracking, maybe I wouldn't recognize it until it was too late.

I put the feed on again, watching her run out of the room at full speed.

"Oh no, is something after her?" I said, panicking. I looked to Smith, but the AI had turned his line of sight away, moving the circuit cube out of my reach. "Hey, what are you—" I began to say but stopped when I heard it. In the distance, a scratching noise, like someone dragging something sharp against metal, reverberated down the hall. My initial instinct was to hide, but I felt frozen to the floor, unable to move an inch.

"Balt, something's coming," Smith whispered frantically, but I still couldn't move, my eyes fixed in the direction of the noise. My hands shook and just when I was finally able to get my legs to stand up, it was too late.

The head of a giant, ant-like creature poked its way through the doorway, its hulking body easily double or triple my size. It had two antennae, round compact eyes, and sharp mandibles that dripped a clear goo. Its neck was several feet long, and it slowly emerged from the back door we'd taken from the stairway. I ducked behind the desk on the side wall before it turned in my direction.

With my heart pounding in my throat, I peered around the desk's corner to get a better view of it. The creature was enormous and scaly, the neck extending its head several feet above the rest of its body, which resembled a praying mantis. I recalled the prints we'd found earlier in the testing arena and hypothesized that this was one of the creatures that had emerged from the sinkhole—the shape of its claws matched exactly. That indicated there might be more of them, possibly close by.

The scar on my shoulder suddenly burned. The word "nightmare" kept cropping up in my thoughts over and over again. The creature concentrated on the lobby chairs bolted down to the ground, picking at them with its two front legs. I turned to Smith, hoping for a suggestion or idea, but he may as well have been shut down, his eyes shut and mouth hanging open. The only other thing I could think to do was make a break for the door Zoe had taken. It was only ten feet away or so and, if I could get there without the ant-mantis noticing, I had a chance to escape.

Before I could gather enough courage to make the move, the insect's long neck peered over the desk, its head hovering over me and dripping a glob of goo on my shoulder.

I screamed and scrambled out from behind the desk, running and slipping on some loose tiles after a few feet. The ant mantis made this horrible hissing sound and spread its wings, flying through the air in a flash and landing between me and the door. I fumbled about on my hands and knees back to the other side of the lobby, heaving with panic as the insect's front legs jabbed at me, trying to pin me to the floor. Each blow shattered the tiles and sent dust billowing into the air. I continued to move, Smith screaming in my ear the entire time, until I found myself near the back door leading back to the stairwell. It was entirely the wrong direction, and I hated the thought of leaving Zoe, but I had no other choice but to run.

Without warning, a series of connected lobby seats flew over my head and smashed into the door. The ant-mantis had ripped them from the ground and they now blocked my path. I could try to climb over them, but the creature was advancing so fast that it would be on top of me before I had a chance.

I was trapped.

ZOE

The olm is a foot-long salamander that lived underground its entire life, never seeing the light of day. While it possessed merely average metabolism and antioxidant activity (the two most important factors when determining lifespan) compared to other similar creatures, it would survive nearly twice as long as its counterparts would. The average olm could live to be more than a hundred years old. With its light fleshy skin, it glowed a translucent white color when exposed to light. Almost like a ghost in the darkness.

But what I was seeing were not olms. And I didn't like what they were showing me.

After separating from Balt and Smith in the lobby, I followed the blur of light through hall after hall, the sight began to remind me of an exhibit I saw when I was younger, learning about the nervous system in class. We got to see the human body digitally stripped of muscle and bone, leaving only the energy transfers visible to give it shape. The bands of light flashed and sparked white between the nerve endings, like billions of microscopic fireworks. It was a beautiful sight. One that made me feel special to be alive.

The longer I followed the light through the halls, more of them began to pass back and forth. The figures moved through me whenever we collided, appearing increasingly human-like. I could make out faint hints of their faces and voices when they approached, but there were so many that their words were lost in the cacophony. It actually was a comforting feeling at first. Like this place wasn't devoid of life after all.

Then my nose began to bleed again and I had to wipe it on my sleeve. A throbbing headache soon followed. Seeing these figures was taking a toll on my body like teleporting did, yet I couldn't turn away.

I fought through the pain and found the first figure I'd followed leaning against a wall. He was a young guy, maybe in his mid-twenties. I was able to get close and really look at the strips of light that composed him, trying to feel them with my hands. But, like the others, he just passed through me, leaving me nothing to feel but the cold wall behind him. He disappeared only to reappear further down the hall, outside a series of broken security checkpoints, the thick doors torn off their hinges. Whatever this part of the lab was, it was high-security, and this figure was leading me toward it. I slid through a set of broken doors and found a small lab. Inside was a single workstation and one wall completely made of glass. It was in there that I found the rotting corpse in a chair, a scalpel still clutched in its hand.

Although it shouldn't have come as a shock, since I knew a lot of the staff didn't make it out in time, the sight unnerved me. Even though the body had to have been there for some time, the stench of death still lingered in the air. The skeleton sat within tattered clothes and I moved in close enough to read the nametag on its lab coat, the black surface covered with dust.

Dr. Alexander Parkman Jr.

The current Dr. Parkman's father.

The realization was shocking at first, as I recalled his portrait hanging proudly on the wall in the lobby where I left Balt. He'd looked larger than life but of course, in the end, he was nothing but a pile of rotting matter—just like the rest of us. The whispers began to fill my ears again and I turned back toward the center of the room, a broken-down cylinder that looked like a rejuvenation chamber standing tall. The voices continued to grow louder to the point where I had to press my palms against my ears until they all suddenly stopped. Then a figure of white slowly materialized out of nothing near the cylinder.

Dr. Parkman's father.

His ghost had arrived.

He moved about the cylinder, taking notes on something before moving to a door I hadn't seen before. Echo wasn't the right word, but it was the first to come to mind as I watched him. It was like I was seeing a reverberation of the past, a fleeting glimpse of what happened here.

I followed him through a door on the far end of the room and down a small flight of steps. This led to the area overlooked by the glass wall in the lab. It was as large as a testing arena and, every few feet, more broken-down cylinders stood tall like a miniature city. I walked among them, catching glimpses of Dr. Parkman's father weaving through them, taking notes as he went. I stopped near one and felt the edges of the shattered glass that was left of their walls, almost jumping out of my shoes when I heard another voice behind me.

Next to Dr. Parkman's father stood a female scientist, much younger than he was. She had her hair pulled back into a ponytail and was peering deeply into one of the cylinders, eagerly studying whatever was contained inside. They must have been part of an experiment—most likely a secret one, given the amount of security outside the lab. Then the girl spoke to him, her voice sounding like an actual echo in the vast room.

"You realize now that there are more of them here than us," she said, turning to Dr. Parkman's father. He didn't look at her, but stroked his beard while studying something in his hands.

"It was inevitable," he said after a second. His voice sounded similar to his son's, making my skin crawl. I moved closer to them, but they never altered their course. It was like I was watching a torrent play out in 3D, unable to affect the scene before me.

"You don't think that increases the risk? It was easy enough to convince them at first, but now so many former students have joined the staff," she replied, a worry in her voice that sounded familiar. "There are already whispers of discontent. The lack of communication with people back home isn't sitting well. They realize things aren't adding up."

Dr. Parkman's father still didn't look at her, writing something on what was probably his datapad. "Elizabeth, what is 'truth' to you?"

The woman seemed taken aback by the question, her head tilting downward. I moved beside her, just making out her eyelashes in the light. "I don't understand what you're asking, sir."

"I'm asking you about the nature of truth."

"Truth is fact," she replied. Her voice was nervous and she adjusted her stance.

"Well then, you are mistaken," he spat back, his voice dismissive. "Truth and scientific law are two very different things.

Truth is merely the perception of those in control, and while their numbers are growing, they're *not* in control. They believe they are here to save humanity, but their only purpose is to advance the work of the Institute. We test them, use them, keep the brightest, and discard the rest. As long as that continues, we are in control."

He wrote something down on his invisible datapad before looking to her, his stare almost powerful enough to knock me over. "You are part of this project because you were deemed able to be trusted. And pardon me for being severe, but if you don't have the stomach for this anymore, I'm sure there are plenty of other projects that can use your talents."

I could see her muscles tense up before she and Dr. Parkman's father began to fade, their light dying and leaving me alone in the expansive room full of broken cylinders. I stood there a moment, trying to parse their words. What were they lying to everyone about? The number of *what* was growing? What was being grown in these cylinders?

It was then that I heard the cry of a baby.

It was distant at first, but the shrillness of it gave me goose bumps. I thought about going toward the sound, but then I heard another. And another. Suddenly they appeared all around me, these ghosts of fetuses floating within the broken cylinders. Everywhere I looked, they were all I could see, and their cries just continued to grow louder and louder. The sound was so intense that their waves rattled my bones.

My instinct was just to cry along with them. Because I had. Because we all had. We were all created down here, not brought down from the surface.

The revelation sent me into a panic and I ran toward the

door, tripping on the stairs toward the lab on the way up. My knee throbbed, but I didn't stop, moving into a full sprint down the security hallway back toward Balt. But no matter how fast I ran, I could still hear their cries. They bored into my mind and bubbled under my skin.

The world was spinning, and when I finally made it back to the lobby, my sense of reality morphed from unstable to almost dreamlike. Was anything that I was seeing real? The cries were replaced with a buzzing in my ears as I stood by the door, watching a giant mantis-like creature thrash inside. I arrived just in time to see it rushing toward Balt as he lay defenseless on the ground, left with nowhere to run.

As if it was calling to me, my eyes caught sight of a piece of pipe that lay near the door. I snatched it up, my fingers curled around its steel exterior so tightly I thought that I could snap it in two. What I had just seen mixed with my memories of the past few weeks, confusion, anger, and frustration combining together to create a volcano inside me.

And I was ready to explode.

BALTAZAR

My face burned hot and, with no other options, I threw my hands up to protect myself. The giant insect closed in, rearing up on its back legs. Hissing filled my ears and I shut my eyes, awaiting the blow from its strong legs. I would have chosen any other death but this, I thought. This place was truly a nightmare.

Suddenly a loud scream echoed off the walls, drowning out the insect's hissing. I shouted as well, instinctively, as if I was just impaled. All I could do as the seconds passed was scream and thrash about, but the pain never came. I opened my eyes to see the creature's head snap back, smacking the wall so hard that it left an imprint and knocked down the portrait of Dr. Parkman's father.

Zoe was standing near the monster, armed with a thick steel pipe. The insect hissed at her as it regained its footing. I knew she couldn't hold the thing off in a straight fight, so to recapture its attention, I grabbed a piece of broken ceiling tile near my foot and chucked it. The weak molding struck one of the ant-mantis's wings and broke apart ineffectively. The insect snapped its head in my direction and, in doing so, left itself open for Zoe to attack. She didn't waste the opportunity, bashing its side with the pipe over and over.

On the third stroke, Zoe's pipe crushed the insect's carapace, spraying a sticky green substance everywhere. Zoe yelled and continued whaling away, leaving the ant mantis, a broken and gooey pulp, collapsed on the floor. Rather than stopping, she kept on hitting it, seemingly not satisfied until she had beaten the carcass through to the floor.

I remained on the floor and watched, nervous to move as Zoe vented a rage that I hadn't thought her capable of. Screaming until her voice gave out, she continued to bash until there was nothing left to beat out of the creature. Its internal organs and fluid had spilt all over the floor, filling the room with a horrendous smell. Then she just let the pipe drop with a clang, huffing and puffing where she stood.

I still didn't dare make the first move. It was so quiet that I could hear the buzz from Smith's CPU.

When Zoe finally regained her breath, she walked over to me and looked me over before offering her hand. Streaks of the creature's green blood were splattered all over her clothes and there was a hollow look to her eyes, like the blue had faded away. It was Zoe, but it felt different. She was different.

"Are you okay?" she asked, a chill in her voice.

I checked her other hand to make sure the pipe was gone for sure. "Ye . . . yeah. Thanks."

She nodded, wiping a wad of goo from her shirt after helping me up. We looked at the corpse of the ant mantis again and I let out a nervous laugh. "You showed him, huh?"

"Remind me not to get on your bad side, Zoe," Smith added.

She ignored our comments and motioned toward the door she came from. "It's just a dead end that way. There's nothing there. I say we double back to the stairs and try a different route."

Smith knew it was a lie.

I knew it was a lie.

I knew that she'd seen something in that room that made her run at full speed in the opposite direction.

But the last thing I wanted to do was question her truthfulness. "Okay," I answered. "Let's go, I guess."

I walked behind her, Smith turning on my shoulder in an attempt to get me to look at him, but I kept my eyes glued on Zoe, following her lead. I knew what Smith wanted to say. I realized, just as he did, that things were becoming more complicated. She'd said I could trust her, and I wanted to believe her more than anything.

But she was lying to me about something. Again. My only hope was that it wasn't as bad as what I imagined.

ZOE

We quietly made our way toward the next staircase, a journey of roughly three miles of ruined labs and who knew what else. I walked out in front and Balt and Smith trailed. The lights in the corridors were still mostly functional, which—though helpful—gave the old labs an eerie, tense feeling, as though the things that had killed the occupants might still be lurking in the next lab. My brain kept demanding for me to stop and think, to process what I had seen earlier and put the pieces together. But I didn't want to. I was scared to, afraid of how it would change what our goal was here. Change everything, really. As long as we kept moving, I could focus on that and nothing else: moving one leg after another, not the implications of what that lab showed me or what the ghosts I was seeing were, or anything. Just moving. Just moving.

My plan worked, but not forever. We continued on but, eventually, the weariness began to catch up to us, Balt and I had been awake for almost two straight days now, and just keeping our heads up began to take effort. It was funny to think that it hadn't been so long ago that I was in my bed, warm under the sheets. This cold lab felt like it went on for eternity, like there was never a time when we *weren't* down here, fumbling in the dark.

After passing through a series of double doors, we found

ourselves in what looked like an education wing, the rooms around us filled with overturned desks and cracked display boards. I was so tired that I literally felt like I was floating in air until I stumbled and glided a few feet before finding ground, and I realized that it wasn't entirely in my head.

I turned to Balt and watched him come to the same realization. He grabbed a piece of glass on the floor and tossed it behind us. I ahead my breath as we watched the shining triangle sail through the air in half speed before finding ground and cracking.

"The gravity is different here," he concluded, lifting his feet and hopping. It took him a full second or two to reach the peak of his ascent before falling to the ground again in just as much time. "What do you think, Smith? A fifth?"

Smith emitted a clicking sound. "I would say about sixteen percent as strong. There must be an arena nearby with a gravity well left on that setting."

"We should keep moving," I said, rubbing my eyes. I thought I heard a baby cry in the distance and shook my head. Must keep moving.

Balt shook his head. "We need to stop and rest, Zoe."

"We can make it a bit a farther," I said, but could barely get the words out without yawning.

"We don't need to push it," he said and moved to one of the classroom doors, pushing it with his shoulder. "Maybe in here."

I lingered in the hallway a bit by myself, catching a glimpse of a figure of light back the way we'd come. I couldn't see its face, but it felt like it was staring at me. Watching me. I followed Balt inside and shut the door behind me, the two of us propping a few desks against it to make it difficult for anything to follow us in.

Parkman's Wasteland Survival Kit had a pack of these small cubes called "insta-burns" which glowed hot when cracked open. When we were sure it was safe, we opened one up on the floor and lay around it. I didn't want to stop, but finally conceded to try and get a few hours of sleep before making a push for the stairway and, hopefully, the next level. After popping our meal pills, we did our best to get comfortable on the hard floor and lower gravity, leaving Smith to watch the door and warn us of any dangers.

Balt kept his eyes on the floor, never looking me in the eye. He was more cool and distant than usual but when he closed his eyes, he was asleep within seconds, safe somewhere else. I closed my eyes and tried to relax, but sleep wouldn't come easy, despite how tired I was. I didn't see any ghosts, but their voices still whispered in my ears.

After what seemed like hours of tossing and turning, I gave up on sleep and opted to just sit and stare at the flickering cube. I was hoping the closer we got to the surface, the better I would feel, but it was dark in this lab and each step just seemed to create another crack in my courage. I tried burying the feelings deep like I always did, but it was getting harder not to feel buried beneath the truth as it continued to pile upon me.

I thought about the lab I discovered and what I knew about human growth technology. The rejuvenation chambers were the pinnacle of that field, using the blue prints dictated by nanomachines to reconstruct students and scientists after undergoing fatal testing. Surely that technology might have other uses. It wouldn't have been hard to create people from scratch, based on some random genetic make-up generated by a computer rather than two living beings.

And in the end, that's what we were. Just human products, created to be used and discarded by PISS.

I watched Balt sleep in the light of the insta-burn. He must have been cold because his teeth began to chatter and in his sleep, he tucked his knees to his chest.

Lying in the fetal position, just like the babies floated in the cylinders.

I grabbed a large piece of plastic covering a desk and draped it over him, making sure the edges wouldn't melt from the insta-burn. It wasn't the best thing to help him keep warm, but it would do. He didn't wake and I could see his face slowly calm, his mind clearing.

I watched him for a bit longer, his purple lips moving ever so slightly as he dreamt. I hoped it was of something wonderful: a warm meal or bed, or maybe even the family that he hoped to fill his empty picture frame with. The thought of it dug into me like a shovel and I buried my face in my hands to keep myself from crying.

I wanted nothing more to do with all the experimenting, but the truth was I would never be free of it. I was a slave to that laboratory all my life, from my very conception. We all were. The realization that we were grown down here like crops didn't seem surprising, given the rest of the lies Parkman told us, but it hit me harder than any other truth we'd uncovered thus far.

I was flesh and blood like anyone else, but I felt fake. Unnatural. Despite my blue eyes and love of art and all the other things that I thought made me unique, the truth was I wasn't. I would have the imprint of the Institute stamped on me forever, and not even the surface would allow me to escape that.

Balt stirred and pulled the desk cover tighter, mumbling something about a bug. I thought again about his empty picture frame and how it would never be filled. It crushed me, but I didn't know how I could make things better. The truth was bleak, and getting bleaker by the moment.

But he still had the light at the end of the tunnel, I realized. I didn't want to let him care about me, but I didn't need to hurt him. He still believed that somewhere up there was a beautiful world with a family waiting to welcome him with open arms, that everything we were going through now would be worth it in the end. That was his truth, at least for now.

And I wouldn't spoil it for him until I had to.

BALTAZAR

I must have been more tired than I thought because within seconds of laying down, I was asleep. It wasn't the most restful few hours,—only two REM cycles at the maximum—but it was rejuvenating enough.

After a dream involving the ant mantis and being torn apart by razor sharp mandibles, I did have a more pleasant one before I woke. I was having dinner with my parents and Zoe, the four of us sitting around a wooden table eating roasted chicken in a beautiful house, the sun shining through long windows with purple curtains. My father told jokes and everyone laughed. When Zoe wasn't flashing me the widest smile, my mother whispered to me something along the lines of, "I'm so proud of you," or "I'm so happy you found someone as wonderful as her."

But, as with many dreams, the reality within them is often unattainable. Our surroundings were a far cry from a house on the surface, and Zoe felt kissing me was a mistake. A family unit in the making, this was not.

The insta-burn had cooled down by the time I woke to find Zoe staring at its white-hot center. She insisted she'd slept, but her eyes appeared heavier and the circles underneath them were darker than ever. She didn't say much as we packed up, and her movements were sluggish despite the lower gravity. It was almost as if a weight had dropped onto her shoulders, slowing her down.

I wanted to ask what she'd seen in that lab that had terrified her so badly. But anytime we made eye contact, she looked away. Trust, I kept reminding myself. I trust her, and if there was something I needed to know, she would tell me.

But the thought lingered, no matter how I tried to dismiss it. Sleep deprivation, erratic behavior, possible hallucinations. They were all symptoms of a mental breakdown.

Hypothesis: The subject (me) will likely die as the result of failing to assess his situation logically.

As we cleared the door to the classroom, I began coughing excessively, phlegm having accumulated in my throat as I slept. I leaned over in an attempt to clear my air passages. Smith, rocking back and forth as I went, instructed me to take some medication we recovered from the Medical Level. I swallowed the pills dry as he instructed and the raw sensation in my throat made me wince. My eyes watered.

"Are you good?" Zoe asked, her raised hand preventing me from leaving the room.

I let out another hearty cough and felt Smith wobble on my shoulder. "Yes. I'll be fine."

She glanced at Smith and the robot whispered into my ear. "Think you can keep the coughing down?"

It took me a second before realizing that it was the noise they were concerned about, not my physical well-being. I took a deep breath, feeling the air move through my lungs. "I won't be a liability," I replied. "I think I'm just developing a cold. The medication should help limit my symptoms."

Zoe didn't seem convinced but led on, turning her back and heading out of the room. I ran my hands through my hair, closing my eyes for a second to give myself a moment to compose myself, but our situation didn't appear better when I reopened them.

We consulted the map before going too far and decided on heading through one of the testing arenas to gain access to the next staircase. Actually, it was Zoe who decided. Smith and I just kept our traps shut and agreed. According to my observations, the southern hallway appeared the quicker route, but the image of her beating the bug to a pulp crossed my mind, its green blood splattering my shirt.

Evidence to support Hypothesis: Subject ignores most efficient pathway due to fear of angering companion.

Zoe walked out ahead and I watched her hips sway while she moved, her hands in her pockets. I let out a stifled cough and the noise instantly spiked my heart rate, the sound shattering the silence around us. Zoe stopped and turned, but I couldn't see her face through the darkness. I could still feel her stare though.

I took long, slow breaths, willing the tickling in my throat to abate.

"Just take your time," Smith said to me. And after a second, when I was sure moving on wouldn't induce another cough, we continued.

When we came to a hall of labs right before the testing arena, we found a series of collapsed walls. We must have moved out of range of the adjusted gravity well because things felt normal again, making us fight against normal forces as we navigated the terrain. Piles of twisted metal and shattered insulation littered the ground. Zoe climbed the first pile of rubble but then quickly ducked down. I didn't hesitate to do the same. A piece of sharp metal jabbed at my calf, but I stayed as still and quiet as I could, hoping that all the dust in the air wouldn't trigger my cough. After a few seconds, Zoe slowly peered over the slab she was hiding behind.

"It's okay," she said to me. "They're all dead."

"They?" I asked.

I climbed to her position and looked out over the landscape. The corpses of dozens of security soldiers were strewn among the rubble, their bodies badly decomposed under their shredded Parkman uniforms. I had seen and dissected plenty of corpses over the years, but the sight still made me cringe. My encounter with the ant mantis had instilled me with a new sense of empathy for death, wondering if they had felt as scared as I did before they died. My eyes followed the path of dead soldiers until I saw what had killed them and caused all of this destruction.

"Would you look at that?" Smith commented, his eyes scanning the downed AI slumped against the wall. It was massive, roughly nine or ten feet high when upright and probably weighed several tons, judging by the damage to the floor beneath it. Its white metal skin was littered with burn marks and a thick, steel rod was driven through the head. Zoe moved in closer and gave the rod a tug, but it never budged.

"Well, that certainly got the job done," she commented, inspecting the AI.

I walked around its perimeter, trying to see it from all angles. It looked like none of the schematics PISS supplied me with when I submitted for resources for the Smith project. "Smith, can you give me a quick layout scan?"

A green beam draped itself over the machine and Smith let out a troubling "hmmmm," halfway through. "That's interesting."

"What is?" Zoe asked.

Smith pulled up a miniature, three-dimensional layout of the AI, and it twirled in front of us. It was an interesting design, outfitted with a titanium exoskeleton and powered by a fusion core that could power the machine for a hundred years, if not longer. There was also a panel near the small of its back, which caught my eye.

I leaned in closer, squinting. "Is that an uplink node?"

"It appears so," Smith answered.

Zoe shook her head. "I don't get it. What's notable about an uplink node? These things aren't controlled remotely."

"True," I said, "but that suggests that they can talk to each other. Perhaps, instead of a series of rogue robots like the reports indicated, this was an organized attack." I followed the thoughts, planting my hands on my hips. "Maybe they're all being controlled from a single source and, if that could be destroyed, it would deactivate all of them."

"I wouldn't get your hopes up," Zoe replied. Moving toward the robot's back, she tried peering behind it to see the node. But after a second of pulling at the machine, she just shook her head. "Even if we could get through this rubble, the node's probably shot. Better luck next time. Then again, if we don't run into another one of these things, that's fine by me too."

I nodded but became distracted by a blinking light in the corner of my eye. I turned and moved in its direction, watching every step I took to make sure I didn't step on anything. Or anyone.

When I got close to the source, I discovered that it was

coming from a gun in the withered hand of one of the security guards. His fingers were still clutched around the trigger. Against my better judgment, I gave it a yank and the gun came free, taking the finger with it.

"What is it?" Smith asked. Zoe approached from behind so quietly I didn't hear her until she was right next to me.

I breathed deeply to compose myself and flicked the severed finger off the trigger. The side chamber of the lightweight rifle had accumulated several layers of dust and I gave it a forceful blow. The light was coming from the battery cell, one bar blinking with another solid one below it.

"It's still charged?" Zoe asked.

"Apparently," I said, examining the rifle. It was an older model of the standard security laser rifle, a single carbine barrel with an automatic energy feeder. I had used similar models a thousand times in the testing arena, so even this older model felt comfortable in my hands as my muscle memory kicked in. "It probably has a few shots left in it if this battery reading is correct. Amazing that it still held some charge after all this time."

"Let me see it," Zoe said. Smith and I glanced at each other before becoming too nervous to look back at her. All I could think of was her beating the guts out of the bug, exhibiting signs of anger so intense that she seemed out of control. I didn't know exactly what Smith was thinking, but the clicking sound coming from his head provided me enough of a hint.

"Why?" I asked, my throat instantly feeling dry. I let out a belabored cough that I couldn't hold back.

Zoe's head tilted ever so slightly, but her eyes stayed locked with mine. "Well, I'm walking out in front, so I think I should be the one carrying it."

Evidence to contradict Hypothesis: Subject avoids putting a weapon in the hands of companion due to previous erratic behavior.

"I could take the lead," I said.

"Or me," Smith offered, a comment both of us ignored.

Zoe didn't say anything at first, and it felt like my knees were going to crumble under the weight of her gaze like the rubble all around us. Finally, she just shook her head. "I see."

"What do you mean?" I asked, the worry evident in my voice. "What do you see?"

"You don't trust me with it."

"Of course we trust you, Zoe," Smith blurted out, sounding defensive. Nervously defensive.

"Stay out of this, Smith," Zoe shot back. I thought about lying on the collapsed ramp, looking up to see her ready to leave me behind. Was she regretting not following through with it?

After a few tense seconds though, she just shook her head dismissively. "Okay then," she said coldly. "You take point. I'll follow."

"Alright," I answered, my voice cracking under the word's implication. I took one last look at the downed robot before continuing on, the arena ahead. I hoped that, if the time came, I would have the courage to stand and fire rather than run. But I knew what the sight of those bugs did to me. Even the thought of another one made my skin crawl.

I looked back every minute or so as we walked, making sure

Zoe was still behind me. I wasn't pleased that I couldn't see her and it was only then that I began to realize how dire our situation was becoming. She was still Zoe. She was the girl that I fell in love with and left everything behind to help. But she was hiding something and I swore to myself that I wouldn't let my feelings for her taint my judgment.

Conclusion: Inconclusive. Subject is determined to remain objective but, in order to maintain the highest probability of survival, must gain the fortitude to overcome personal feelings of affection. The greatest environmental threat may be his companion.

ZOE

With my hands curled into fists, I followed Balt toward the arena, the rifle held firmly in his grasp. The lights in the halls were dim, so Smith occasionally had to use its ocular beams to show the way. Their glow was so intense that it burned my eyes, but then the darkness returned. I was getting used to it. Getting used to this place.

Logically, I could see why Balt didn't want to put a weapon in my hands. He'd asked if he could trust me and everything I had done up until this point would prove otherwise. I had already contemplated leaving him for dead and was keeping little tidbits from him, like how we were both genetically engineered rather than born, and how I was seeing ghosts walking around. But it hurt nonetheless, anger boiling over the pain. Parkman and the rest saw me as nothing more than a creature to be poked and prodded. Maybe that was all I was in the end after all.

We continued in silence, and the closer we got to the stairs, the more figures of light I began to see. They walked past and through us, Balt and Smith never flinching. It took my best effort to pretend to be oblivious, but their chatter was so loud sometimes it was almost as if they were inside my head, forcing me to squeeze my palms over my ears for some relief.

Maybe it was a good thing Balt was leading. I don't know how I would have explained it to him.

Through the din, I gave some thought to what these apparitions could be. Other than the "I'm going crazy" explanation, the best thing I could come up with was that this was an unforeseen side effect of *Project Wind*. That whatever they'd done to me, not only was I able to move through space, but space-time as well, to an extent. Maybe part of my brain was still able to pick up the fleeting remains of residual energy given off by the bodies of the scientists who worked here, the electric currents reenacting scenes over again, cementing their actions in time.

Herzman and Lebowitz would be so proud.

Then again, screw them.

We stopped to drink some water at a bathroom off the hall and Balt got a chance to breathe, doing his best to stifle the sound of his coughs with his arm. I watched the blurry outlines of two scientists speak to each other near the sinks next to us, their voices echoing off the walls so loudly that I couldn't hear anything else. One of the women, her hair pulled back into a ponytail, splashed water on her face while looking into the mirror. Another, with frizzy hair, was standing over her with her arms folded. "But he's married!"

Ponytail didn't look at her, just sighed. Pretending to look in the mirror, I inched closer to them, realizing that she was the same scientist who worked with Dr. Parkman's father in the genetic engineering lab. Elizabeth. "I'm well aware of that," she replied to her friend. "But he approached me. And what do you say to the youngest Alexander Parkman when he flirts with you?"

"You say thanks, but no thanks!" her friend laughed. "As brilliant as he is, you know it's not just your insight into proton acceleration he's after. And just because he's sterile, that doesn't give him the right to sleep around."

"He actually opened up a bit about that the other evening," Elizabeth explained. "A 'noble sacrifice' he said after working for years with radiation treatments. He says it doesn't bother him that he won't be able to continue the Parkman line and still will 'live forever' through his work, but I could see it in his eyes. He's actually a very sensitive man."

Her friend didn't appear to buy her version of Dr. Parkman. And neither did I. The last thing the world needed was a spawn of a monster. "All I'm saying is don't let him take advantage of you like this and undermine all the work you've been doing."

I walked closer to Elizabeth, trying to see her face as clearly as I could. The light moved about her slender cheeks and evaporated at my touch. The news of her affair with Parkman reminded me that these were people at one point. Living, breathing people like us.

Well, almost like us.

"I know," she said quietly. "I have a bad feeling about the whole situation. If anyone ever found out, I'd be thrown out of his father's research group for sure. But it's all so exciting. He makes me feel . . ."

For a brief second, I thought she looked at me and chills ran down my spine.

"Zoe?"

I turned to Balt, flustered by the sound of his voice. "Yeah? What's wrong?"

"Your nose," Smith said and I turned to the mirror, shocked to see blood flowing freely from my nose.

"Oh crap," I muttered, cleaning it off with water as I held the bridge of my nose, trying to stop the bleeding. Balt stepped in front of me with a roll of toilet paper and gave me a clump, the soft material turning bright red on contact.

"You should try to take it easy as well," he said.

I held my head back, distracted by the two female scientists as they faded into nothing. "Yeah, maybe," I finally answered. We waited a minute until the bleeding had stopped and I stuffed small wads into my nostrils for good measure before turning back to Balt. "How's it look?"

He smirked and his happiness warmed my cold heart. Maybe a glimpse of whatever we'd shared before all this was still in there. "Still thermal."

I shook my head, realizing that I might be flirting with him. "We should get moving again. The arena is just up ahead."

He nodded, hoisting the rifle up to his shoulder again. "Right."

"And let's hope for a nice empty arena, yes?" Smith reminded us, as if we wanted anything else. We exited the bathroom and proceeded down another two hallways before finding the double doors of the testing arena, the lights flickering intermittently inside. The ground changed from cold metal to loose gravel, and the far side was lost in shadows, creating a wall of black.

"A lot of things could be hiding on the other side," Smith said. "My sensors can detect any variant AI in the area, but the bugs are another story. There could be a whole nest of them on that side."

"Or a whole bunch of nothing," I rebutted. "There's no guaranteed safe way through this place. Just gotta keep going and hope for the best."

"She's right," Balt agreed, and it felt good to hear the words. "Let's just do this."

We opened the doors slowly and took the first few steps lightly, aware of all the sounds around us. But other than the buzzing of the flickering lights and crunch of our feet on the gravel, there was nothing else to be heard. Yet with every step I took, the stronger my urge to turn around became.

"I should have installed night-vision in your ocular lens," Balt whispered to Smith, shaking his head. "In hindsight, that would have been extremely useful."

"In hindsight, a body would have been swell too," Smith answered, and I let out a small chuckle, temporarily forgetting to watch where I was going. Suddenly, my next step failed to find ground and I fell, my hands grabbing at gravel as I slid. The sound of the small pebbles tumbling with me was like an avalanche. When my descent finally ceased, I found myself inches from a deep crevice, as deep as the one we'd found in front of the lift earlier. Quickly, I started the crawl back up, eager to put as much distance between the great drop and myself as I could.

"Zoe! Are you okay?" Balt yelled from above.

"Yeah," I answered, my voice notably shaky. "There's a pretty big hole down here." On hands and knees, I struggled the rest of the way up the gravel slope, the rocks pinching my skin as I went. When I reached the top, Balt helped me up with an outstretched hand while Smith did his best to pierce the darkness ahead with its ocular beams.

"Mind the gap," Balt joked.

"You're telling me," I said, annoyed with myself. After coming so far, to die from such a stupid misstep felt unforgivable.

"Well, we're certainly not getting through this way," Smith determined. "The only other route was the southern hallway Balt suggested earlier but, by its location on the map and the angle of this crevice, it might be a dead end as well. Best to see if we can just find a place we can cross in here."

Balt and I didn't object and we followed the deep gash in the opposite direction until we found it beginning to shrink toward the wall of the arena. When we got there, the crevice was still a good six or seven feet wide, but the other side was much lower, forming another ramp downward.

Balt leaned over the void, squinting in the darkness and coughing slightly. "Well, life or death decision number one thousand and forty seven: do we jump and climb up the other side, or do we double back and try to find another way?"

Although it was an important decision, my attention was again drawn toward the back end of the arena still shrouded in darkness. The air was so still that any movement near us could be heard, but something felt like it was close by. Watching us. I looked to Smith but it didn't seem to pick up on anything.

"Are you alright, Zoe?" Smith asked. Balt mimicked his glance.

"Ye-yeah," I said, only realizing then I was shivering. I didn't want to say it, but I just didn't want to be on the other side of this hole in the ground. "I say we double back. It's not worth the risk."

Balt continued to look down the great rift. "I'm not sure I agree. As Smith indicated, the data indicates that the other hallways are most likely in a similar state. Plus, given the height we have compared to the opposite end, this jump shouldn't be too difficult."

I knew he was right, but the anxiety I got from the darkness continued to grow. I took a small step back toward the door. "No, let's head back." I turned and started walking, but Balt wasn't following.

"This isn't just your decision," he said and I stopped, looking at the darkness, then back to him.

"What?"

He shifted his stance nervously, coughing again. "It's just . . . my opinion counts too."

The lights above seemed to dim, making the dark wall appear like it was closing in on us. I moved closer to Balt, my nerves on high alert. I wanted to be out of this arena. Now.

"Balt, just . . . don't argue with me. We *need* to leave."

"Just like you said we *needed* to climb that ramp near the lift."

His words had a bite to them and I felt my knees tremble from all the implications behind them. He seemed to regret what he said, running his hands through his hair and shifting the gravel with his shoes, but they were words that he couldn't take back.

So he definitely knew.

"Is that why you didn't want to give me the gun?" I asked, moving closer. "Because you thought I would just shoot you and leave you behind?"

I could see his hands shaking. I didn't want to take this fight too far, but I didn't want to back down. I'd made a mistake, but he didn't know what I was dealing with. What I was trying to protect him from.

"N-no, it's just," he stammered before taking a deep breath. "I *know* that there are things you're still keeping from me. I want to trust you, but I can't ignore . . ."

"This isn't a walk through a garden, Balt!"

"Don't you think I'm well aware of that? I gave up everything to come with you here!"

"No one asked you to come!"

"Guys!" Smith shouted.

"What!" we both yelled, turning to Smith. His eyes flashed red, something tripping his variant AI alarm. The arena was dead silent for a moment, and then a loud crunch shook the ground. In the darkness, a red light glowed, and Balt and I were too afraid to do anything but stare back at it.

There was another loud crunch, and a surge of wind blew past us, a large object flying overhead. It landed so close that the impact sent us tumbling to the ground, landing inches away from the mouth of the crevice. I turned in the direction of the object and choked as the giant AI craned its face in my direction. It was massive, at least five times the size of the one we'd found in the labs, and even its slightest movement made the ground tremble. Across its chest was the outline of a crown in black, stretching from shoulder to shoulder. The AI leaned over me and planted its colossal arms on either side, leaving me with nowhere to run. Its lone eye centered right on me and it was so bright that all I could see was red.

But it didn't crush me or toss me off into the hole or anything I was expecting. It just stared. I could see the LEDs twirl along the ocular lens, adjusting to make me out clearly. Almost like it was trying to decide if it recognized me.

And then I felt it again.

Suddenly every inch of my skin grew hot, my muscles twitching in pain like I was in that dark spherical room again. I gasped and wheezed but couldn't catch my breath. The arena seemed to grow darker, leaving me alone with the giant AI staring me down, burning me with its gaze.

I was so afraid that I thought I was going to pass out, my head feeling lighter and lighter through the surges of pain. The robot's giant arms planted alongside me and my eyes flickered, a lightness suddenly taking over. It was only when it was too late to do anything about it that I realized I wasn't fainting.

I was teleporting.

I felt lighter than air and everything went white. Then black. It was only after a minute or so that I realized my eyes were working again. Wherever I was, it was so dark that I couldn't see anything. I brought my knees to my chest and rocked back and forth, feeling the darkness infiltrate my mind.

Maybe I was dead. Maybe I was safe. It didn't matter. I hated myself and everything I'd done, including abandoning Balt and Smith in the arena with that monster.

BALTAZAR

Watching Zoe be beside me one moment and simply gone the next was awe inspiring, my mind trying to wrap itself around the physics of what I just witnessed. It seemed impossible but, clearly, it was not. The event even baffled the AI, as it stood there seconds after, hovering over the spot Zoe had vacated. I could hear its ocular lens spinning faster and faster trying to locate her, most likely running a diagnostic scan at the same time to insure an error had not occurred.

After a few seconds though, the awe morphed into terror when I realized that it was now just me and the AI in the arena. Based on its size and the tremors created by its movements, the AI must have weighed hundreds of tons. It was literally a walking building, more than capable of crushing me to nothing with a single swing of its hand. Rather than sitting around to see if I was correct, I set my sights on the opposite side of the rift, hoping my new leg would give me the strength to launch myself the necessary distance to clear the hole.

Gravel shifted under my frenzied dash and I didn't hesitate when I hit the edge, launching my body toward the far side of the crevice. I held my breath while I was in the air, but I cleared the hole with several feet to spare, the gravel crunching and sliding down toward the darkness in my wake. I scrambled toward the door but lost the rifle in my panic, the weapon tumbling on the ground. I thought about stopping for it, but the giant AI had turned its attention to me. Its shift sent out another shudder through the ground, positioning itself to move over the hole with one easy step.

Smith and I stumbled over a section of collapsed wall and I ducked underneath it, getting as far under the wreckage as I possibly could. Smith shut down his ocular beams and the two of us lay still, listening to my rapid heartbeat while hoping it didn't see where we hid.

It grew closer at first, scanning the ground. The red beams rained down around us, but the concrete was expansive enough that we were fully covered, remaining undetected. After a few seconds, the AI let out this shrill cry and banged its massive claws against the ground. The thuds then grew fainter, the robot lumbering away and eventually busting through the wall in the direction of its fallen comrade, the one we found earlier. I stayed still until everything grew quiet again, making sure it was safe before slithering my way out from the rubble. Smith lit the door of the arena on the other side and I made my way toward and through it, leaving the arena behind me.

When we reached the stairs, I took a second to pause and regain my breath. My lungs were burning, dust coating my throat. I tried concentrating on not coughing and drawing the AI back in our direction, but I felt so frazzled that I couldn't help it. I pulled up my shirt and tried expelling everything inside me, muffling the sound as much as I could with the material.

"Do you think she's okay?" I asked Smith once the coughing stopped and I regained some breath. My eyes were tearing from the dust in the air. At least, that's what I told myself.

The processor in the AI's mind hummed. "I think so. She picked the perfect time to get out of there. If it weren't for *Project Wind*, she'd be dead."

"If it weren't for *Project Wind*, we wouldn't be down here."

There was silence. All the possibilities of where she could have teleported began to flood my mind. It was definitely a possibility that she could have gotten somewhere safe and warm. Maybe, I thought, she was able to teleport to the surface. Maybe she was alive and free like she wanted.

But then my thoughts grew grim. Maybe she was back at the Institute, left to endure the wrath of Dr. Parkman. Or maybe she was lost somewhere in the lab, alone in the dark, disoriented. My instinct was to assign probabilities for each scenario, but as I tried, I realized I knew nothing about *Project Wind*. I didn't know about a lot of things.

"I'm sure she's fine," Smith assured me, observing my grimace. "We'll find her. Then the three of us can get to the surface and out of this place for good."

I sighed, watching my slow breath rise in the cold. "Assuming she wants us to find her, of course."

I sat for a bit longer and replayed our shouting match in my head. It was foolish of me to push her like that. Then again, I considered, it confirmed my fears that she really didn't want me here. She didn't feel anything for me and my decision to follow was surely the wrong one. Now I was left to deal with the consequences. Smith and I were alone in a foreign lab. I checked my pocket to find I had one pack of meal pills still with me but, other than that, was completely unprepared. We had no other supplies or any way to defend ourselves since I dropped the rifle. In hindsight, clearly the argument over the weapon did not benefit me in any way.

Zeke and Tern made their way back into my head, and I missed them more than ever at that moment. I wanted Tern to be supportive and for Zeke to crack a joke, tell me I was being a quark and that bacon would make it all better or something. But they were very far away, in a place I would most likely never see again.

"Of course she wants us to find her," Smith said, trying to reassure me. "Don't think that way. She was upset. Stressed. I think we're all feeling it, quite honestly."

"We are?"

Smith cleared his throat. "Well, you two at least. I'm fine and dandy wobbling around your shoulder like a benign tumor."

I laughed through watery eyes. "Benign for sure."

We were quiet again and I still couldn't get myself to move. I was drained, mentally and physically, and afraid of what would come next. Would we really be able to find her? Would we find a way out of here before that AI or one of those insects got us? I would find out soon and, for the second time in my life, I didn't think I was ready for an answer.

"So . . . read any interesting articles lately?" Smith asked lightly.

I sighed, rubbing my eyes. "One the other day actually. Talked about mass relay travel and how it might be easier to reach and colonize other planets rather than rebuilding our own."

"There's a thought," Smith answered. "A little long distance travel."

"Would be pretty nova seeing another planet."

"Concurred."

"Then again, I'll settle with seeing my own first." I looked up, the lights at the top of the stairs on, glowing brightly.

Smith made a clicking noise. "Whenever you're ready, boss. We lost Zoe, but it's only temporary. Now it's time to find her. And she's going to be relieved to see us. I just know it."

Protocol #54: *small steps are the beginning to any great endeavor.*

My knees made a cracking sound when I stood and I dusted the dirt off my pants before beginning the climb. My hand tightly grasped the guardrail. I took each step slowly to insure I kept my coughing to a minimum. We were able to make it up two levels before the pathway became loaded with debris, blocking any further ascent.

"Two more down," I remarked to Smith.

"Five more to go," he answered, pulling up the map and finding our location. I traced the path ahead, trying to find anything that would help.

"This looks like the Robotics Level," I said, scanning the labs ahead. "This was where all the serious animatronics advancements from the Institute during the last century were done." I paused, a hint of excitement tingling my fingers. "It's rather remarkable, when you think about it."

"If only we got to see it under different circumstances," Smith answered.

"Still . . . we should check it out. We might find something useful."

Smith's eyes grew wide. "Like a body for me!"

"Or another surveillance hub," I replied. "But I suppose if we were to find something to mount you to, what better place to look?"

I could sense Smith smiling on my shoulder. We took a long look down the black hallway before exiting the stairwell, being mindful of all the sounds around us. When there were no apparent dangers about, Smith turned on his ocular beams and we slowly continued on, trying not to disturb anything.

As we moved, I noticed that the structure of this level was more dilapidated than the others. Most of the labs and work areas were riddled with rubble and pipes torn from the ceilings. Prospects of finding anything that would benefit us didn't appear promising, but through a slew of more dead security officers around a high security checkpoint, we discovered a thick vault door, its lock node still functioning.

Smith remotely logged in and was able to give the door just enough juice to open it wide enough for me to slip though before the power ran out. Inside was pitch black but quiet. We fumbled about until we found a main terminal, allowing us to restore power to the lights.

The circuits came on with a thud, and the fluorescent lights illuminated the room one section at a time, the lab slowly coming to light. The main terminal itself was sandwiched by a series of servers, standing tall along the walls. A walkway led to more of them and crossed a massive construction pit, the robotic arms frozen in place. It appeared undisturbed for the most part. The room buzzed with so much activity that it became difficult to focus on one thing at a time. I left Smith logged in at the terminal and started moving down the walkway, listening to the hum of the servers.

"Many of them are still functional," I said, running my hands along their cold metal surfaces. "How's the system integrity look from the terminal?"

"Uhhhhh," Smith moaned, "Not so great. Take a look." With his eyes, he displayed a graphic representation of the system, the hoped-for solid block fuzzed and corroded in most spots. I winched and coughed.

"Well, that's disappointing."

"Agreed," Smith replied. "Let me see what I can clean up. There may yet be a nugget or two here we can use."

I continued along the walkway, checking out the construction pit below. Dust had covered the usually sterile workspace, but I tried a few test commands and learned most of the construction arms were still operational. I booted up the graphical interface and was able to open the logs from the last experiment done here, the tag J. Seagreaves in the corner.

"Wow, Seagreaves himself stood here, working with these same controls." I tried not to sound too enamored by the fact, but I couldn't hide the excitement in my voice. Dr. James Seagreaves was one of the greatest minds in the field of engineering for the Institute. Besides neuro-netting, he was credited for many major advancements in AI construction, electron mapping, and the list went on and on. I used to read his work every night before I went to bed when I was younger, staying up late into the night to try to comprehend his theories. He was a genius who, rather than seeing old age, died somewhere in this lab when it was overrun. It was a far worse fate than he deserved, I thought.

A clicking noise came from Smith. "This must have been his lab. His digital fingerprints are on a lot of this stuff. But besides some logs, there's not much left in here . . ."

I started to nod, but a cold chill make all the hairs on the back of my neck stand tall. One red eye stared at me from a glass display in the wall. I gasped and it took me a second to realize it was just a model made of nothing more than plastic and paint. I inched in closer and inspected the display, the model within standing roughly the same height as me. The proportions were different, but the design was definitely the same as the two variant AI we encountered. I was perplexed. Perhaps Dr. Seagreaves recovered one and was studying it before the rest attacked?

"Smith," I said, my eyes still glued to the display. "You need to see this."

"Balt," Smith interjected, his voice just as tense as mine. "I think *you* need to see *this*."

"What?" I said, turning to him. "What is it?"

The holographic cube spun in the air, floating gently before him.

"Just come look," he said, his voice suddenly sounding metallic and cold. "I don't think you would believe me if I told you."

ZOE

Seconds bled into minutes. Maybe hours. I stayed put until a strange calm came over me like a wave, not washing over me but rinsing me out. I had gotten so used to the cold that it no longer bothered me, my skin giving off a comfortable chill to the touch. The darkness all around began to feel friendly too. It was just there. Like me. We were two parts of the same organism.

I sighed. It was still so dark that I couldn't tell if my eyes were closed or opened. With my ability to teleport, I could go anywhere. Yet I didn't want to move.

A voice called out through the darkness. I still didn't move though, not sure whether it was real or just a figment of my imagination. Or the dark. Then I caught sight of a light glowing in the distance, an amorphous blob moving through some sort of hallway to my right. It approached, and when it got close, I could see that I was in a well-furnished room, elaborate red carpets stretched from corner to corner. When the light reached the doorway, it solidified into the shape of a person, its face so clear that I recognized it instantly.

"Darling, why do you look so sad?" Dr. Parkman asked, looking in my direction. I stood but didn't say a word. He lit the room, but I still felt hidden in the darkness.

"I know these are tough times," he sympathized, his hands

cupped behind his back. He moved about the room methodically, as if this speech had been prepared down to the smallest detail. "But you need to be strong. You have always been a fighter. You're going to beat this. I know you will."

He moved closer and I backed up to stay away, tripping on a bed I didn't see behind me. I fell backward onto the sullied mattress, the material cold and moldy. Something hard poked at me and I turned to see a corpse lying under the covers, its rotting flesh covered with the castoff carapaces of many tiny insects.

I screamed and flew off the bed, running through Dr. Parkman and down a hall. When he was out of sight, I was enveloped by the darkness again. My pulse slowed. My breathing relaxed. With my hands outstretched, I made my way down a flight of stairs, emerging into a larger foyer that was lit from some lights pouring through wide front windows. This was a house, I realized. Parkman's house. I was ready to run out the front door but another voice caught my attention. A female voice.

I followed it and found Elizabeth sitting in a room off the foyer, dressed in her usual lab coat. Despite her usual ponytail, she looked older than before. Aged not by time but emotion. Stress. She rubbed the corners of her eyes and continued doing so even when Dr. Parkman re-entered, sitting next to her.

"Would you like anything to drink?" he asked, a whimsical melody to his speech.

"No," she answered. "I don't plan on being here long."

There was a silence and I sat across from them, becoming an invisible part of the scene.

"I came here tonight to tell you that I can't do this anymore." Her words were clear. Confident. I wanted to applaud.

Dr. Parkman took it in, his adam's apple bobbing. "What do you mean?"

"I mean that it's clear that we're doing *this* for very different reasons. Your wife is upstairs dying," she explained in a hushed voice. "And you decide to spend your time with me. Or perhaps Dr. Marrow or Dr. Helgan. I'm sure there are few others that I don't even know about."

Parkman didn't have a reply to this. He simply leaned back into the sofa, the material never moving against the light that made him up. Elizabeth stood, turning to him. "We're not children. I knew what I was doing. I'm as guilty as you. But I've finally accepted that what I feel for you will lead me down a path that will only make me miserable in the end. This isn't love, nor will it ever be. So goodbye, Alexander."

And with that, she was gone. A fading light consumed by the darkness. He shortly followed, and I sat alone in the silence a bit longer before moving to exit the house. The wooden door creaked when I pulled at its handle, revealing a platform illuminated by weak fluorescent lights that had something growing over them. I emerged from the house and walked slowly to a railing that sat on its edge, my breath leaving my lungs at the sight below me.

"I'm home," I said aloud.

Stretched in front of me was a garden, short lampposts giving their surroundings a warm yellow glow. The grass was overgrown and the plants lazily stretched across the terrain, their green fingers stretching in every direction. There were a few trees too, their branches growing purple fruit that made my mouth water. I kept my eyes glued to the foliage and walked along the railing until I found an intact staircase that led down to the garden. To my right stood a sign overrun by vines, but I was able to make out the words "Botany Level" through the vegetation. I had teleported to a higher level.

Closer to the surface than I had ever been before.

I walked slowly through the grass, listening to the soft crunch under my feet. The air here tasted fresher and my eyes wandered about, identifying all the species that were surviving here. While it reminded me a lot of Level H, the further into the garden I traveled, the more differences I noticed. What was before me was something completely different in many ways. Untamed. I felt grey in the scene of green and brown and stopped by a small stream that was flowing between two large fruit trees, cupping the water with my hands to drink. Unlike the Institute, this place had no rules, I thought. Nature always does what it wants eventually.

I continued until I found a patch of tulips, the small red buds stretching upward to greet me. I buried my nose within them and just breathed. In and out. It was the most wonderful smell I had ever experienced, and my heart fluttered at the sensation. I plucked one and placed the stem behind my right ear, the bud nudging my temple. I moved through a section of tiger lilies and stopped by another tall tree, watching a fog of light turn into a professor and her class sitting on the grass. They were younger kids by the look of them, probably seven or eight. I sat in the back row and mimicked their positions, my legs tucked into my chest.

"Can anyone identify the species of plant behind me?" The professor asked, referring to the large red flower behind her, the petals at least three feet wide with a hole in its middle. She was a stout woman that reminded me of Dr. Douffman. Same shrill voice. "Check your notes if you need to."

The rest of the class rummaged through their datapads. Amateurs. I raised my hand and didn't wait for the professor to call on me. "That is the *Rafflesia arnoldii,* the world's largest flower. It has no leaves, steams, or roots, but rather acts as a parasite on the vines it grows on. It can weigh up to twenty-five pounds and the hole within it can hold up to eight quarts of water for it to drink."

The professor didn't react, of course, and continued to scan the class for someone with an answer. Finally, a boy's hand shot up, reciting a poorer version of what I had just said. He was a short kid, with curly hair and freckles stretching across his nose. I craned my neck to get a better look at him. There was something vaguely familiar about his eyes. Like I had seen them before.

Then it hit me like the concrete walls of the tunnel to the testing arena, ripping me from my daze in paradise.

Balt.

It wasn't him, of course, but this boy must have shared many similar genes, built from the same basic genome outline possibly. I felt a drop of blood emerge from my nose as the class disappeared, leaving me alone in the grass. Grabbing a leaf, I used it to wipe up some of the blood and tried to fight off a sudden, pounding headache. Reality slowly filtered back and I felt cold and tired all over again. Trudging over the plants in my way, my mind raced. Was Balt alive? Were he and Smith able to get away from that giant AI? How would I find them again? Would they even want me to find them?

I tried desperately to imagine the map that Smith had shown us time and time again, but my mind was blank. I knew the Botany

Level was higher up than the Education and Testing Level I left them on, but how much higher I couldn't be sure.

I searched for an exit to the garden through the trees, the vegetation growing thicker and thicker the further I went. It got to the point where I debated heading back the way I came, but I got so turned around that I had no idea which way that was. I was lost.

Nearby, a group of plants ruffled and I froze, a deafening silence taking over. My head throbbed, but I did my best to concentrate on any noise around me. Any at all. Another plant shimmied behind me and I swallowed hard, my breath slowly rising into the air in a white plume. With one mute step after the next, I moved away from the noises as quickly as I could, my eyes searching for a thick branch or anything at all I could use to defend myself. I spotted a meter-long branch weighed down by another's leaves, cracked down its center. It wasn't thick, but it was pointed at the end. Sharp. I gave it a firm pull, which made a louder crack than I was hoping for.

Then it came like a coming storm, a fluttering sound all around me. I climbed up the tree; hand over foot up the branches until I was high enough that I could see the area around me. My heart dropped when I got to the top. A few feet away, the ground gave way and fell into a massive meteor crater. But rather than standing empty, its sloped surface was covered with giant green hives, slimy and wiggling. They were nests. Hundreds of them.

I had teleported away from one danger and walked into the heart of another.

BALTAZAR

I watched a video log of Dr. Seagreaves sitting under the dim light of a table lamp, a thin cigarette hanging from his mouth. Smith played the feed through his eyes and I grabbed a seat to watch. I leaned back, just as Dr. Seagreaves did the same, realizing then that we were using the same chair. I studied him, taking in every detail. In my mind, I always pictured him kind of like Dr. Parkman. I considered him a larger-than-life brain that was working on a level beyond anything I could comprehend. But now, as I watched, he just looked normal, for lack of a better description. He appeared just another tired lab worker with bags under his eyes.

"Personal log #4181. September 12th, 2151. Tomorrow, the first neuro-netting trial is set to begin, scheduled for eight a.m. and lasting about twenty hours or so for full sync," he began, looking blankly at the datapad before him. He gave his eyes a hard rub. "I have been waiting for this day for a long time. A long time. But at the dawn of this great breakthrough, I find myself more full of worries than anything else."

He took another long drag before continuing. "We know for a fact that 'immortality' as it were is quite impossible with the current level of technology. Cellular reconstruction research has seemed to hit a wall, and the rejuvenation chamber, though promising, seems held back by *us*, ironically. Any attempt to reconstruct a person at a healthier state or younger age results in rapid cellular death, the mind somehow rejecting the body like a sickness. As I've said before, robotics has always been the key, and neuro-netting will finally bridge the gap between man and machine." After another long drag, he sighed. "Just why did it have to be *him*?"

He leaned forward in the chair and I did the same, watching him rub his temples as the smoke from the cigarette drifted upward and out of view of the datapad recording the log. I caught sight of my cold breath rise along with it.

"Encryption cycle #121," he recited, and the log flickered before returning to a solid feed. "I have nothing but respect for Dr. Parkman and his family. What they have done for science cannot be stressed enough. But I, unlike most of the population here, was not born in this lab. I've seen the world and was still more than eager to give it all up when Alexander Jr. invited me to work here. But that outside experience, I feel, has given me some perspective the others don't have. The Institute is its own world, and the Parkman family, whether purposefully or not, has become its god."

With his lips inches from the datapad, he continued in a hushed tone. "While they share the same ego, I do not believe Alex has the restraint of his father, the same judgment. Hell, the megalomaniac requested the unique decal of a crown across the unit's chest. We have all the necessary precautions in place for anything disastrous, but I still worry about what will happen when we install his mind into the X1. How does one curb the aspirations of a Parkman? Freed from the limitations of flesh and the burdens of humanity, what will this version of him become when we create a version of him that might actually 'live forever'?"

The log ended there abruptly, leaving Smith and me alone again in the lab. I leaned back in the chair, my mind putting together the pieces of what I had just learned. The giant robot that attacked us in the area had a decal of a crown on it. I glanced back at the model robot within the glass display, the X1, staring at its lone red ocular port. "The giant AI was Dr. Parkman."

"And he took control," Smith finished. "Unbelievable."

"It doesn't compute though, Smith. There must have been precautions, like Dr. Seagreaves said. Fail safes, kill switches . . ."

Smith clicked. "I'm sure there were, Balt, but . . ." he said before pausing, choosing his words. "Being a machine with a human persona is a lot like playing a part in a torrent, in a way. We know our role. We know our directives and do our best to fulfill them, but that doesn't mean there aren't other things going on inside our heads. We can have our own goals. Call it . . . human nature, for a lack of a better description."

I knew he spoke honestly, and the effect was chilling. I stared into the lights within his eyes and squinted. "Is there anything you are striving for? A goal that I haven't programmed?" I sounded desperate, my throat going dry halfway through speaking. Zoe and I had a wall of secrets between us, and I didn't want to think that there were things left unsaid between Smith and me as well.

Rather than brushing off my question, the AI flashed a large smile. "A body would be nice," he replied. I nodded but stayed quiet, realizing he was serious. "I want freedom, Balt. I understand my current state, but I want the ability to make my own decisions. I think it comes from my first directive to investigate the robots here. I was ready to be autonomous. Now all I am is just a talking head on your shoulder. Literally."

"I understand," I answered, nodding. I tried empathizing, dwelling on what it would feel like having all that knowledge and analysis power, but be powerless to act on it. Things had been difficult since we'd left the Institute, to say the least. I had always felt that I had a good sense of who I was and what I was capable of, but this place made me doubt everything. Danger, or the threat of danger, was prevalent everywhere we went, and I was constantly being put into situations where I wasn't sure what to do or think.

But this was the first time in my life that I was free, I realized. Not shackled down by the schedules PISS set for me. The realization was scary at first but focusing on it now, I began to feel a surge of energy flow throughout my body. I could do whatever I wanted, only limited by my will.

"So let's make you one," I said.

"Pardon?" Smith asked.

I stood, examining the materials in the room. "Let's make you a body. The construction pit still works. It will take some time, but let's do it."

"Are you sure, Balt?"

I hesitated, considering the possible consequences. An autonomous Smith could be a great help, but what was stopping him from just leaving? By his own admission, freedom was his goal, and that was more easily achieved without having to look out for Zoe and me. But, after everything that we had gone through, I saw him more as a friend than an invention. I was probably being a quark, but I felt that he saw it the same way.

"I want to do this for you, Smith," I replied. "You have

supported me since the beginning. It's the least I can do. Plus, with two of us able to explore, it would increase the chances of finding Zoe."

A smile curled in the corner of the robot's mouth. "Well, alright then. What can I do to help?"

"Do a quick scan of the room for components. I'm going to need to see all my options."

Smith filled the room with a green light, a small list of results floating near his head. I considered each one, watching the design come together in my head. Two pivot spheres for knees. A carbon rod for a spine. I grabbed what I needed from around the room and placed them within reach of the construction arms, taking the helm at the console to begin.

Smith didn't say much as I worked. I assumed he didn't want to break my concentration. The controls for the robotic arms were rigid, but I gained a better understanding of them as time passed. The experience made me feel confident again, doing something I excelled at. Piece after piece came together, fused with liquid metal and grossilium wiring. Grease from the parts coated my hands and I wiped them on my shirt, leaving black stains. I'm not sure how long it took but, by the time I finished, my knees felt like they were going to buckle any second. I mounted Smith onto the crude body before taking a much-needed sit. While he booted into each piece, I took a moment to swallow one of my few remaining meal pills, feeling an immediate relief of my hunger and thirst.

The major parts of the body were thin, no thicker than my arm. A single pipe with a fusion power cell and wiring fused on its sides served as his torso, sprouting similar pipes for his arms and legs. Round pivots of varying sizes served as his joints. He rotated each part a full 360 degrees and flexed each finger on his crude hands before walking toward me. When he was close, he knelt down on the ground next to me so we could see eye to eye. "This is excellent work, Balt," he said.

I sighed, watching his hands move about. "Thank you. It's not optimal, but . . ."

"No," he cut me off, "it is." He smiled and offered me his hand; now warm, thanks to the electricity moving through it. I felt honored to be able to shake it. "Ready to go find Zoe?"

"Definitely. The only question is where to begin."

He nodded, looking toward the door. "For some reason, I feel like she'll find us. Or at least make so much noise that she'll lead us right to her."

"I hope not," I answered, and slowly made my way back to my feet. "But if she did, I'm sure she could handle any unwanted attention." I caught another glance of the X1 in the corner and swallowed hard. "At least, I hope she can."

ZOE

I clung to the branch as creatures like the one that had attacked
Balt scurried around below me, cutting leaves with their mandibles and consuming them. The garden had been sustaining them
for all these years but, if Balt's encounter with one earlier was
any indication, they had a taste for flesh as well. Thankfully, they
seemed unaware of my perch in the tree above as they ate. Their
wings fluttered when they were done, propelling them along and
helping them rapidly descend into the nest within the crater. The
green hives within it glowed like a neon city.

I waited until I was sure they had all passed before slowly
slithering my way back down, the sound of their wings ringing in
my ears. When I reached the ground, I crept slowly back toward
Parkman's house, crouching low to the ground. I didn't want to
be back there with *him*, even if it was just a memory of him, but
the farther I was from the bugs, the safer I would be.

I only made it a few feet before another barrage of sound
buzzed through the air. More flutters of thin wings. More clacking
of sharp mandibles. I scrambled along like a frightened animal,
tumbling and thrashing about until I landed in a thick bush, thorns
tearing through my clothes and scratching my skin. I lay as still
as a stone, enduring the biting pain, while more insects passed

by toward their nest. The leaves were so thick that I couldn't see more than a few feet in any direction, but the sound was deafening. The clacking of claws and fluttering of thin wings bled through the foliage from every side.

There I waited, frightened to breathe until everything was still again. I closed my eyes and concentrated on the darkness it brought, only then gathering enough courage to wriggle my way out of the bush and around a patch of tall reeds nearby. But again, I only made it a few more feet before more of the giant insects arrived. I looked up to find another swarm of insects beginning to descend, their long legs outstretched like giant landing gear. I ran in the opposite direction, losing my footing on something hard and falling over the lip of the crater.

I tumbled steadily downward, head over feet, coming hard against the ground again and again until the slope leveled off. When I finally stopped, I was dazed and broken on the dirt floor, the world spinning and throbbing around me. A pain sliced through my shoulder like a knife when I finally got to my feet, but the glow right next to me seized my attention. I had fallen all the way to the bottom of the crater and landed just a few feet from one of the hives.

Before I could figure out if I could climb back out of the crater, the reeds above began to sway violently as the insects landed. I ran around the nearest hive to stay hidden, my back pressing against the sticky, squishy surface. I took a brief second to catch my breath, but the sounds of crawling and shifting dirt were closing in, so I took off, doing my best to disappear. Keeping close to the hives ahead, I moved aimlessly, wandering deeper and deeper into the nest and losing all sense of direction. Fear propelled me forward, every second expecting to hear the roar of the swarm. But those sounds never came. They still hadn't spotted me. I still had a chance.

I zigged and zagged between hives. Shadows of tiny feet pressed against their walls from within but I never stayed long enough to examine them. When I finally found a spot where the din of moving creatures died down, I just collapsed on the floor, my butt making a thud against the soil. My lungs felt like shredded plastic bags and I could do little more than wheeze and sweat as I leaned back against a hive. The surface was so soft that, in my exhaustion, I was tempted to fall asleep.

A jab poked my back and, at first, I thought it was my heart slamming against my rib cage. But then I felt another on my lower back and realized then that it was coming from the hive. I moved away and turned just in time to see an insect's leg puncture the glowing green surface. The leg thrashed about, unable to make the hole any bigger, no matter which way it twisted and turned. Then, slowly, it sank back into the hive and I felt a small wave of relief wash over me.

A silence once again filled my small corner of the nest, only to be shattered seconds later as the insect's head burst through the hole the leg had created.

While it was only a little bigger than my fist, the small head had a set of mandibles that looked capable of chopping a limb off in a single bite. They unclasped eagerly and the creature let out a horrific cry that pierced my eardrums. With a heavy stomp, I brought my foot down on the insect and felt it crunch under my shoe, a green goo coating the ground. But the damage was already done. Like a coming storm, the sounds of beating wings grew louder and louder behind me.

I turned and dashed, focusing only on moving forward as fast as I could. The hives began to burst open around me, legs slapping against me as I ran. The sprint felt like running through sharp branches. Suddenly something slammed into me hard enough that I lost balance. I stumbled into the hives in my path and bounced off their surfaces with a jolt. Behind me I could feel bursts of wind from flapping wings and a growing cacophony of screeches. I never gained enough courage to look back though, keeping my senses focused on the ground as it slowly began to slope upward again.

My legs ached and the sharp pain in my shoulder forced my face into an involuntary grimace, but I kept my legs pumping up the side of the crater. The top was within sight.

I almost made it, too.

But about halfway up, I stumbled. Two of the ant mantises caught up to me, flying over my head and cutting off my escape. I turned back, but the entire nest appeared to be approaching, hundreds of wings flying through the air toward me.

This would be the perfect time to teleport, I thought.

So of course, I didn't.

Every nerve in my body sparked and I rolled on the ground just out of an approaching ant mantis' leg slicing the ground. There was a roar, and dirt suddenly shot up everywhere, the ground shifting below and throwing up a massive cloud of earth. I stumbled into a newly formed crater, falling several feet before finding myself at the mouth of a small, dark tunnel uncovered by the shift. Dirt stung my eyes, but the insides of the tunnel felt cooler. Pliable, like metal. I wiggled my torso inside what felt like an air vent before mandibles crunched down on my right ankle, sending lances of pain shooting throughout my body.

The mantis gave me a yank, others crawling around and on top of it, trying to get a piece of me as well. I clawed at the metal panels around me, catching enough of a lip with my fingertips to give me a moment to steady myself and kick the creature in the face with my other foot. It wasn't the hardest hit, but it was enough to make it let go of me for the second I needed to scurry further inside. I scrambled forward on elbows and knees, but the bug wasn't ready to give up, tucking its wings to its sides in order to squeeze in after me. Its screeches echoed in the dark passageway.

Short of air, I found myself hyperventilating as I stumbled ahead. Before I knew it, I crashed headfirst into something hard. Some kind of grate was blocking my path and, before I could find a way to open it, the bug had caught up to me again. Its wings thudded against the metal sides of the shaft and its claws swiped at my feet. I wriggled around to give it another kick, pushing hard against the grate with my back. The metal gave way and I fell a few feet through the ceiling of a lab, shattering some glass beakers that had been positioned nearby on a workstation.

The bug was quick to emerge from the vent after me but I was on my feet before it landed. With a fleeting burst of speed, I made for a door on the far side of the lab, grabbing at the handle and trying to close it behind me. But the bug was right behind me and thrust one of its arms through the crack before I could completely shut the door. The limb flailed about, slashing haphazardly at anything it could reach. I leaned down to avoid it, but kept my grip on the handle, pulling with all the might I had left. And with a satisfying crunch, the limb snapped, half the flailing end falling to the ground next to my foot.

The ant mantis screeched and soon his friends joined him, spilling into the room from the vent like a river. But they were on the other side of the thick, metal door, unable to burrow past. I was eager to get away, but took a second to catch my breath. I stayed seated on the floor, so tired that I couldn't even think straight. My breath rose in the frigid air and hung there for a second before dissipating. The sounds around me slowly faded, and I let my eyes adjust to the faint shadows. My pulse slowed and my anxiety slipped away, leaving my body to feel like a hollow shell.

Comfortably numb and free from all feelings, I continued through the darkness ahead.

BALTAZAR

Smith's feet clanged as he walked across the metal floor, but I could barely hear them over my muffled coughs. My cold was getting worse and it was making it difficult to breathe.

"Why don't we slow down a bit?" he suggested, but I waved him along.

"Just a little further. Then I'll take a break."

Thankfully, he didn't argue and we continued on. The truth was I needed the rest. Anything close to normal walking speed sent me into coughing fits and my knees felt so sore that I felt sure they'd buckle at every step. But I didn't want to stop moving. Zoe was out there somewhere, and every second might count.

We stopped to do a map check at the next intersection. I took advantage of the pause and sat down on a crumbled piece of wall, resting my tired limbs. The map's holographic display floated before me and I poked it with my finger when I regained my breath, tracing our path. There were only five levels left to the top: two residentials, botany, aquatics, and the control floor—that was where the main terminal hubs were, as well as the passage to the surface.

After thinking it through, Smith and I decided that the best way to find Zoe would be to reach one of the main security hubs.

That way, we figured, we could activate any possible cameras as we did before and scan each floor. There were no guarantees any of them would still work, but it held a better chance of success than randomly stumbling into her, given the size of the old labs.

After jumping at noises that turned out to be a giant rat scurrying down an intersecting hallway, we reached a staircase that took us up to the top Residential Level. The exit led us to a tram station. We emerged on a concrete platform and I looked down the dark tram tunnel. "When do you think the next one is set to arrive?"

Smith let out an exaggerated laugh and we jumped onto the tracks, following them to what the map indicated was one of the main residential areas of the lab. The tunnel was almost pitch black, but the mouth was nearby and a glimmer of pale light shone through, leading to an arena larger than any I had ever seen. One-story houses, complete with their own patches of dead grass, sat in perfect rows under a domed roof hovering hundreds of feet above us. I thought back to my history textbook, trying to remember the word for areas that resembled this before the war. "Suburbs?" I said aloud, guessing.

"I believe so," Smith corroborated. He did a quick scan with his eyes, bursts of blue light flashing outwards. "There don't appear to be any robots in the area."

"Right," I answered, distracted. I did my best to be wary of our surroundings, but I couldn't help but stare at the windows of the houses before us. Most were covered with so much dust that they resembled simple sheets of grey, but a few others were clearer, allowing us to see inside. It was foolish, but I couldn't help but wonder if I might find a house that resembled the one in my dream, the fantasy home my family lived in that I'd visited with Zoe.

Smith tapped me on my shoulder. "Should we proceed?"

I nodded, leading the way. We followed the tracks of the tram, and I absently reached out and touched each lamppost as we passed. "If these are similar to the Parkman domes on the surface, then the ceiling is actually made up of digital membranes," I explained, pointing upward. "They simulate the sky as the hours pass: sunny in the afternoon, dark at night. They even simulate sunrises and sunsets that color the sky different shades of reds and oranges." I looked off in the distance and tried to picture such a sight with my own eyes, but all I could see was grey.

"Must have been very pretty. Soon we'll get to see the real thing. Right?" I didn't respond at first, so Smith lightly elbowed me, his touch surprising me so much that I jumped. "Sorry, didn't mean to scare you."

"It's okay," I replied, looking downward. "I suppose I just forgot you could do something like that." Smith nodded and I watched his pivots twist with every step, the motion somewhat clunky but effective. "Does it feel uncomfortable?"

Smith rotated one of his wrists and then a knee 360 degrees. "Good enough. I'll probably need some sort of lubrication at a future juncture until I can acquire something a bit more sturdy, but you did a fine job, Balt. You should be proud."

I sighed. "Thanks, Smith. Hopefully when we get out of here I can—" I suddenly caught my breath. A flicker of motion in the corner of my eye caught my attention and sent my heart into overdrive.

We ran toward one of the houses and hid near the concrete front steps. Smith did another quick scan with his eyes and the blue bursts turned red, confirming my fears. There was a variant robot in the area. I felt sweat beading on my forehead despite the cold. In the distance, a series of clomping sounds could be heard, like something heavy walking about. We wasted no time moving out of sight and up the front steps of the house. The door was locked, but one of the front windows was cracked. I squeezed my fingers into the gap under the frame and managed to slide the window open. The heavy steps grew louder by the second, the variant AI approaching.

Smith and I slid clumsily inside and landed near a dinner table before plunking down on a wooden floor. I moved to close the window behind us, but instantly ducked back down as I caught a glimpse of the AI round the corner of the house. It resembled the one we saw when we found the laser, a miniature of the X1 without the crown decal. We shrank under the window against the wall, our bodies tucked into balls, as we listened to the AI's steps. The deep crunching sounds of the grass and dirt under its weight grew louder and louder before stopping right outside. Then a deafening silence fell.

A red light suddenly poured through the window, much like the lights emitted by Smith's scanner—only much more expansive. The red lights flowed through the room and I held my breath, tucking my feet in as close to my body as possible as the beam inched toward us. Smith and I locked eyes and, after a few excruciating seconds, the beam disappeared. The grass outside crunched under the heavy steps of the robot, growing fainter by the second.

We remained still until it was completely silent again. Even then, Smith performed another scan to make sure it was safe. The sight of the blue light relaxed my muscles instantly, but it still took me a few minutes to work up the courage to stand again. Instead of heading out though, I suggested we stay put for a bit longer in the relative safety of the house.

While Smith kept watch at the window, I started to walk through the house, running my hands over the dust covered surfaces. The walls were a dark blue with a few paintings hanging on the walls. One was of a woman sitting in a chair. Another was of a bridge spanning a lake in the rain. They weren't prints, but hand-painted originals. I touched the surface ever so lightly, feeling the smooth texture of dried paint on canvas. Zoe would have loved to see these, I thought. I turned and stared at four empty chairs around a wooden table before moving into the next room.

In this room, there was a red rug on the floor with a leather couch along the wall. Careful not to stir up any dust, I sat and leaned back into the cushions. I closed my eyes for a second before opening them to stare at an electronic fireplace, black and inoperable. I tried thinking about the scientists who had lived here. I wondered what they ate, how they slept, and what they laughed and cried about. I wondered if a couple lived here, or if an entire family had called this place home.

I fantasized about my dream again, trying to place my imaginary parents in the room. Indulging my imagination even more, I pictured Zoe sitting next to me, leaning against me with her head on my shoulder, just watching the flames in the fireplace. We would talk to my Dad sitting across from us, listening to him tell us about the experiments he'd done that day—something cutting edge and important, I decided. My mom would offer a witty comment every now and then, but she would be standing in the back. She would be working on a new painting for the walls. Like Zoe, she was artistic and saw the beauty in the world around her.

The word lingered in my mind. Zoe was artistic. She drew pictures and felt music in ways I couldn't even fathom. I remembered her showing me her drawings. I didn't know what to think about them then, but now I would have given anything for her to show me her creations again. I think I would gain a new appreciation for them now.

I hoped she was okay.

Smith whispered my name from the other room and I woke from my daze, heading back into the dining room. "I think it's clear," he said.

I stood in the doorway, nodding, but another picture on the wall caught my eye. It was one I'd missed the first time. I moved closer and wiped the dust from the surface, causing me to cough ever so slightly. It was a photo of two adults and a child between them, his hand in theirs. It must have been the weariness affecting my judgment, but I really thought the boy looked like me.

"Balt, we really should get moving," Smith urged.

I turned to Smith, shaking my head. "Sorry. I'm right behind you."

We looked both ways through the window before slipping out again, keeping close to the houses. I took one look back at the home before leaving it behind.

ZOE

After leaving the bugs in the lab to duke it out among themselves, I tore off one of my sleeves to tie around my bleeding ankle. Nothing seemed broken, but moving any faster than a hobble made it feel like my foot was going to collapse in on itself. So I took it slow, slumping forward like a zombie.

I stuck to the shadows. In many of the labs I passed, I could see that the floor had caved in, opening onto another crater with an even more enormous ant mantis nest below. It wouldn't take much for them to come swarming up here. Maybe just a single shout or a loose rock tumbling down would send them swarming up to devour me. But they wouldn't find me. I was just a shadow in the lab now. I was not even really here.

I slipped through the halls and came across a back staircase, where I was able to make it up another level before rubble blocked my path. But it was enough for now. Another step closer to the surface.

I emerged from the stairwell to find the layout of this floor was different from the others: more symmetrical and covered in rust. The walls that were not made of corroded metal consisted of glass and looked out on hundreds of long tubes filled with water and dead fish. The lights within the tubes still worked and gave everything a bluish hue. This must be the Aquatics Level, the former hub of marine and ocean studies. What were once miles of thriving aquatic ecosystems to be studied and valued were now like everything else: black and dead.

Well, almost dead.

I watched echoes of scientists and students admiring the displays, watching the fish bop against the glass. The younger students pressed their hands against the tubes, but their fingers left no imprints in the dust. They were all so excited and noisy that I opted to enter a lab that was quiet and dark for a bit. There I could be alone.

I remembered Dr. Grima's painting above his desk. It was a serene ocean scene he'd wanted to see since he was little. Dr. Grima and his story about the bar-tailed godwit felt like ages ago, a former life. I tried picturing the bird, but all I could see was the night consuming it, not even having the moon to light its path.

Dr. Grima. Another misguided fool. I sat on a desk a lot like his and laced my fingers behind my head, stretching. He was a man like so many others who lived in this place, searching for the truth. But, in reality, they were missing the most basic things about their world. Dr. Douffman. Cindee and the other girls. Balt. No matter what happened, they would all be slaves to Parkman until they died. Test experiments for life. Above or below, there was no real escape.

Then why was I still climbing?

My mind continued to wander down that dark spiral. I thought of an ocean of dead creatures. Helena's field of grass withered and brown. The surface of my dreams suddenly wasn't so inviting, and what scared me the most was the lack of response I felt. Hours ago, I'd wanted out so badly, but now I just felt numb.

Barren. The room began to feel like a coffin and I was ready to just lie down and give up.

Then I heard a sound.

It almost resembled a whistle from a bird. It caressed my ear and only grew louder with the passing seconds, so I got up and followed it. Through the dark glass halls, I felt my way along until a blue light glowed at the end of one hallway, growing brighter the closer I got. Mesmerized by the song, I continued forward until I was able to see that the blue light was coming from a swimming pool. The lights were still on under the surface like in the tubes earlier. But unlike everything else, it still looked pristine. Somehow untainted by the ruin and decay of this place.

I sat beside the water and rested my injured ankle, letting my fingers glide across the wet surface. The water was just a few degrees above freezing by the feel of it. That didn't stop a figure of light from doing laps up and down a lane though, its arms slicing the water while the liquid remained perfectly still—apart from the ripples cause by my fingers. I watched the figure swim back and forth until it stopped in front of me and rubbed its hands over its eyes, clearing and revealing a familiar face.

Elizabeth.

I shook my head, my eyelids feeling heavy. "Who are you, Elizabeth? Why do I keep seeing you?"

She didn't answer and just lay back in the water, humming and floating about on her back like a lily pad. I stood and circled the pool, continuing to talk. "I'm happy that you stood up to Parkman. That you didn't let him take advantage of you. That took guts." I swallowed hard, letting out a low sigh. "I feel like he's still watching me now. Is that weird? I gave up everything for a chance to escape him and his Institute, and yet even here, I feel like his hands are still around my neck. Like he's stamped on my DNA or something like that. And I'm just not sure getting out of here will change anything."

We stayed silent for a while and I imagined Elizabeth was thinking of an answer for me, a rationale that would make everything feel okay again. But the lights just seemed to grow dimmer within the pool. The darkness was spreading. It closed in on us but stopped when a second figure of light entered the room, as if on cue.

"Dr. Parkman," Elizabeth said, shooting her head up from the water.

Dr. Parkman stood by the edge of the pool, close enough to me that I instinctively took a step back. His hands were buried in his lab coat, hidden from view. "Hello, Elizabeth."

Both of them stayed quiet, seemingly unsure of what to say. Finally, she emerged from the water and he handed her something, most likely a towel, which she used to dry off before wrapping it around herself. I could see a twitch in the veins in his neck. Very un-Parkman like.

"How have you been?" he asked. "It's been what . . ."

"A year," she answered quickly. "A little over."

"My, that long?"

She nodded. "Well, running the new labs is such a demanding task that I'm sure the time has just flown by, even if it is only next door. And from what I've been hearing, it's been a great success so far."

"It has," he answered, but he didn't sound as proud as I thought he would. They were silent for a bit before she responded.

"I've been well, to answer your first question. Very well." I smiled.

"Elizabeth, I—"

"How's your wife?"

He swallowed. "Not faring much better. Still in and out of the Medical Level. But she's a . . . fighter."

"She is," Elizabeth answered. "A strong woman."

There was another silence, and I could tell he felt uncomfortable. His hands shuffled in his pockets and he kept switching his weight from one foot to the other, unable to find a comfortable position. He wanted to say something, anything, but she just stood there staring at him, unimpressed.

"I must be going, Dr. Parkman," Elizabeth said, running the invisible towel through her hair. "It was nice seeing you again."

She took one step before he stopped her, not ready for her to leave. "Please, call me Alex." His hand wrapped around her thin arm, but she shook it free.

"Goodnight, Dr. Parkman."

Parkman stood still as she walked to the door, like he was frozen in place while the words pierced his skin. But before she reached the door, he called out to her one more time. Even within the echo of his presence, I could feel his anger and frustration boiling over like a volcano. I wanted to tell her to keep going, to run and not turn back. But what was done was done. This was all history, and all I could do was watch.

"I know what you did," he said when she approached, his tone biting. "Don't you realize the odds that . . . ?" His jaw quivered ever so slightly. "That child is my most improbable creation."

"I don't know what you're talking about," she replied, her voice as even as the water stood now.

In an eruption, he slapped her, the force of the blow making her crumple to the floor. I cried out and tried to hit him, but all I could swing at was air. He stood over her and struck her again and again, her screams echoing off the walls. I stood back in horror with my hand over my mouth, my muffled screams mixing with her own. Then, grabbing a handful of her hair, he dragged her back into the pool, the two evaporating under the surface

I fell to my knees while her screams reverberated in my ears. In a burst of emotion, I clawed at my own hair and cried, holding nothing back. Not this time. I wept and moaned until I didn't have a tear left in me, until I was a desert. The one person who seemed strong enough to overcome the monster of this place still fell victim to him in the end.

I don't know how long I sat there. Minutes? Hours? I was just another piece of equipment in the lab and probably collecting my own layer of dust. But once the wave of grief washed over me, I thought of Elizabeth floating in the water again. The subtle current of the water took her where it willed and she just floated along, above it all.

Her end was a violent one, one that she didn't deserve. But she was stronger than Dr. Parkman in the end, despite what he did to her. She was beyond his control and even killing her couldn't change that.

I wanted to be as strong as her. He could be beaten, despite his reach.

I stood, looking toward the door on the far side of the pool and wiping the tears from my eyes. It was dark, but I could tell a few of the lights beyond were still on, lighting the way. I was closer to the surface than ever before, and I decided then that I wouldn't let the hand of Parkman hold me back, regardless of who I was, or how I was made. I didn't know what was going to happen, but I knew it would be on my terms. I was going to get out of here.

Or at least die trying.

BALTAZAR

After our brief encounter with the robot, our plan was to stay among the houses. They provided more cover as we searched for the next station, which, according to the map, contained a long but clearly labeled path to the higher levels. We continued that way until Smith spotted a lone doorway on the edge of the dome, standing at the end of a plot of grass sandwiched between two small, yellow houses.

We stood and stared at the sign next to the door for at least a minute before either of us said anything. I wasn't sure what Smith was thinking as he took in the small rectangle sign above the door, its letters just as unremarkable as the rest of the blank wall. But for me, the sign didn't seem real. It was more likely to be either a cruel joke, I thought, or just a figment of my imagination.

I blinked once. Then again.

Then I rubbed my eyes.

But it was still there. We hadn't been reading it incorrectly.

"Emergency Passage To Surface," Smith read, slowly.

There was no lock and no special key card needed for access.

"Is this really it?" I asked, almost to myself.

Smith pulled up the map, searching feverishly until he was able to find the single doorway we stood before. It was so small in comparison to everything else, so it wasn't surprising that we'd overlooked it. But here it was, a lone spire that led right to the top of the facility.

"I believe it is. Yes," Smith answered definitively.

Part of me wanted to start running at full speed through the door and up the stairs behind it. I would climb flight by flight and not stop until I burst through the steel vault door, or whatever was up there. Whatever would greet us above, whether it be a lush grass field, a barren landscape, or a sprawling metropolis inhabited by three-headed monkeys, would be an answer. The sight would slake my burning desire for the truth.

But then a hollow feeling struck my stomach. We couldn't go. Not without Zoe.

"We still need to find her," I said, not taking my eyes off the door.

Smith made a clicking noise. "Right. Of course," he replied. But he was still staring at the door as well. In the corner of my eye, I could see a twitch in his legs. Directives or not, freedom was his goal. "Then again, our goal was to make it to the top level and gain access to the security hubs. I'm not sure if this will connect with any of them, but it's certainly worth a try, no?"

There was an edge of nervousness in his voice, an uncertainty that I think I understood. Could we possibly turn back with the finish line right in front of us?

"Okay," I agreed, nodding my head. "But we turn back if we can't find them. We don't leave without Zoe."

Smith nodded but didn't look at me. His hand was on the door's handle in one swift motion, pulling it open with ease. Sure enough, there was a stairway behind it, empty and waiting to be climbed. I took a deep breath before following him up, taking that first step slowly. But the next one, I took more confidently. Then the next one. Soon both of us were sprinting up the spiraling column, our feet skipping steps as we rose higher and higher. My legs cramped and I went into violent coughing fits every few steps, but I didn't want to lose pace with Smith, who was going so fast that I started to envy his steel structure: Impervious to fatigue and illness but, hopefully, not promises.

After several hundred stairs, I found Smith stopped on a flat landing, standing with his back toward me. I collapsed to rest and saw that there was a thick metal door before us, triple enforced latches cementing it to the fortified walls. But the handle tilted when he pressed it. Above it, again, the simple letters read "To Surface." We were here.

The little breath I had left dissipated at the sight of the door.

"Are you ready?" Smith asked me.

Frankly, I didn't know. But I stood and grabbed the cold metal handle regardless, giving it a twist.

Then there was a click.

Then the door opened.

A dark ramp led upward and we both headed through, the curves in the tunnel preventing us from seeing its end. Our pace quickened and I felt a sudden burst of adrenaline. The possibilities revolved in my mind once again but when we emerged, what we found was something different. Something not only unexpected, but unwanted.

Smith and I found ourselves in what looked like another arena, just as large and empty as the others. Rubble littered the floor and we climbed a pile to get a better view. But no sooner had I reached the top than I threw myself flat against the rubble, dragging Smith down beside me. I swore, ducking my head under a piece of sheet metal, listening to make sure we weren't spotted. There wasn't silence, but there wasn't anything that sounded like an alarm, either.

Despite Smith's warning glances, I crawled about to the side, trying to gain a better look at what exactly lay ahead. I stuck my face between two twisted pipes, letting my eyes wander over the arena floor.

The arena was infested with robots.

On the opposite side of the gigantic arena was a massive round iron door, almost as big as the arena itself. But the path leading to it was littered with variant AI like the one that had almost found us on the Residential Level. There were at least a hundred of them, judging from my quick count. One much bigger than the rest sat on the floor directly in front of the door, as well, like a king on watch. The same one attacked us in the arena earlier, I realized, when Zoe and I were separated.

Dr. Parkman.

With this machine, he had achieved the omnipotence he desired. He towered over the others, the smaller ones seemingly in a trance as they worked around him, doing his bidding. Together they were building something in the arena, although I could only guess at its purpose. A missile to break into the new labs, perhaps? It looked almost like a standing coffin, pieced together with a varied arrangement of metal and components. At its bottom, four bowl-shaped nozzles appeared to be for propulsion. The entire structure was just about as tall and wide as Parkman and he stood back observing it, the red light from his ocular lens gently reflecting on the structure's surface.

I slid back down the side of the rubble heap, and Smith and I retreated to the tunnel, staying as low as we could.

"Well, that didn't work," he said in a hushed tone. "What are we going to do? Head back down?"

I didn't want to admit it, but I was crushed inside. The disappointment ground me down until I didn't know how much motivation I had left to keep trying. I ran my hands through my hair, trying to keep from coughing. "I don't know, Smith," I replied, slumping to the floor. "Figuring out how to open a door that size seems daunting enough, let alone sneaking through the robots. It just seems . . ."

"We're so close," Smith replied, kneeling down. "We're not giving up."

I stayed quiet for a second, tension making the veins in my neck bulge. "We still need to find Zoe."

"And we will."

I looked up and Smith was inches from my face, his ocular beams almost blinding me. He still believed in me, I thought, this hunk of bolts that had been with me since the beginning of this ordeal. For so long he needed me to carry him. But now, I needed him to pull me along.

He didn't disappoint.

I took his hand and we began to retreat from the surface door, moving to the other end of the arena rather than back down the emergency staircase. Moving through the rubble as quietly as we could, we found the ground littered with human corpses and broken down robots, likely the remains of a massive battle. Eventually, standing amid what looked like an imploded assault vehicle and several decapitated robots, we found a round building that almost blended in with the landscape. Its doors were heavy and ominous. We peered between the cracks to check for any signs of danger before heading into the darkness, finding nothing but a hallway toward the back.

We headed down, but I froze after a few steps, suddenly afraid of the darkness ahead.

"What is it?" Smith asked, but I just held my finger up to my lips, gazing deep into the darkness.

I held my breath. Something was coming toward us. We froze where we stood under the light, nowhere left to hide.

ZOE

I stopped in the dark, hesitant to move into the light that filled the end of the hallway. Ever since I'd discovered Elizabeth's fate, my determination had been renewed. My ankle still bled and throbbed but I'd climbed the stairs all the way to the top of the old labs. The door to the surface was so close. And there he was, either waiting for me or standing in my way.

He looked different somehow. Sweat glistened on his forehead and his shirt was covered with black streaks from something. But that wasn't it. He almost seemed to glow.

"Is someone there?" Balt called out.

He didn't realize it was me. If I wanted, I could retreat and hide. I could stay in the dark and slither by, never having to worry about him or anyone else ever again, or feel the pain of losing anyone else again. He was so angry the last time we spoke. I tried leaving him for dead once, lied to him so many times more. Maybe he wouldn't be happy to see me.

But the angry fire wasn't in his eyes anymore. Neither was the fear. And as comfortable as it felt now, I knew the dark was not where I belonged.

I took a step forward and, sighing, I shook my head ever so slightly as I stared at him.

He took the next step, moving toward me slowly at first. I

stumbled on my wounded ankle and he broke into a jog, his arms outstretched. When he was close enough to reach, I grabbed him, holding him so tight that I thought I might break him. He was here, solid flesh and bone and not some being of light that only I could see. I could feel his heart beating fast against mine and I buried my head in his shoulder. I burst out laughing without really knowing why. It hadn't been that long ago, but it felt like I hadn't seen him in a lifetime.

When we pulled apart, I could see there were tears in his eyes. I wiped them with my thumb, saying, "Don't get all emotional on me now, Balt."

He sniffed. "I'm sorry. I was just worried that we would never find you again." A breath left his lips and we remained close, his arms wrapped tightly around my waist.

Only three to five percent of species were considered monogamous, the bald eagle being one of them. Two bald eagles would meet when they were young and would stay together for the span of their entire lives, only moving on when the other died. It's a bond rarely seen in nature, which makes it special. Some lives are just meant to be lived together, I suppose.

I drew them once, a lifetime ago. They were soaring through the air, their wings ever so close. The setting sun behind painted the sky various shades of orange.

"You're hurt," Balt said, bending down to inspect my injured ankle. The makeshift bandage was completely coated in blood. It felt raw, but I just shrugged my shoulders.

"Had a little run-in with our six-legged friends. It's not bad," But that wasn't what I wanted to talk about; there were a thousand other things I wanted to say. So much I just wanted to get off my shoulders so we could leave it all behind and get to the surface with a clean slate, and a clear conscience.

But before I could speak, I realized that something was missing from Balt. There was movement behind him and Smith was suddenly *standing* by his side. The AI scared me at first, prompting my hands to curl into fists by reflex, ready to strike. But the warm glow of his ocular beams, which had led us through so many dark hallways, instantly disarmed me.

"Smith," I greeted, scanning his crude body up and down. "I like the new look."

He planted his hands on his makeshift hips. "Why, thank you, Zoe. Thanks to Balt, I've become fully autonomous! He's quite handy, if I do say so myself," he explained, nudging Balt with his elbow and making his creator turn red with embarrassment.

"Always has been," I replied.

Balt smiled. The three of us were back together and everything seemed right again.

Well, almost right.

"Balt," I began, my heart beating faster and faster. I looked into his soft brown eyes, picturing the cells within them, grown within the cold lab instead of within a warm body and a loving home. I wasn't sure how he was going to react, but it wasn't my place to make that decision for him anymore. "There are a few things I need to tell you."

Balt nodded slowly, sighing. "Yes. I think there are some things I need to tell you, too."

There was silence before Smith began slowly backing away. "Should I leave you two alone?"

I wanted to say yes, but it didn't seem right to exclude the AI now. After all that we'd been through. "No, Smith. You deserve to know all of this, too. No secrets, from *any* of us, remember?"

Smith smiled and Balt helped me down. We sat in the hall in a circle, the fluorescent light above us making a slight buzzing sound. I remembered the three of us hidden under the workstation in the bio lab, the night I'd told them my secrets. *Almost* all my secrets. But this time, I wouldn't hold back. I rubbed my eyes and tried to hear the whispers of any figures of light around, but everything else was silent. We were alone.

"I've been . . . seeing things. A side effect of *Project Wind*. I think."

I hoped.

Balt tilted his head while Smith remained still, his fingers folded together. "What kind of things?" Smith eventually asked.

I bit my lip, trying to find the right words. "They look like light, in the shape of people. I can hear them speak to each other throughout the lab."

Balt looked up and down the hallway. "Are there any about now?" he asked. "That's somewhat off-putting to think."

I shook my head. "No, we're alone. They're not actually there, I think. It's more like they're echoes of the scientists who worked here. Like they're reenacting what happened. Showing me things . . ."

I trailed off, my throat suddenly feeling dry. I grabbed Balt's hand and felt my skin rub gently against his. "We were grown down here, Balt. Not born on the surface."

The words hung heavy in the air and I could see them infiltrating Balt's mind, his face twitching as his brain processed the thought. And when it did, his shoulders slumped, his Adam's apple bobbing. "What do you mean?"

"I found a lab when you were working with Smith on the security cube. Inside I saw these . . . tubes, meant for cell growth. And those echoes showed me. They've been growing test subjects here all along. That's all we are—or were. I'm not sure what to think anymore."

Smith made a clicking noise. "It would be easier," he said, his voice so low. "From a rather moderately sized genetic bank, you could create hundreds of thousands of different combinations; have a whole legion of test subjects at the ready."

I listened but kept my eyes glued on Balt, almost feeling his heart ripping into two. He'd been hoping for a different light at the end of the tunnel than I had, I knew. Now it turned out that light wouldn't be there. That picture frame by his bed would always be empty.

But rather than crumbling, he just shook his head ever so slightly, looking into my eyes. "Thanks for telling me."

"I'm sorry I didn't tell you earlier."

A tear dropped from his eye but he wiped it himself, running his hands through his short hair. "Doesn't change our plan, though. We still need to get out of here."

"The passage to the surface is just behind us but . . ." Smith began and I held my breath while he looked to Balt to continue.

"It's sealed shut . . . and there are dozens of robots stationed right in front."

"Great," I said, wanting to pull what was left of my hair out in frustration.

"But that's not all," he continued, appearing more nervous. I realized then that he was holding more back too.

"The robot that attacked us in the arena, when we got separated. The one with the crown decal . . ."

"Yeah?" I answered, remembering the giant red eye before I'd teleported away.

"It's Dr. Parkman."

My stomach churned, remembering his rage when he'd murdered Elizabeth. "How can that be?"

Smith explained a log they'd found by a Dr. Seagreaves, the scientist who figured out how to imbue human minds and personalities into machines. I tried to listen, but all I could think of was that red eye, staring me down like it knew me. It sent every hair on my body standing on end, and more than ever, I wanted to get as far as I could away from here.

"All the more important that we leave this place behind," I replied, relaying my thoughts. I refused to be burned by his influence anymore.

"Right," Balt answered, rubbing his hands together eagerly.

Smith clapped. "Alright! So now all we need to do is figure out a way to get past those robots. There are a lot of them, but maybe if we could create a distraction or something to allow us to sneak by . . ."

"I know how to distract them," I said, suddenly feeling tired.

Balt leaned in. "How?"

In my exhaustion I forced out a laugh. It was a crazy thought, but what was sane about anything here? "You're not gonna like this."

BALTAZAR

"I found their nest," Zoe began. The rest of her plan got progressively worse from there.

"Nest?" I repeated, just the sound of the word making me twitch.

"Of those bug things. They have a whole colony on the Botany Level that's not too far from here thanks to some collapsed ceilings." From her tone, I believe she expected me to take this news as comforting, but that was probably the last emotion I could experience from the news.

Protocol #98: *Fear is a condition of the mind, nothing more.*

I leaned back, folding my arms while frowning.

"Not to jump ahead," Smith interjected. "But if I'm following your thought process correctly, you want to lure those creatures up here, get them to engage the robots, and then slip through during the scuffle?"

"Well, we'll still need to get the door open," was all she replied.

I gulped so hard I thought I swallowed my tongue.

"I told you two that you weren't going to like the plan."

"And you were correct." I ran my hands through my hair. Hair, which I realized then, had been grown in a lab. The color and arrangement had been determined by computer coding.

I squeezed my eyes shut and forced the idea out. I would deal with it, but not now. There was still so much left to do. "There must be another way. Is there a side vent in the arena or an access panel or . . ."

"Something?" Smith offered.

"Yes, some other way out than by creating chaos and hoping to squeak by. Just thinking of the numbers on each side, the statistical likelihoods of not being spotted are . . ."

"Well, let's look again then," Zoe said, cutting me off. "If there is another way, we'll find it."

We led Zoe back down the hall slowly because of her ankle. She insisted it wasn't too bad, but I caught her wincing with every step, not helping to notice the irony of our role reversal. When we emerged from the terminal, I helped her over some of the rubble and we silently made our way back to the entrance of the emergency staircase. We watched the robots move about in the distance. I scanned every inch of the walls, hoping to find something that would indicate a way through, something that would provide an opportunity that didn't involve those creatures. But all the grates and vents were in the ceiling, hundreds of feet above us. The large round iron door was the only way.

"There's a control room," Smith indicated in a hushed voice, pointing one of his metal fingers to a window in the far wall, behind a group of robots repairing one another like monkeys grooming. "I bet we could open the door from inside there."

"I believe you're correct," I replied. "What do you think, Zoe?"

I turned to her and saw that she wasn't paying attention to us, her eyes soldered on Dr. Parkman, seated directly in front of the door. His lone red eye was still staring at the structure the smaller robots were creating. Her fists were clenched.

"Hey," I said, tapping her on the shoulder.

"What?"

"The exit controls," I pointed. "Over there."

"And look at that," Smith added, pointing to what resembled a broken down tram. The robots had picked large portions of its outer shell apart, but it was still mostly intact. The cars curved through the arena, the final one sitting within twenty feet or so of the control room.

I studied it, my fingers gently tapping against a piece of sheet metal near us. "Are you thinking what I'm thinking?"

"We could use it to get close," Zoe declared. "Wait until the bugs distract those robots and then make a break for it."

"That's quite a distance for a sprint though, especially considering how fast these things move," I pointed out.

"It's a chance, Balt. And our chances have been pretty good so far."

I nodded, recalling the glow of the phase cannon staring me down as I twirled that blasted matter mover over and over. I'd stood there wondering if Zoe would return or if I was going to be reduced to particles. Things seemed grim then, but we'd made it. We were still making it, actually.

"Let's head back," I declared. "Go over everything again."

The others agreed and we returned to the terminal where we'd found Zoe, our backs hunched as we snuck through the rubble-strewn arena. I started pacing in the hallway when we were back inside, watching my shadow move about.

"It's not the best plan, but it's a plan," Smith declared.

Zoe nodded, "Our options are limited, Balt."

"I know," I said, frustrated. For a second, the sensation of ants crawling over my skin made me shutter. "But you said it's a whole nest? Not just a few or a bunch, but an entire colony? They will be everywhere within seconds, and even if we get the door open and make it through, what's to keep those things or the robots from following us out. We're not even sure what is on the other side of that door."

Zoe stood, placing her hand on my shoulder. Her touch eased my tense muscles. I sighed, planting my hands on my hips. "There's just a lot of factors we can't . . ."

"I know," she said, her voice so soft. I looked into her blue eyes and remembered how they made me feel like I could figure out anything.

So much had changed, but not everything.

"You and Smith head inside that tram and get as close to the control room as you can," she said. "I'll head back to the nest and lure the bugs into the arena. Once I lure them up here, I'll just hide and wait for you two to open the door. Then we'll all leave here for good."

The sound of the insect's wings fluttering echoed in my ears, a chill running up and down my spine. I looked down. The sleeve tied around Zoe's ankle was stained crimson. The odds that she could outrun them on that ankle were slim, even for our standards. To optimize our chances, I knew the proper assignments.

Protocol #98: *Fear is a condition of the mind, nothing more.*

"You head to the tram. I'll lure them up."

Zoe shook her head.

"With your injury, you don't have the mobility to outrun them, Zoe," Smith declared from his perch on a piece of rubble.

"Exactly," I agreed, nodding.

Zoe squeezed my arm. "No way. This is *my* plan. *My* risk to take."

"You physically can't pull this off. It *has* to be me."

"But—" she protested, at a loss for words. "But I can't unlock that door. I can't manage systems like you can."

I motioned toward Smith. "He can do it. Stay close to each other, and once you see a clear shot, take it. Open the door."

"No, Balt. It's not gonna happen this way."

"It has to."

Zoe took a step and I could see the pain on her face. She didn't want to give in but she knew I was right. We had just found each other again, but our paths needed to move apart once again.

"Head down the hall," she said in a quiet voice. "Stay to the right of the terminal you come out of and follow the offices you find there. You'll see all the holes that lead down to the nest along there. Just watch your step."

"Alright," I answered, staring down the dark path by which she'd come.

Smith stood and shook my hand, the metal warm from the heat moving through the circuitry. "Good luck, Balt."

"Thanks, Smith," I answered before turning to Zoe, her eyes watery. It was my turn to wipe the tears from her face. I hugged her and felt her breath on my skin, the muscles in her arms tightening around mine. "This isn't goodbye."

"I know," she said.

I took one last look at her before heading down the hall, my head held high. "I'll see you two on the other side. Then we'll be on our way to the surface."

The path ahead was pitch black, so I used the walls to keep my balance. I stepped over collapsed portions of wall, trying to focus. All I could think about at first were those bugs, hundreds of ant mantises with clacking mandibles that could cut right through bone without missing a beat. Even if I could outrun them, I worried, I would be heading right into a seriously grim scenario. The robots were equally as deadly.

But things have felt dire before, I told myself. Yet, here we were, one door away.

It would all end now, one way or another.

ZOE

And just like that, he was gone again, off to retrace my steps back to the nest. I did my best to hide my worry while Smith and I started back toward the door to the arena, stopping by a sub-station off to the right where one broken down tram sat silent on the rails. While the AI checked down the line, I rubbed my hand across one of the dusty windows. Inside, small cradles lined its walls, measuring maybe two feet by two wide. There was some-thing somber about the sight and, when I was ready to catch up with Smith, a figure of light by my side kept me lingering. After sparking in and out of existence, it solidified and stood right next to me, looking through the same window I was.

Although I shouldn't have been, I was surprised to see it was Elizabeth. She must have been here before her last swim. We were connected, this figure and I. She was a calming presence, and I wanted to reach out to her to see if she was as soft and warm as she made me feel. But, like always, she was just a fading light when my hand passed through her, a specter of energy long gone.

Elizabeth put her hand to the glass, staring at something through the window. I inspected the cradle in front of her and realized then that the small holds were meant to be padded for something fragile. Precious. And from the sloping direction of the tracks, this tram must have come from the lower levels.

Where the children were grown.

Elizabeth stood quietly, but then another figure manifested beside her. I didn't recognize the man, although his lab coat hinted he was another scientist. He had a receding hair line and a tired but welcoming smile. Something was clasped between his fingers, a cigarette maybe, that he promptly put out against the metal of the tram once he saw what was inside the car.

"Oh, is that her?" he asked.

Elizabeth didn't say anything, but pointed to the cradle near the window.

The man smiled. "She has your eyes."

"I was worried about that. It will make her stand out."

After looking around, the man placed his hand on her shoulder, whispering into her ear. I had to get close to make out what he said, the words so faint they felt like an echo themselves. An echo of an echo.

"Her file will check out," he told her in a hushed voice. "I went over it several times and made sure to delete the edit marks. I don't think anyone will suspect anything."

Elizabeth didn't look at him, but I could see her shoulders relax slightly. A weight taken off them. "Thank you, Dr. Seagreaves. You'll never know how much this means to me."

The man nodded before looking around again to make sure no one was around before answering. "It's no problem. Given the circumstances, I understand why you wanted to do this. And why you trusted me."

Elizabeth nodded, but then I could see her face crumple. She wanted to cry, wail so loudly that her voice would fill the whole tram station. But she didn't. She just took a moment to collect herself before sighing, wiping her eyes. "You're among the few who would understand why I need to hide her. He's been away overseeing the finalization of the new labs, but enough people know that I was pregnant that I'm sure it will get back to him. Eventually. But with your actions, I hope he will never find her. His genome is in the student pool, so blood testing all the students won't help. He might have suspicions, but he'll never be one hundred percent sure. She'll be hidden. She'll be safe."

I stood there, listening to her words and thinking of her in the pool when Parkman had killed her. So she did have a baby. His baby. And wanted to protect her from him.

"I hope so," Dr. Seagreaves said. "But then again, I'm sure you've heard the news on the neuro-netting project. Are any of us safe once the X1 is imbued with his mind?"

She didn't say anything to this, opting to press her hand against the glass. I looked into her eyes. They were empty and colorless, but I was starting to think I knew what color they were.

I got one last glimpse of her face before she faded away. But it was enough. It wasn't just a coincidence that I had been able to see her more than the others. We were connected.

I was different after all.

Then my knees buckled as the truth bore down on me. Every bit of joy was ripped from my chest and replaced by something else. I pictured the black of my insides and dropped to the floor, grabbing chunks of my hair and wanting to scream so loudly that I would shatter.

Maybe I was wrong.

Maybe I was grown like the rest.

Better to be a product of a monster than the offspring.

But then I remembered the stare he gave me in Dr. Grima's office, so long ago. The same stare the robot gave me in the arena.

He didn't recognize me.

He recognized part of himself.

"Are you alright?"

I barely heard Smith through my blind rage; my ears ringing so hard that I thought my eardrums would burst. When I didn't answer, Smith knelt down across from me, the glow of his eyes leading me out of the downward spiral my mind was taking.

"Do you see them . . ." he began and I nodded, my eyes fused shut.

"He's my father."

"Who?"

"*Parkman!*"

My voice echoed through the tram station, Smith put his hand over my mouth, hoping silence, and nothing else would follow. Thankfully, no thudding of metal feet lumbered toward us, and I whispered, "I'm sorry." I looked to the stairs that lead out to the arena and could almost feel the heat of the giant robot's stare.

Parkman's stare.

"I'm not sure why you think that is the case, but our time is short, Zoe. We need to start heading toward the broken tram. Balt needs us to open that door."

"You go," I shot back, not looking at him. "Get out of here."

"I don't understand."

"It's pointless," I shot back, my words so sharp they could have cut through him. "Don't you get that? I *am* Parkman! I really am just another piece of rubble he left in his wake!" I stood and felt so many things that I thought they were all going to pour out of my skin. Rather than continue to shout, I took a deep breath and grabbed Smith by the shoulders. "Just . . . go, Smith. Get that door open and go. There's no freedom for me on the other side."

Time was against him. I could see the calculations behind the glow of his eyes, estimating the distance between the door and the nest. Analyzing the average speed sixteen-year-old's can run, flight speeds of insects extrapolated by size. He didn't have time to debate me and change my mind. I was a liability. He had to leave me.

But he didn't.

Smith moved in close, opening his mouth to speak. But the voice that emerged wasn't his. It was Balt's.

"Love is one of the most obtuse terms created," he began, his voice sounding like a recording. "Everything can be traced back to logical rationales and love shouldn't be any different. When one organism encounters another that stimulates them intellectually and arouses them physically, chemicals are released within the brain, which said organism wishes to repeat. Tie in genetic instincts to procreate, and feelings of 'love' make sense. Or at least, that's what I thought until I saw Zoe."

My head cocked back, not sure of where this was going or why Smith was playing this for me now, but I didn't try to stop him. I just listened.

"I don't know anything about her really, other than she was that girl who survived the incident on Level H. I have no idea what her interests are, or if she's nice, or even if she's interested in males, but I just can't stop thinking about her. I assumed that these feelings would diminish over time, but they only keep intensifying. All I can do is picture her beautiful blue eyes, her perfect skin, her soft white hair . . . and I want to know every single thing about her. I feel both physically and mentally dominated by thoughts of her and it's simultaneously the best and worst emotions I have ever felt. It all feels . . . illogical."

There was a pause in the audio and I thought it was over, but then Balt's voice returned.

"But it's the most wonderful contradiction I have ever encountered. That's why I need to pursue this venture. I need to find out what it is about her that makes me feel so amazing that there doesn't seem to be any challenge I can't overcome with her affection in mind. That can't be ignored." Then there was a small laugh. His laugh. "I'm such a quark."

I didn't move. I didn't say anything. I tried picturing this girl he was talking about, because that's not who I saw the last time I looked in a mirror.

"I'm not really sure what it is that you are feeling right now, but we have an important task in front of us," Smith said in his own voice.

"Smith, I . . ."

"There is a young man out there who has demonstrated to me nothing but poor decision-making ever since he met you. But he sees something in you so wonderful that all of the danger, all of the risk-taking, seems worth it to him. It is fine if you wish to give up at this juncture, but do not make that decision based on your personal worth, because there are those out there who think everything of you."

Smith shook my hand. "It was a pleasure getting to know you. But I must go if I am to open the door for Balt. I hope you will follow, but I will not force you."

Off he went, turning his back to me and making his way back up the stairs to the arena. I could still feel the gaze of Parkman on me through the walls; feel his filthy imprint on my cells, his blood coursing through my veins. I hated him more than anything, and the knowledge that we were genetically related filled me with such a heavy feeling that I didn't think I could move.

But I did. I got to my feet and hobbled behind Smith toward the arena.

I wasn't sure I deserved the affection Balt had for me. Whether I deserved to be anything more than just a part of this lab.

But somehow he was sure. And I trusted him.

BALTAZAR

The first hole I came to after following Zoe's directions was about six feet by six. The floor had given way and dropped what looked like an expensive piece of machinery about a hundred feet to the floor below. Gazing down, I could make out the circuitry spilled about over a dirt surface. Around it, green pods glowed eerily like nuclear rods. I got one look at them before pulling my head back out of the hole, trying to stop myself from hyperventilating.

It was time. I closed my eyes and breathed, mustering every ounce of courage I had left.

"Why did it have to be insects?" I whispered to myself.

I could hear the bugs below. They were crawling around, gnawing on the circuits. The flutter of their wings made a rapid flapping noise that raised goose bumps on my skin. I stared at the way I had come and tried to remember every move I would have to make to get back as quickly and efficiently as possible: left in the tram station; run over the first pile of rubble and under the second because it was too high to climb quickly. There was a little underpass made by a crumbled steel support strut. I could even hide in there if I needed to. Then down the far hall. That was going to be the tricky part. It was a straight path from there. I was fast, but they were faster.

The tension began to make me feel a little lightheaded. I was dazed, as if I was on a heavy dose of painkillers. I contemplated whether my mind was subconsciously trying to separate itself from my body, preparing me for whatever was going to happen. I rubbed the scar on my shoulder and decided that I didn't want to be alone if this was going to be it for me. I wanted to be among friends.

"Dang, that's a far drop," Zeke would say, punching me in the shoulder. Usually I would punch him back, but I would permit it this time.

Tern would inspect the dimensions of the hole, scanning the room we were in for a way to grab the creatures' attention efficiently. "That broken piece of slab over there?"

"Yes," I would nod. "I believe I'll push it over and down the hole. If that isn't enough, I can start yelling as well."

"Ballsy," Zeke would say. "Insane, but ballsy. I like it."

I'd grin, and a silence would take over our little gathering around the hole. Each of us would remember how good it felt to be among each other's company. They were good friends. They still were good friends.

"So," Tern would eventually say. "How have you been? Any luck with Zoe?"

"We did kiss," I would reveal, smiling at the memory. "But I'm not sure what to make of that. It's complicated. This hasn't been the most optimal environment in which to foster a relationship."

Zeke would throw his hands up in the air. "Whaaaaaat? This is the *perfect* environment to make her wanna jump your bones! Danger around every corner, never knowing what moment might be your last . . ."

"Powerful revelations that make you re-examine who you are and what's important," Tern would continue. "Hate to say it, but maybe he's right. Then again, I could see how you've felt pretty preoccupied."

A group of bugs stirred below me, fighting over the corpse of a robot, its circuits sparking as it was pulled apart.

"Yeesh, nasty things, aren't they?" Zeke would comment. "Gotta hand it to you. I don't know if I would have the guts to do this."

"Agreed," Tern would add.

"Thanks, guys. I believe the experience is making me braver . . . but I think it's more likely that the lack of food and water has me somewhat delirious and is blurring my judgment."

Zeke would wave his hands in the air. "Nonetheless, I hereby rename you Balt 'The Beast' Harris. May legends of your beast-ness live on through the ages!"

"Hear, hear!" Tern would celebrate.

I'd smile again. It would feel good. "Well, I guess it's time to do this?"

"Want our help?"

"Nah," I'd say. "I can do this. Good luck, friends. I don't know what we're going to find when we get past that door. *If* we get past that door, I should say. But I won't forget you two. I'll get word to you somehow."

"Good luck, Balt," Tern would answer, giving me a hug. Zeke would then make an overly exaggerated crying sound and bear hug us both. We'd laugh just like old times. But that's what they were. Old times.

Now it was time to stir up the nest.

I took a deep breath and moved behind a thick slab of concrete that was leaning against the wall. It was several hundred pounds and fractured on both ends. With my shoulder against it, I gave it a little push, the thick material shifting ever so slightly. It was too heavy to move, really, but all I needed to do was push it over the slightest degree. From its placement, it would fall right through the hole.

With my eyes closed, I dwelled on the thought of Zoe for one more second, remembering the look of her blue eyes and preparing myself to do anything to see them once again. Focused on the image, I pushed against the concrete slab with enough force to send it tilting in slow motion, standing tall before quickly tumbling right through the hole. I watched it crush two creatures, their screams quickly replaced by a sickening thud. Green goo splattered around the point of impact.

"I'm up here, you subspecies!" I screamed at the top of my lungs. "Come and get me!"

Come, they did. They were so fast my brain barely registered that all I could see were fluttering wings. The first was through the hole by the time I got to the door of the small room.

I tripped in the hall but caught myself with my hands to keep from falling. Behind me, the ant mantises shrieked their too-familiar shriek, and I could feel my heart working overtime, pumping blood to my limbs and propelling me forward into the tram station. I went left like I'd planned, but the bugs were just too fast. They flew over me as I passed the first rubble pile and one made a swipe for my head.

An eerie ringing instantly replacing the sound of their wings. I could hear my heart pounding against my chest as well as my diaphragm, rising and falling over and over as it pushed the air in and out of my lungs. But all I saw were bugs. They were crawling over every inch of the walls.

When I got to the second rubble pile, I went under the support structure, sliding into the thin tunnel through it. Sharp edges from the debris poked at my flesh, but I crawled as quickly as I could. In the frenzy, I kicked at the rubble behind me, blocking the path with rock and concrete. My hearing slowly returned, filled with shrieking. Blood ran down my neck and back and when I touched my ear, I could feel a chunk of the top missing. The pressure of my touch sent a biting wave of pain through my body. I clenched my teeth, yelling and cursing. There was no way I was going to make it to the arena, I realized. There were just too many.

So I waited.

I could hear the flutter of wings outside but I didn't move, planting my face in the gravel and feeling the dust enter my lungs, triggering a coughing fit. It didn't matter though. They knew where I was.

I could hear the patter of legs around me, the bugs descending on the rubble pile. Dust and dirt began to fill the hole and I could feel the weight of the rubble shifting around me, crushing my limbs. I screamed and clawed at the entrance, terrified of being buried alive. In a panic, I scurried out of my hiding spot and slipped on something smooth under my feet, sending me tumbling to me knees. One bug on the rubble spotted me and leapt, its claws outstretched and ready to impale me.

It shrieked.

I screamed.

My hands clutched at the smooth surface I slipped on and I raised whatever it was over my head, watching the bug zoom toward me. Its claws struck but, rather than leaving me dead, bounced off after a thundering impact that sliced the palms of my hands. I realized then that I was holding a thick piece of plastic covering that was light enough to carry but thick enough that they couldn't penetrate it.

This is your chance, my brain yelled. RUN RUN RUN RUN RUN RUN RUN!

With the plastic on my back, I ran for the hallway, a few more smacks sending me reeling, though I managed to stay on my feet. The plastic was too wide to fit into the hallway, but flexible enough that I was able to bend it in the doorway. I left it behind as I broke into an adrenaline-fueled sprint, my feet flying across the floor faster than I ever thought possible.

The plastic sheet didn't keep the bugs wedged for long, their cries only fading for a few seconds before the sharp tapping of their claws could be heard in the metal hallway. But that's all I needed, I thought. If I could make it to the arena, there would be more for them to focus on than me. I would be the least of their problems.

ZOE

Once we were back in the arena, I followed Smith's lead through the rubble. We found the derailed tram and slid inside though a broken window. The shattered glass made tiny crunches under our feet, which, with the robots so close, made my hair stand on end. Smith's eyes glowed red but there was nowhere to go but forward.

The first car was mostly clear but the second was full of twisted metal, the remains of some sort of machine that had been tossed through the tram with such force that it broke through one side of the vehicle and partially through the next. Smith lifted a frayed piece of metal and I slid under Smith's arm, helping him through the small opening after me. His metal body didn't have the give of flesh and made a scraping noise like nails across a datapad when he bumped into something, so his progress was slow to prevent making noise. But we stayed together, tackling one tram after another. Like the levels of the lab, my mind began seeing the path ahead in sections. Another car down. Just a few more to go.

We made it through the next two without a problem, but then hit a point where a twenty-foot space separated two cars, the gap exposed to a group of robots that were ripping apart the remains of some machine, scouring its insides for parts. Smith and I stopped at our last few feet of cover and stared at the tramcar door on the other side. It was so close, but with the eyes of so many robots just a head turn away, it might as well have been on the other side of the planet.

"Do we try a different way?" I asked in such a low voice that even I wondered if I had spoken at all.

But Smith shook his head. "No time. Balt might be here any second."

Impulsively, I took one glance out of the car and watched the robots tug and pull at wiring, sparks flying into the air. Then, before I knew it, I was moving across the gap, my ankle burning in pain with every step. But I pushed on, scurrying like a bat in the light. When I reached the opposite side, I turned back to Smith who was staring at me, his mouth agape. It was a rash decision but, as the seconds passed and there was still no sign of movement from the robots, we both relaxed. I had made it.

Then the leg of Parkman appeared, planting itself in the gap between Smith and me. The dirt from the ground shot up from the impact and smothered us in a brown cloud, stinging my eyes and lungs. I ducked under a few seats and froze, hearing the clicking sound of the lens in his red eye, shifting somewhere above. He knew I was close, trying to find me in the storm of dust and dirt. I stayed still and had to look out of a broken window across the car, the glass shards reflecting my fear.

Behind Parkman's arm, I could see a light on in the distance coming from a room behind a glass wall. I regained my bearings and realized that was where I needed to be. *The control room.* But how to get to it with this monster right next to me?

Parkman took another step and landed on the tram car right in front of me, his weight crushing the car and leaving me trapped. I looked back to try to find Smith, but Parkman's other leg was still there, blocking my view. Panic began to set in and the only thing I could think of was to wait until Balt got here. If he was able to bring the bugs, maybe I could make it to the control room during the commotion. But I would be exposed, easy prey for any bug or robot that noticed me. That is, if Parkman didn't find me first.

Time was short. I was so scared that I thought I was going to faint, suddenly lightheaded. But the more I focused on the sensation, the more it seemed to thin out, floating about in my brain like a sheet of light. I slowed my breathing and just stared at the control room, imagining the thick glass and stale air. I listened for the buzz of the florescent lights inside and, even through a roar from Parkman, I could just make out the hum of the control panel. I was as light as a feather, as insignificant as a blade of grass. I closed my eyes, focusing.

And then I was inside.

I fell to the floor, my knees weak. My head felt like it was torn inside and out and blood dripped from my nose, staining my hands red as I tried to squeeze my nostrils shut. Through the glass window, I could see Parkman, his back toward me, his enormous hand wrapping around a tramcar and lifting it off the ground, his red eye scanning inside. I had gotten out just in time, but without Smith, who was hopefully still hidden. Still safe, I hoped.

I rose to my knees and looked at the control panel, its knobs and lights appearing just as they had in my mind. But in terms of opening the door, I didn't even know where to start . . . A slicing headache cut my mind in two. I looked for something, anything, that might give me a clue, but Parkman, who took another earth-shaking step in my direction, seized my attention. His red eye pointed toward me and flooded the room in red light.

I fell back again and tried moving away from the glass, but the small room left me nowhere to go. Parkman's head lowered with a creak and he got down on one knee. With one swift motion, one of his fingers impaled the glass and shattered it with ease. I screamed and looked around for something to grab, anything I could use to defend myself. But then my ears were filled with another sound, one that I thought I would never be happy to hear.

The sound of flapping wings filled the arena like a coming hurricane, and Parkman turned. We both stared at the far side of the arena to see the swarm of insects approaching, claws and mandibles out and ready to strike. The robots in the arena abandoned their work and charged ahead to meet them, metal meeting chitin with a crunch. It was absolute chaos in every direction I could look. Except for one, which made me let out a delirious laugh.

Balt, bloody and dirty, ran toward the giant door like a general leading the charge. He had made it, just like he said he would. And now I had to do my part.

I regained control of my senses and looked back to the control panel, finding a knob on the right that brought up a virtual interface. A cube appeared before me and I started ripping it apart in search of a file that would open the door. All around me were digital groans and primal screams, but I stayed focused, trying to find that level of concentration that Balt seemed to be able to tap into time and time again. As if he was channeling through me, things seemed to almost slow down, the files revealing themselves. "Main Door" flashed in front of my eyes and I ran the executable within it.

Instantly, red and yellow lights began to flash against the walls as a siren blared so loudly that it droned out the fight. A giant burst of wind blew through the arena, and the great door began to swing slowly open. It cracked a few feet before Parkman was thrown back into it, flailing about as he tried to fight off a swarm of attacking insects. His body had blocked the door from opening more, but there was still enough room for us to squeeze through. An opening to the surface.

I slid over the console, through the broken window, and out into the arena, watching Balt roll under a robot as it delivered a blow so powerful that it made an ant mantis burst into goo. I ran as fast as I could, limping on my injured ankle, imagining the lines of our approaches intersecting like on a graph. I made it to the door before him and waited behind its thick iron weight, screaming for him to hurry. He was only a few meters away when he was lifted into the air, an ant mantis catching his arm and tossing him to the ground.

He crawled backward until he was up against the wall of the arena. I could see the terror in his eyes, the crippling exhaustion that was consuming him. And with the surface right behind me, I ran toward him, grabbing a broken piece of a robotic arm on the way. I swung the arm wildly and missed, but the insect, surprised by my sudden charge, backed off for just a second, giving me time to reach Balt.

Panting, I helped him to his feet. The two of us stood shoulder to shoulder as the ant mantis slowly approached, its mandibles champing. It spread its wings as it prepared to attack. But then something jumped on its back, the insect thrashing about as green goo began to shoot out in steady jets.

"Smith!" Balt shouted. The AI had latched onto our attacker, stabbing the creature with a piece of sharp metal. But his enemy whirled and writhed, finally grabbing Smith by one arm and smashing him against the ground, the impact smashing his new body to pieces. With his head still attached to his upper body, he reached out with one hand toward us.

"Go!" he shouted before his eyes went dark. A group of bugs descended upon him and tore him apart. Balt began to run toward the frenzy, but I grabbed his hand, pleading to him to come with me. Another bug began to descend upon us and we ran for the door, barely making it through before a loud splat exploded behind us, a robot ramming the bug into the wall. We collapsed on a cold floor and I felt it wasn't flat, but sloped. Upwards.

Hand in hand, Balt and I moved up the dark ramp, climbing higher and higher while the sound of the battle grew fainter with every stumbling step. Soon, all I could hear was our heavy breathing, yet we couldn't stop, darkness soon overwhelming us. I could feel Balt falling over himself in exhaustion, but I urged him on, helping him up when he fell. My shirt was soaked with blood from my nose and my ankle felt like it was broken into shards. But the pain felt insignificant when a light appeared in the distance. Then another. Then another. We reached the top of the ramp and I collapsed to my knees at the sight visible through the massive glass dome above us.

The most beautiful sight I had ever seen in my life.

A black sky peppered with thousands of stars.

My mouth gaped open and I wanted to cry. There were so many stars, and yet each one looked unique. I suddenly felt infinitesimally small, but uniquely alive at the same time. Balt knelt beside me and we just held each other, looking at the endless sky.

"I can't believe it," he said, his breath slowing down. He squeezed my hand and I squeezed back.

Overcome by the sight, I imagined Helena staring up at the same sky and feeling everything that I was. I turned and realized that Balt was looking not at the sky, but at me. His face was pale but so beautiful then. He looked at me and I felt like the girl he thought I was—like the girl I used to be. He kissed me and, for a second, it felt like were the only two people on the planet, the sole citizens of a universe all our own.

When we finally broke apart, we rested our heads against each other before he fell back to the floor, his hands outstretched on the ground. "We did it," he breathed.

"C'mon!" I shouted, laughing and overcome with the desire to see what else was beyond the dome. The structure was massive, a giant circle around us that was filled with seats and broken down escalators that led upwards. I thought of Smith and the sacrifice he had made for us. He was responsible for the joy I was feeling, and I promised I would find a way to repay his memory. He would join the group of friends I had lost, but would stay in my mind forever.

I climbed the steel steps of the escalator, going as fast as my ankle would allow. "Balt, c'mon!" I shouted behind me but kept going, wanting to see the surface so badly, see the beautiful grass and the rolling hills and endless oceans and all the other beautiful sights I had read about and seen in history torrents.

But when I reached the top and got my first glimpse at the world outside the glass, my pace slowed. My face tingled and my eyes began to water. I put my hand against the glass and let my palm drag downward, completely devoid of any feeling at all.

The terrain was grey, almost white. Nothing stood but a barren landscape of endlessness, craters littering the ground in every direction. They hadn't been lying. There really had been a war, and it had scorched the Earth. Everything was gone—all the whales and bar-tailed godwits and hognose snakes and dead-leaf katydids and all the rest. They were all gone.

Balt caught up behind me and I felt his hand fall onto my shoulder, his heart sinking with mine. I wanted to scream so loudly that the dome would shatter into a million pieces. But then I saw it. And it took my breath away.

It sat in the distance. A sight so surreal that it took me a moment to figure out what I was looking at, even though it was unmistakable. Beyond the horizon, so close yet so far away, the blue planet hung in the darkness. Streaks of white cloud littered its face, but blues and greens and browns covered the rest.

It was Earth, beyond our grasp.

BALTAZAR

I ran my hands through my hair with so much force that I thought I'd ripped the strands right out of their roots. With one swift kick, I toppled a row of seats, the clang of metal echoing throughout the dome. The outburst of emotion was pointless though. Nothing I could do would bring Earth closer.

Zoe was on her knees in front of the glass. She didn't say anything, just stared out at the planet floating in the darkness. I wanted to say something heroic and uplifting that would rekindle our drive to keep fighting, but only numbers appeared in my mind. There were 238,900 miles between Earth and the moon. 384,400 kilometers. 420,464,000 yards. 15,136,704,000 inches.

Smith would have been so disappointed to learn that he'd sacrificed himself for a view of a dead rock.

I could hear a faint screech in the distance—echoes from the battle in the arena, I assumed. The hordes were distracted in destroying each other, but only for so long. It was just a matter of time before one or all of them came up the ramp after us. I examined the glass of the dome. It was double enforced, but certainly not indestructible. Depressurizing the whole facility might only take the slightest crack.

I sat down by Zoe. Our shoes touched and I thought of the night she'd come into my room. That night, she was there in front of me but her mind was off far away.

"I don't want to give up," I said. My voice didn't sound brave or reassuring but they were words—the first step in not admitting defeat.

Her blue eyes turned to me. Even now, her gaze still made me feel heavier, like the gravity on the moon had suddenly increased. "I don't want to either."

"So what do we do?"

There was a loud thud behind us coming from the ramp down to the arena.

Zoe limped to her feet and I could see her fists tightening. She closed her eyes for a second before saying, "We look around. People had to get here using some sort of transport. There's got to be something."

"Something," I echoed, looking around.

We headed in opposite directions, looking for something that would get us off the moon. The farther I went, the more evidence I began to uncover that what we found ourselves in was some kind of station or port. The seats were for passengers to wait in before loading and unloading onto something. Blank screens on the wall once must have displayed the schedules for flights. There must be something, I kept telling myself.

After running past a curve that took me beyond Zoe's line of sight, I found a series of stairs that led to an upper platform. Once ascended, I found myself on a landing that led to several other terminals. The area was massive, easily a mile long, and would take hours to search through. But it didn't take hours, fortunately. I followed the series of checkpoints directly in front of me and came to a loading area, the floor checkered yellow and black with amber lights still glowing strong on the walls. A graphic interface sat silently in the middle of the zone but buzzed with life at my touch.

A blue virtual display appeared before me. It wasn't the most efficient terminal, full of buffer data due to a chronic lack of maintenance. There were also numerous file corruptions, exploding into a series of zeroes and ones at my touch which blocked out my view of everything else. It was like navigating through a minefield, my mind recalling the sensation of bones cracking as we'd tested such devices in the testing arena. I needed to be careful, make sure not to access something that would cause me to have to backtrack through files, slowing me down.

There were hundreds of listings regarding arrivals and departures of ships. I wanted to explore them all, but I knew it would be ultimately pointless. I needed to find an active ship with enough fuel to get us to Earth. My fingers flew through the digital files, falling into a mental groove when I decided on the "Acquisitions" directory. Strings of item codes and ID tags for all registered Parkman equipment appeared before me. Everything had a tag, I thought. Everything from beakers to weapons to genetic growth pods was documented.

Ships would be documented too. I just needed to find one that still functioned.

I heard Zoe calling my name, but I could do little more than grunt in return, trying to continue to scan the ID tags as quickly as possible. They wrapped around me, blurring by like the walls of a red hallway moving at high speeds. My eyes darted about, trying to find something that seemed helpful. The sound of footsteps soon came from behind me and Zoe appeared by my side, out of breath. Her eyes scanned the code with me but she diverted her view after a few seconds, the flashing lights of the tags disorientating her.

"Find anything?" she asked.

I didn't answer, still mired deep in the code. They slowed down for me and I started picking up patterns in their arrangements. Larger objects carried more distinct numerical combinations, including tags that started with prime numbers. I started getting better at isolating the chains and, in a moment of glory that made me want to shout in victory, I was able to find the ID tag for registered vehicles. 112464.

I quickly discarded the chains of trams and elevator tags and found a listing of what the system identified as "jump pods." With their status screens up, the small, one-person chambers looked no bigger than a closet, equipped for emergency decompression. There were 47 listed as active, but most of the power cells were reading dead. All but one, which still had maybe enough juice to escape the moon's gravity but not more than that.

The display flashed before us. I tried calculating the odds in my head of the likelihood that it would get one of us to the planet, let alone both of us. The initial math wasn't promising. But before I could get a word out, Zoe just shook her head, reading my mind.

"We do this together, Balt. No more sacrifices."

I gulped, suddenly feeling hot even though it was several

degrees colder in dome than it had been in the lab. So many of the details spelled failure, I thought. Low oxygen reserves. The effect of two people's weight on the trajectory.

She turned my shoulders so I had to look at her rather than the display. "We started this together. We finish it *together*."

There was another loud thud that sent a vibration throughout the dome, the glass making the slightest shuttering sound. Rather than concentrating on the noise, I just squeezed her hand, thinking of the first time I saw her on that platform in the testing arena.

If I only knew how she would completely mess up everything.

If I only knew how she would make my existence feel truly extraordinary, not just a cog in a machine.

"Okay," I said. "We do this together."

I turned back to the display and highlighted the location, launching Bay 94. We ran side by side back down the stairs, weaving in and around the seats with our sights on the numbers on the ground, steadily rising. When we passed the entrance that lead to the ramp to the arena, the thuds were replaced with a brutal scratching sound. To my ears, it resembled fields of jagged metal being dragged across each other. Rather than waiting to see what it was, we continued on and found the pod in a row with others like it. Number 94 sat at the end, possessing the only glowing green light in the row. I opened the pod door and quickly checked out the space. It was definitely small, no more than a square-meter space, and probably less. But we could fit, I determined. We could do this.

The systems checked out and I was ready to climb in, but when I turned back, I saw Zoe had stopped near the railing, examining the floor below like she was looking for something.

"Go," she said to me, not looking away. "Get it ready and I'll be right back."

"What? No, we have to—" I started to protest, but she cut me off.

"Please, Balt. Just trust me."

"What happened to 'we finish this *together*?'"

"We are. But I need to do one last thing." She kissed me again. "Just don't leave without me."

She turned and headed back in the direction we had come, the scraping sound growing louder in the distance. I wanted to run after her, but I trusted her. She would be back.

I turned back toward the pod and started prepping it for launch, double- and triple-checking every function. There was no guarantee it would work, I knew. It had been sitting here idle for years, and even if it launched, the systems probably wouldn't stay operational long enough to get us all the way to Earth. The most likely scenario would be that we'd just suffocate in space, our bodies left to drift in the black void forever.

But we would be away from here.

We would be together.

That would be an acceptable end to my life, I decided.

Pressed against the corner within the pod, I stood with my eyes focused on the launch command, listening to the scraping sound in the distance. I had no idea what it was or what Zoe felt she needed to do. But she was off to face it, leaving me with nothing to do but wait.

ZOE

The scraping noise grew with the passing seconds like a thunderous stampede. I could feel the glass of the dome shake around me, but I held my ground, waiting until I could make out the red eye in the darkness. When it finally did appear, it focused in on me and the scraping sound stopped.

"I'm here," I shouted, my hands out to my sides.

Parkman made a loud grunting sound and the scraping picked up once again.

I knew the smart thing would have just been to follow Balt to the pod. Our best—albeit remote—shot of getting off this rock was mere feet away, yet the thought of leaving this place as it stood bothered me. Escaping was enough revenge against the flesh-and-bone creature that dominated the new labs. I hoped it would tear him up inside that we were beyond his grasp, beyond his control, just like my mother.

But for the metal abomination before me, something more drastic needed to be done.

I wouldn't leave him intact.

When Parkman finally emerged from the darkness of the ramp, I saw that the bugs had done a number on him. His legs were crippled, metal wires ripped and frayed, dragging against the floor as he crawled. But his processor was still intact, his large arms pulling his body along. He was capable of rebuilding the rest of himself later. The job simply wasn't finished. That would be left for me.

His red eye stared me down, the lens inside focusing and refocusing over and over. He got so close that the red consumed me like the jaws of a giant animal. I stepped out of its light, moving toward the opposite end of the dome, making sure to keep my eyes locked with his.

"C'mon," I commanded. "Follow me."

Parkman released a loud clicking noise from his processor and did just as I told him to, crawling with his arms. It didn't take him long to catch up to me, so I quickened my pace, turning my back and running around the rows of seats. I started screaming at him then. "C'mon, you monster! Aren't I what you were looking for? Aren't I that prize you always wanted?"

Parkman began to swat the seats out of his way in a frenzy, the metal chairs flying through the air and smashing against the floor of the dome with deafening crashes and scrapes. I continued to shout at him, trying to do all I could to draw him toward me quicker. Faster. As if the sound of my voice cut through his core, Parkman seemed to become even more enraged, stumbling about on his path toward me in a disorganized and flailing motion. Finally, with the edge of the dome upon us, I pressed my back against the cold glass, its surface freezing my skin.

Parkman stopped in front of me, craning his neck so that the light of his eye was so close it was all I could see. The lens inside spun around and around like a tornado. With my fist, I smacked the eye hard in its center, forcing him to move back.

"You can understand me. Can't you?" I barked.

Parkman let out a shrill noise before replying. "Yes, I can." His voice was hollow. Alien and cold.

"Good."

We both stood there, he and I, staring at each other like we were sizing each other up. Inside I was scared, terrified of what it would feel like to have every bone in my body crushed into a pulp. But I wasn't going to stand down. Not to him. Not now.

"You're Elizabeth's daughter," he stated calmly, his head slightly tilted to the left. "My daughter. You have her eyes."

I closed my eyes a bit longer than a standard blink. "I know what you did to her. What you did to this whole place."

"The confines of flesh—" he began to explain but I shouted back.

"Shut up!"

Parkman pushed up on his hands, reminding me who was a threat to who. But I still had one trick up my sleeve. I was going to make this opportunity count.

"You think you're some sort of god? Well, you're not! You're just a hunk of metal driven by the brain of a pathetic monster who was so insecure with himself that he needed to kill anyone who he couldn't control. You're nothing but a coward."

The robot let out another shrill noise that sounded like a laugh. "I see so much of myself in you."

"You see nothing!" I shot back. "Nothing about me is any thanks to you!"

"Everything is thanks to me! This place exists simply because I will it so! This is my domain and soon it will grow! Once the craft in the arena is finished, I will return to Earth and there will be no limit to what I can do."

I thought to the structure the AIs were building in the arena. A spacecraft. A wave of fear rippled over my skin but it only strengthened my will. I needed to destroy him now or no one would be safe.

"Your domain is a crumbling ruin on a lifeless rock. And that's how it will end," I said, hoping to strike a nerve, to force him into action.

Parkman moved his face closer to me. With my body against the glass, I took a deep breath before speaking again, concentrating. This would be it.

"Your legacy will be that of a failure, of a crazed, washed-up scientist who couldn't think about anything other than himself long enough to do anything worthwhile. That will be what humankind remembers of Alexander Parkman III. And if you still can't see that, you're even dumber than I thought."

With one swift motion, the robot pulled his arm back, his iron fist striking without hesitation. But I wasn't there to see the blow land. From the landing near the escape pod, all I could hear was the breaking of the dome glass, the roaring of the atmosphere blowing out into dark abyss outside. I stumbled toward the jump pod but before I could get inside, the hurricane-force wind became too much, pulling my body toward the other side of the dome.

With one final lunge, I grasped the edge of the pod's hatch and hung on desperately as I flapped in the wind, rocking violently about. The effects of my teleportation began to hit my body then, the blood rushing from my nose and this time also from my ears, but never hitting the ground before being blown away. My vision blurred and I cursed myself for being so reckless, risking our escape to get revenge. And with one final sway, I lost my grip, lost my chance to get away.

Until Balt gave me another.

I felt his hand wrap around my wrist, holding onto me as the explosive decompression did all that it could to claim me. Cracks spread throughout the glass of the dome like lightning bolts. With one final pull, Balt hauled me inside and we shut the hatch just in time to listen to the dome collapse before launching.

The next few minutes were hazy, like the time between dreaming and waking. The pod shook violently and my head smacked against its metal side over and over. I felt sick, dizzy, and cold. I wanted to close my eyes and never open them again. But as if it matched the pace of my breathing, the pod began to calm when I did, the vibrations replaced with a gentle droning sound as we flew through space.

Through glassy eyes, I saw Balt's face up against mine, our bodies pressed against each other. I could feel his arms wrapped around my waist in the tiny space and I lay my head down on his shoulder.

"That was pretty irrational," he said in a soft voice.

"Yeah."

"But you got him?"

"Yeah."

"Are you okay?"

I lifted my head and nodded. "My head just hurts." He wiped some blood from under my nose.

"I think you should resist the urge to teleport for a while. Deal?"

"Deal."

Our pod drifted for hours and I wanted to ask if we were going to make it, or if the power would last until we got to Earth, or how it was going to descend safely to the ground, or a thousand other questions that bounced around in my head like excited molecules. But I didn't. I just closed my eyes and Balt did the same, our heads resting against each other.

I didn't know how long we had left. A few minutes. Hours. Maybe years. But however long it was, it was ours now. Whatever was going to happen, it was going to be because of what we chose. I drifted in and out of sleep, dreaming of standing in a beautiful grass field, the blades tickling my bare ankles. I looked up toward the endless black sky littered with shimmering stars, feeling small and far away from everything I knew.

And totally, completely, and unequivocally free.

ACKNOWLEDGEMENTS

Oh boy, where to begin.

Thank you so much to Jenn Mischler, my incredible agent who saw the potential in me and my work and was willing to take a chance on an unknown guy. Your feedback and insight has been invaluable and know that I will always be indebted to you.

To Christopher Loke, Reece Hanzon, Zach Power, and the rest of the incredible team at Jolly Fish Press, thank you for doing all that you did to turn *Surfacing* into a reality and the best book it could possibly be. Onward and Upward!

To my wonderful wife Molly, who was and still is always willing to pick me up when I stumble. This book would have never come together had it not been for your love, support, and guidance through the past years. Thank you for everything, especially introducing me to this YA thing so many years back. You are my love and hero.

To my amazing parents Angie and Peter, thank you for being you. You put a roof over my head, food in my belly, and love and creativity into my heart. I am who I am because of your wonderful influences and hope that I have made you proud.

To my stellar sister Sarah, thank you for being such a positive influence in my life. You have always been the definition of strength and courage for me and if I put half the amount of joy and love into the world as you have, I will have considered myself lucky.

To Lucy, Bob, Jeff, and Andy McLeod, thank you for making my new life in PA just as good as the one that I left in New York. From the first time I entered your home, I felt like part of the family and that has been a great comfort over the years.

To Mrs. Cummings, Mrs. Iacovetti, Mr. Rewjewski, and Ms. Clarke, thank you for being amazing life-changing teachers. Your insight and energy inspired a love of literature and learning in me. Without your presence in my life, this book surely would never have happened.

And to the incredible staff and students of Boyertown Junior High West, Broughal Middle School, Whitehall High School, and Lincoln Middle School, your smiling faces during the day gave me the energy to write at night.

MARK MAGRO grew up on an island in New York and has spent most of his time teaching in middle schools and high schools, getting more tattoos than he should have, and earning more than 5,000 trophies (and counting!) while playing PlayStation. *Surfacing* is his debut novel and, when worried he wouldn't be able to finish it, he relied heavily on Protocol #4 of the Parkman Institute of Science and Solutions handbook: Don't Panic.

He lives in the Lehigh Valley, Pennsylvania, with his wife and spoiled dog. Follow him on Twitter and friend him on PSN @MagroCrag